Plague U

The Intern Diaries Series- Book 2

D. C. Gomez

GOMEZ EXPEDITIONS

Cover design by Christine Gerardi Designs

ISBN: 978-1-7321369-0-8 for Paperback Editions

Published by Gomez Expeditions

Request to publish work from this book should be sent to: author@dcgomez-author.com

For all the people who still believe dreams can come true:
this book is for you.

Chapter One

According to some studies, people have more heart attacks and strokes on Mondays than any other day of the week. It seems that the Monday-morning blues are truly dangerous for your health. I agreed with that sentiment, at least today.

I usually didn't have much to complain about in my job. It wasn't like I needed to punch a clock Monday through Friday, or as if I lived in a cubicle world. I had a unique position; I was Death's Intern for North America. I might need to explain that a bit, since that sounds like I am an assassin or mercenary of some kind. We, myself and the other interns, are not allowed to kill.

I literally work for Death, the being that takes your soul to its afterlife. Death's job is simple: she delivers souls to their final destination. She is like the UPS for the soul world. Most people wonder why I refer to Death as she. Death, as it turns out, appears to each person differently. Death takes whatever form the person imagines her to be; which, at times, can be confusing or disconcerting for some of us. For me, Death appears as a tall, beautiful woman with long, silky, brown hair who is always perfectly dressed. It is probably a blessing that nobody else could see my version besides Death and me, since Death resembles my dead mother.

If Death's job is so simple, why would she need Interns? In the eight months that I have worked for her, I've learned a couple reasons Interns are required. One, if anyone attempts to interfere with Death's delivery system, it is our job to find them and stop them. And two, sometimes people die and they don't realize it. When this happens, it is our job to assist them to the Afterlife. Most of my time is spend doing number two.

Having to chase this ghost around the park was the reason for my Monday-morning blues. Here I was, Isis Black, running laps at Spring Lake Park in Texarkana, chasing the soul of a track and field runner who didn't know he was dead. Did I mention it was six-thirty in the morning? I was having flashbacks of being in the Army.

On most occasions, I am attractive—or at least exotic-looking—with long, black hair, a mocha complexion, and about five feet, nine inches tall. This morning, I was a hot mess. Spring Lake Park had a trail around the park that claimed to be a mile and three quarters. Summer started early in East Texas and for late May, the temperature was quickly rising. My long hair was stuck to my head, and I was pouring sweat.

"Isis, this is his fourth lap. You better hurry!" Bob shouted at me. He was sitting on the tailgate of his truck, "The Beast," with our boss, Death. If I weren't mistaken, they were drinking coffee while I ran like a maniac behind this ghost.

"Thanks for pointing it out!" I yelled back, slightly out of breath. Bob had parked by the baseball fields near the doggy park area. The park had different sections and this side had an entrance on the service road parallel to Interstate 30. Thirty made it easy to get to many places in Texarkana.

"If you can talk, you're not running fast enough!" I heard him yell from behind. I considered giving him a sign with my finger but remembered Death was there. Bob was spending way too much time with Constantine and he was starting to sound like him. Constantine was the Guardian, the trainer of all Interns and Death's Right-Hand person. He was also a five-thousand-year-old talking Maine Coon cat—welcome to my life. But I had to admit Bob was right. I needed to pick up the pace.

Our runner had a particular pattern. He did four laps around the park and then he was gone. According to Death, he'd died right after finishing his last lap at record speed. He was so excited by his new personal record that he missed the fact that he had died and he never saw Death. Every day, runners and walkers were being haunted by the presence of this ghost. We were running downhill now, heading toward the spring and he was picking up the pace. I had been chasing him for two laps and I was not going to lose him now. I took off at full sprint, hoping to cut him off before he hit the bridge.

I wasn't sure if I was imagining things, but I had the horrible feeling my dead runner thought we were racing. He was getting faster. I was so busy trying to catch up that I failed to see the flock of geese coming at me. I wasn't sure if it was the geese or the lone duck that did it, but I ended up head-first in the water. While the outside temperatures were rising, the water was still freezing. Last fall, the city had cleared the natural spring of debris and dirt, so now the lake was deep in some areas. I was standing in water up to my shoulders. My dear, dead runner looked over his shoulder and laughed. Lucky for him, he was already dead.

"Stop!" I screamed, as loud as my voice would allow. The ghost stopped. I wasn't sure who was more surprised, me or him.

As Death's Interns, we had the power to see and touch the souls of the dead. We were also "gifted"—I'm still debating that one—with the third eye: the power to see into the supernatural world. That gift was a blessing and a curse because sometimes the things you saw were nasty.

Could we control the dead? I wasn't sure of that. I dragged myself out of the water and walked over to the soul—Constantine hated it when I called them ghosts.

"Do I know you? You've been following me for a while. Are you also training?"

It wasn't fair. He wasn't even winded. I was hoping the physical laws didn't apply to ghosts and he just had that extra advantage.

"You don't know me, but my boss is here to take you home." I found it was best to keep it simple and to the point. The first time I'd tried to retrieve a lost soul, the lady beat me with her purse for fifteen minutes in the middle of Los Angeles. I was surprised I wasn't sent to an insane asylum, since nobody else could see what was happening while I was covering myself and ducking like a lunatic.

"Home? Dear, I live down the street from here."

Before he could turn around, I grabbed his arm. The second lesson I'd learned about retrieving souls was the sooner I touched them, the faster reality clicked. Not sure what it was about my touch, but it grounded them. He froze and started looking around. I knew the look; he realized he was dead. I prayed that his afterlife was filled with running paths in the sky.

"Are you ready?" I'd also learned to keep conversations short. Tears were rolling down his cheeks. I slowly laced my fingers with his and started walking him back in the direction we had come. I was the last human being a soul would ever be touched by, so I never hurried.

"When did I die? How is my family?" His voice was barely audible. I was grateful for Death's gift of being able to hear him.

"Three weeks ago. Your family is coping with your loss. You were loved by many." We were almost the same height, so I didn't have to look up to see directly into his eyes. "They will be fine. It's time for you to go home." I squeezed his hand again.

"Three weeks? What have I been doing all this time?" He looked even more lost.

"Oh, the usual ghost stuff—scaring the hell out of every runner in Texarkana."

At that, he laughed. It was a full laugh that reached his eyes. The world felt a little emptier when souls like these were gone.

"So, what took you so long to get me?"

I could tell he was teasing. I couldn't help but play along. I looked at him, pretending to be highly offended, trying to hide my smile. "Hey now, it took us a while to track your running pattern. It wasn't like you ran at the same time every day. By the time we got here, you were gone."

He gave me a devilish grin. "I like keeping people on their feet."

I glanced up. He looked proud of himself. I just smiled.

We walked in silence the remainder of the trail. My dead runner looked around in wonder as if he was seeing everything for the first time. Spring Lake Park had a quaint magic to it. It was in the middle of town, on the Texas side. Texarkana, Texas, has a sister city on the Arkansas side—Texarkana, Arkansas. One street, called State Line, divides the cities. Maybe it wasn't the most original name for a street, but it worked. For most people from big cities, Texarkana was a small town with nothing to do. For me, it had that small-town charm, where people waved at you on the street, men opened doors for you, and store owners still believed in being pleasant.

I led him toward Bob's truck. Death slowly turned around to face us and my dead runner stopped.

"Death."

That was all he said. It was hard to explain, but I knew how he felt. The first time I met Death, I knew without being told who I was facing. I am convinced that some unconscious part of our brain recognizes her essence.

When Death was around, time stood still. The noises of the world faded and nothing else mattered.

Death handed Bob her cup and walked toward us. My dead runner looked stunned and I was afraid he was going to start running again.

"It's OK. You're ready," I whispered to him as I gave his hand one more squeeze. He looked at me and slowly nodded.

"Thank you, Isis," Death said. She took his hand. I was always amazed how gentle she was with each soul. Regardless of what their afterlife would be, she took full responsibility for them and exuded compassion. She smiled at the runner and he took a deep breath and visibly relaxed.

"Do I want to know why you're wet?" Death asked me.

"A goose attacked me." I was embarrassed. It was hard not to be when I looked like I had been dragged through hell and Death was wearing a three-piece skirt suit from Oscar de la Renta. Hey, just because I don't dress up doesn't mean I don't know designers.

"I can see that. By the looks of it, they won," Death replied with a smile and started to walk away with the runner.

"Death, wait. Question—can I control the dead?"

"To some extent. You do have some of my powers. In the same capacity that you can make a living person do certain things, you can make the dead follow your commands." Death was still smiling at me; I was staring at her with my mouth wide open.

"Why have I been running all over the country chasing them then?" I was not happy about this and my wet hair drooped over my eyes, aggravating me more.

"That is an excellent question, dear. I figured you enjoyed it. It was in your manual." Death winked at me. I received the intern's manual on my first day on the job. It probably didn't help that I still hadn't read it. Obviously,

Death knew that already. "Besides, dear, not a bad practice. Your power doesn't always work on everyone, especially if they are recently dead." She winked one more time and turned around. Death and runner boy took three steps and they were gone.

I walked over to Bob, who handed me a towel and a cup of hot chocolate.

"Thank you so much, Bob." I started drying my hair with one hand while I held the mug in the other. I refused to let go of my hot chocolate. Bob made the best hot chocolate in the city. "You know, you could have helped me over there."

Bob gave me his million-dollar smile.

"You looked like you had everything under control. Besides, you're the Intern here. I'm just the driver. If I step too far away from Death, I won't be able to see the guy—or lady." Bob smiled again and it was so hard to be mad at him. I gave him my most evil glare, but looking like a wet poodle, it did not have much effect.

I was staring over the rim of my mug at Bob as he drank his coffee and looked off in the direction where Death had just vanished. I was still in awe over his transformation, or, better stated, recovery. Bob was my first friend in Texarkana. When we met, he was a homeless veteran suffering from PTSD and severe paranoia. After he'd been kidnapped by witches and made it through that mess, Death and Constantine offered him a job with us. Bob had witnessed the supernatural and was left shattered. The validation that the horrors he faced were real and he wasn't crazy helped him collect the pieces of his shattered self and heal. He reminded me of Psalm 23—Even though I walk through the valley of the shadow of Death, I will fear no evil.

He was a new man and genuinely feared no evil. His six-foot frame had filled in. His sandy-blond hair was neatly combed in a high and tight, military-style haircut. It was hard now to tell how old he was, maybe forty. But the most shocking change was in his sea-green eyes. They were no longer haunted. They shone with mischievousness and humor all the time. If Constantine was the evil dictator of our little family, Bob had become our Yoda. He was always cool, calm, and collected—and always fashionable.

Bob was staring toward the park. I glanced over in the same direction.

"What's going on?" I wasn't sure what I was looking at. A young guy was walking very awkwardly across the park.

"I have no idea. He is human, right?"

I glanced at Bob and then back at the guy. "If you can see him, I have a feeling he's alive. Human, that might be questionable." Recently, I had found out that just because something looked human, it didn't make it so. "Should we help him?"

I tried to take a step forward, but Bob stopped me. Before I could complain, the guy grabbed a squirrel that happened to be nearby. The man's speed and accuracy were almost inhuman. He took a bite out of the squirrel.

"Oh my God!" I gasped. That was a new one for me.

"Isis, get in the truck, now." Bob pushed me toward the passenger side and then ran to the driver's side. He didn't have to tell me twice. I was spooked. And I worked for Death.

Bob started the truck and was backing it up even before I managed to close the door. Bob threw the shift into drive faster than a drag racer. I looked out of the back window just in time to see the guy staring at us.

"Bob, hurry!"

That was all he needed. We were out of the park in less than three seconds and heading toward Reapers.

Chapter Two

Bob pulled The Beast into its designated space inside of Reapers Incorporated, otherwise known as Reapers, for short. This was our headquarters in North America. Since I had moved to Texarkana, running away from my past, Death's team was forced to follow. The way the recruitment process for Death's Interns worked was simple. If you killed the previous intern, you became the next candidate. It wasn't until recently I found out that the selection was not automatic. Death had the final approval of the candidate. I had accidentally killed Trek, the previous North American Intern. While trying to climb out of a New York City fire exit in a crowded apartment, I accidently pushed him off the ladder. I didn't know he was there till I heard the screams. Now the job was mine. As strange as the job seems, it does have some incredible benefits, including a significant salary, free room and board, food, transportation, and even a clothing allowance.

Reapers is located in the Business Park in Nash, Texas. From the outside, it doesn't look exceptional; it is a large metal building, three stories tall. The only weird distinction, if that, is the sign outside that read Reapers Incorporated in red, Gothic letters. On the inside, it is a different story. The first floor contains a shooting range, a gym area that I honestly hate, a new mechanic's workshop for all the vehicles, and Bob's quarters. He has a large master bedroom and living area. The entrances to Reapers are secured by all sorts of scanners, metal detectors, and spells.

Come to think of it, the entire building is a huge bomb shelter. The building was designed to withstand spells, ghosts, supernatural attacks, and, of course, human's bombs. While the first floor is mostly a training area, the team has an apartment up on the second floor. The apartment is almost a third the length of the building and is separated into two main areas—the shared space and the bedrooms. The shared space, called the loft, has a fabulous kitchen, which is the first thing you see when you walk in. Right next to the kitchen is a dining area, now with a much more significant table since Bob had moved in. The far corner is the command center. It has large monitors arranged around Bartholomew's computers.

The last member of our newly formed family is Bartholomew. I wasn't sure how but Death is his guardian. Bartholomew is a genius and, at twelve years of age, the best-supply sergeant and gun dealer I have ever met. There is nothing he cannot procure, either equipment or information. Bartholomew is going through a growth spurt and is now five feet, six inches. His brown, curly hair is still messy and at times, it hides his hazel eyes.

Bartholomew and Constantine had designed Reapers before I accepted the job. They were only expecting me, so the apartment had just three bedrooms. Bob was not offended by this at all. If anything, I was sure he loved his area downstairs. The main bedrooms in the apartment are in the back with a doorway right off the kitchen. I hated to admit it, but my bedroom, with its huge bath and walk-in closet, is my little haven. Trust me, working for Death has its perks.

The Beast's parking space is between The Camaro, formerly called Bumblebee, and Ladybug. Constantine had named his yellow Camaro Bumblebee, and recently received a TM violation notice, long story. He is still angry about it, so we are only allowed it call it The Camaro. Ladybug is my midnight-blue Mini Cooper. Bartholomew had a hard time taking in the name since the Mini isn't red. After a while, he couldn't fight it. The Mini is as cute as a ladybug, so the name stuck. At the far end of the garage area is Death's pale greenish/yellowish mustang, the Death-mobile. I am not brave enough to even take the cover off.

Bob turned The Beast off. The 'Beast' moniker is a bit of a contradiction; it is a 1980s white Toyota regular cab truck. In comparison to most vehicles in Texarkana, it is tiny. I wasn't too impressed at first until Bob and Bartholomew finished upgrading it. The engine in that truck is to die for.

Bob and I walked into the loft to find Constantine napping in the command center area on top of the black-leather couch. That couch is the most comfortable piece of furniture in the apartment. We are all in love with it. Constantine looked up at us and did his cat stretches. Bob walked over to the sink and started washing all the empty mugs he had brought up. Bob is always thoughtful. Now that he is adjusting back to "normal" life–whatever that means when you worked for Death–he has developed an obsession with cooking. He is addicted to the Food Network. Bob is the Barefoot Contessa's number one fan.

"Isis, do I want to know why you're wet?" Constantine had jumped on the kitchen island and was sniffing me suspiciously. "Why do you smell fishy?"

"She fell in the lake chasing the runner." Sometimes, Bob can be a little too helpful for my taste.

"Thanks, Bob." I gave him another evil glare that he totally ignored. Instead, he just smiled wickedly.

"That sucks." That was a very calm remark for Constantine. "Did you at least get him?"

"Yes. I eventually yelled at him to stop and was able to grab him." I made sure not to make eye contact when I said that.

"You didn't try that from the beginning?" Constantine's voice had taken on a confused tone.

"I didn't know I could do that," I said, trying to look innocent.

"Girl, please don't tell me you still haven't read that manual." Constantine was now staring at me like I had stolen his lunch.

"I've been busy." I was pleading now and sounded pitiful.

"Busy, busy, my tail." He glared at me then turned toward Bob. "You got the soul, but why are you two looking so disturbed?"

Constantine and I were now both looking at Bob. I had no idea how he was going to explain the guy.

"The runner wasn't the problem. It was this weird guy we saw when we were leaving."

I could tell Bob was struggling to find the words to explain.

"That is not very specific. Tons of weird guys run around Spring Lake Park. You know its history." Constantine had taken his Sphinx pose as he spoke.

"He was different, even for Spring Lake. He took a bite out of a squirrel that was still alive."

"You didn't tell me they had an Ozzy concert at the park."

I rolled my eyes. Constantine was an encyclopedia of pop culture and he used his references at the worst possible time. On the other hand, when you were as old as he was, I was sure he didn't care.

"I wish. He was almost zombie-like." Bob was looking perplexed and I was afraid to hear the answer to this.

"Don't say the Z word," Constantine growled.

"Please tell me you're kidding. Do we have zombies in the world?" I couldn't help it. I had seen World War Z and that was one group of supernatural creatures I could live without.

"Didn't you hear what I said? We do not say the Z word." Constantine growled at me this time.

"Sorry, but you're kidding." I was still pleading.

"Unfortunately, no. There are very few things that land on Death's bad list; those 'things' are one of them." Constantine looked very thoughtful.

"Death has a bad list?" I was grateful Bob had asked the question. Bob was Constantine's favorite human and he could get away with anything. Those two had become inseparable. It was a bit creepy.

"Well, everyone has one. Death's list is fairly short: vampires, necromancers, and anything that doesn't stay dead. Oh, I almost forgot, and that alchemist guy. He is a special one." Constantine was very casual when he delivered his little speech.

"Vampires? Really?" I didn't care about some alchemist guy unless he planned to eat my soul, but vampires were a whole different story. My job was getting more difficult. I was starting not to like Mondays anymore.

"Girl, please!" Constantine had a way of saying the word girl so it sounded like an insult it was almost like he was calling me dumb, maybe he was. "Where do you think all those stories come from? For every myth, there is a touch of truth to it."

"Fair enough, but you didn't say the Z word. Is it not on the list?"

"The zombies," Constantine said, looking around before he said the word, "are not technically the problem. They are not self-created. You need a necromancer to raise them. Death has an automatic death sentence for anyone raising the dead and you are supposed to carry it out. See why we don't want any of them running around?"

My mouth went dry and I just stared at Constantine. I am supposed to kill people. Oh, wow. As I remember,

Constantine told me we had five simple rules as Interns and they were simple: one, you could not tell anyone you worked for Death. This one should be deleted since everyone knew I worked for Death before I walked into the room. Two, you could not kill anyone unless it was in self-defense. Three, you could not contact Death unless you were dying. Four, being an Intern was my primary job. Other jobs could not interfere with this one. Five, any romantic relationship could not interfere with this job. Becoming an executioner was not one of the rules and I was terrified. I had never killed anyone, not even while serving in the military. I was in the Army band with the 82nd Airborne Division.

"How often do necromancers appear?" Oh, thank God Bob asked the question. I was still stunned.

"There are not many around. The ones remaining have gone underground, hence the reason we probably do not have a Z problem. It's probably somebody on drugs."

Constantine wasn't very convincing.

"I know this is against the rules, but shouldn't we call Death?" I didn't want to, but this was way over my head.

"No! At no cost do we call the boss unless we are one-hundred-percent sure." Constantine had jumped up and looked like he was ready to pounce.

I was saved from replying when Bartholomew entered the room. He was covered in grease and carrying a package. I hadn't seen him downstairs, so he was probably in the shooting range or in his new makeshift shop. He was too busy looking at some schematics to even make eye contact. I looked over at Bob, who shook his head, confused.

"Hi, Bart, how are you?" I tried.

"Hi, Isis. Here, this came in for you." He handed me the package, barely looking up.

"Hey, big guy. What are you working on?" Bob asked Bartholomew while I struggled to open my package.

"My robot is getting stuck and I can't figure out why." Bartholomew was still barely looking at us. This was unusual since he was the most social and caring person in the group.

"What robot?" I asked Bartholomew as I pulled a blowgun from the package. Attached was a small card that said, "Welcome to the family. Glad you are still alive. Jose."

"Doesn't anyone ever pay any attention to me? Remember I signed up for the College Bowl robotics competition."

Oh God, I forgot that Texarkana was hosting a competition between all the universities and colleges in the area. While Texarkana did not have a college football team, it planned to have all other events to include chess, debate, and, of course, robotics.

"I'm sorry, Bart. Is that this weekend?" I was trying to calm him down. I had never seen Bart so upset before.

"Hellooo, Memorial weekend!"

Wow, Bartholomew was becoming a very moody preteen. We were in trouble.

"Is that this weekend?" Poor Bob was going to get it by the way Bartholomew looked at him. "Calm down, big guy. We just found a zombie in the park and were a bit preoccupied."

"There are no zombies in the park. Stop saying that." Constantine's fur was standing up on end. This was getting intense.

"Don't you dare ruin this for me! I'm the youngest person competing. I have a lot to prove." Bartholomew was ready to scream.

"OK, everyone, calm down now. No more 'zombie' talk till we find out what's going on. Bart, I'm pretty sure you'll be fine. If anything, you'll destroy everyone. Breathe."

Now that I thought about it, twelve-year-old boys with unlimited budgets will be noticed.

"I've got work to do." Without another word, he stomped out.

"Constantine, is it wise to have him compete? Wouldn't that draw a lot of attention to us?"

"Are you planning to tell him no?" We looked at each other and I knew he was right.

"Good point, his wrath might be worse." I was staring out the glass panel that faced the right side of the balcony. It had a clear view of the first floor as well as the stairs leading down. Bartholomew looked pissed. I didn't know he was so competitive.

"Isis, what did you get this time?" Bob was looking at me expectantly. That was one thing I loved about him now, never dwelled very long on stuff.

"A blowgun, and by the looks of it, it's from South America."

Bob walked over to look at the blowgun. Death's Interns were a peculiar breed. Due to the high mortality rate, interns waited at least six months before welcoming others to the family.

"I really like Jose. That's one busy boy." Constantine sounded like a proud parent.

"How many is this now? Three?" Bob was playing with the blowgun as he talked.

"Four, if you count the penguin picture I got from the Bob in Antarctica. I also got a sword from Asia and the magic gourd from Africa. No clue how to use that one." I guess as part of the welcoming letter you also received a gift, some of them odd.

"You got a penguin picture?" I was glad Bob asked and that he was as confused as me. "Antarctica Bob is special, but what do you expect when you live all the way down there alone? Besides, he has the most seniority."

Constantine looked thoughtful, which always terrifies me. "Isis, what are your plans for this week?"

"I was planning to investigate the guy at the park. Help Abuelita out with food, the usual. Why?" My hackles were going up in nervous anticipation at what Constantine might be plotting.

"Isis, you need a life," Constantine said in a very matter-of-fact way.

"What? I have a life." I looked at Bob for moral support, but he wasn't looking at me.

"When was the last time you went on a date?"

Was Constantine kidding? He was back into his Sphinx pose.

"I've been busy, between Abuelita and this job." I did not like this conversation at all.

"Isis, you don't have any regular shifts anymore. You need some distraction, so we set you up on a date for Wednesday. Only lunch, but it'll be great."

Constantine had a weird grin on his feline face and Bob was staring at the floor. I was stunned.

"Constantine, did you bump your head or something? I'm not going on a blind date. That's crazy." I didn't know what else to say.

"You'll be fine. I made you an appointment to see Patty as well. Get a facial, a manicure. The whole nine yards." He was looking at me like this was normal. I was going to choke him. "Isis, you are becoming a hermit and losing touch with the world. Dealing with souls all the time is not good for a human. You need some normal interactions even if they are horrible. So, you're going on a date and that's an order. I don't need you going postal on us." Without another word, he jumped down and headed out the kitty door.

"Can he order me to date?" I looked at Bob for support.

"If you work for Death, I guess so. Don't worry too much, Isis. It's only one date. How bad could it be? Besides, the guy works for the postal service and he's harmless." Bob handed me the blowgun and patted my shoulders. "Isis, we just worry about you."

"Thanks." My day had officially gotten worse. "I'll take a shower and head over to Abuelita's to help out."

Bob smiled and headed out the door. Was my life so bad that I needed to be set up on a blind date by a cat?

Chapter Three

I drove Ladybug down to Abuelita's. I was still in a horrible mood. Abuelita's was a small—OK more like a hole-in-the-wall—Tex-Mex restaurant located on Highway 82 between Nash and Texarkana. While the place was little, it had the best food in town. The owner was Abuelita, so she wasn't very original with her naming. Abuelita enjoyed being a grandmother and was proud of it since Abuelita meant "grandma" in Spanish. Abuelita was about five feet eleven, with gorgeous silver hair and curvaceous body. For a woman in her sixties—I was pretty sure that was her age—she looked incredible. There was something earthy about her that reminded me of my godmother, the fabulous woman who'd raised me. Abuelita described herself as a modern-day medicine woman. Constantine preferred the term practicing sorceress aka witch.

The restaurant was closed at this hour. Usually, Abuelita's was only open for dinner during the week and had lunch and dinner hours during the weekend. In the past few months, business had increased. According to Abuelita, rumors spread that Death's rookie Intern was working at her place and the entire supernatural community in the four states area was coming out en masse. That was the main reason why I was no longer working my regular hours. I never expected to be so upset about losing a waitress job, but I enjoyed the job and my regular clients. Unfortunately, after three different incidents where thugs challenged me to a fight, Bob, Constantine, and Abuelita all decided it wasn't safe for the clients or me. Death's Interns had a reputation for being "tough," and everyone wanted to test their skills against me.

Fortunately, Abuelita's business didn't suffer from all the fights. On the contrary, its popularity increased and many continued to come in hopes of a show. Abuelita also expanded into home catering. At first, it was aimed at her elderly clients that were no longer able to drive. Then the news spread and now Abuelita was catering parties and office meetings. This new addition to the business meant Abuelita was always working. As Constantine pointed out, I didn't have much of a life, so I came over a lot to help—or maybe just hide. I didn't eat meat by choice, but I loved the smell of Abuelita's kitchen. To ensure no lunatics followed me, I varied the hours I went to Abuelita's each day.

It was a late Monday morning and the place was deserted, thank the Lord. I parked behind the building next to Abuelita's Cadillac. She was a bit eccentric, but nobody could deny she had great taste. I walked in through the back kitchen entrance. I still had my keys to the place, even though I was no longer waitressing. If I hadn't seen the crazy scene in front of me before, I would have panicked. Abuelita looked like a mad scientist. There were pots on both of her large stoves. Steam was coming out of half of them and she was mixing some bowl as if the ingredients were on fire. Then again with Abuelita, that was possible.

"Isis, honey. Can you stir that pot over there, please? Don't let the rice burn now." Abuelita had this crazy ability to know who was in the room even without seeing them. After all this time, I was used to it.

"Yes, ma'am." I walked over the pot and stirred the rice. I glanced at the other pots, where tamales were steaming, frijoles were simmering, and something sweet was boiling. "New recipe?" I asked, pointing at the boiling pot.

"Sweetie, you will never believe this. I met a Dominican the other day." She was so excited that she stopped mixing for a moment.

I was a little confused. "A Dominican? Like a Catholic priest or like Dominican from the DR?" Honestly, this was a valid question in my mind. I had never heard of a Dominican from the Dominican Republic this far down in Texas. Most were in New England or New York City.

"Really? She rolled her eyes at me as she spoke, trying to look serious. "One from the island, of course."

"You met a Dominican in Texarkana. Was he or she lost?" I was in awe.

"It was a guy, and honestly I thought the same thing. He was previously in service in the army and got a job at the depot. But that's not the point. He was telling me about this dessert his mother used to make. I had to try it." She was back to mixing with the delight only chefs and cooks get.

"That's interesting. So, what's the dish? I know you're dying to tell me."

Abuelita burst into a huge smile at my question. She really couldn't wait to tell me.

"It's like a sweet empanada, made with guava and cream cheese. They are a bit smaller and lighter. So, I'm hoping to perfect them for the College Bowl. Trying to see if we can compete with those stupid fried pies. Everyone is raving about them lately."

I couldn't help but smile as I shook my head. Abuelita was getting as competitive as Bartholomew. This College Bowl was going to be the death of my people. I started stirring the frijoles absently.

"Isis, are you OK?" Abuelita's voice sounded worried.

"I guess." I was making my rounds around all the pots, trying to avoid looking directly at Abuelita.

"Well, that's convincing. Let me hear it, child." Her crazy mixing had stopped and she now had a giant ball of dough in her bowl. She washed her hands and grabbed her cutting board to put her dough on.

"Agh. Constantine says I have no life and set me up on a blind date." I let the words spill as quickly as possible. Abuelita stopped kneading and looked at me. She raised an eyebrow in response.

"Did he? How do you feel about it?" She slowly started kneading the dough while paying close attention to me.

"I have a life, just not a social one. Do you know how hard it is to go out when you're chasing souls all over North America? What happened to the whole light thing?"

Abuelita looked at me, confused. Obviously, my quick change in topic lost her.

"You know, the light or tunnel people are supposed to see when they die. It seems nobody notices it. Maybe we need a marching band or some fireworks to tell people they are dead. That way I don't spend all my time chasing ghosts. How am I supposed to have a so-called life?"

"Is that really what's bothering you?" At least this time, she pretended not to be so curious about my weird meltdown. "While you are on that side, please start a couple of bowls of salad. We got deliveries shortly." I walked over to the industrial size fridge and pulled out my ingredients. At least my hands would be busy chopping veggies while I was ranting to Abuelita.

"Honestly, what kind of small talk am I supposed to have? How am I supposed to answer when some poor human asks me what I do for a living? I can't tell them I work for Death, even if it wasn't one of the rules. I don't have a nice side job, like Eric, who can claim to be a cop and is dating." At least when I was a waitress, I could use that as an excuse. I was pouting.

"Eric is dating?" That was all Abuelita got from my whole speech. I turned my head to face her. She had moved the pot with the sweet concoction over. I guessed that was the guava.

"Yeah, according to Bart he is dating some 'hot blonde' that was a former Miss Texarkana." I even did the air quotations over the "hot blonde" part. Eric was Reapers' designated martial arts expert and trainer. I had to admit Eric was one sexy man—or should I say, witch. The man made his uniform look good.

"Texarkana has lots of hot blondes, dear. But are you OK?" She gave me a very odd look. I wasn't sure what it meant.

"Yeah, why wouldn't I be? I don't get the obsession for me to start dating. Is not like I haven't tried, but is really hard with my line of work. It's like I have the plague or something. It's just not fair. Everyone had a semi-normal life—even Bob, who looked like a young Daniel Craig.

"Isis, it has nothing to do with your dating status and more to do with your interactions. You are spending too much time with the dead. That's not healthy."

I was in the middle of destroying a tomato when her words hit me.

"What do you mean?" I glanced at Abuelita after analyzing the ruins of my tomato. I needed to stop taking out my anger on veggies or my salad was going to become soup.

"Isis, even if you are Death's Intern, you are still human like the rest of us. If you spend too much time with the supernatural world, it's easy to lose sight of your own humanity. Constantine just wants some balance for you. Besides, they probably did a full background check and a financial analysis on that poor boy already. He's probably safe." She gave me a devious smile.

"You seem pretty sure about that." I was wondering what Abuelita wasn't telling me. She looked around the kitchen nervously.

"You can't be too careful these days. After last fall, I had Bartholomew run the same checks on Angelito's new girl. I'm not taking any chances." My mouth dropped. Angelito was Abuelita's only grandson. A beautiful twenty-two-year-old, over six feet tall and very muscular. He fancied himself a ladies' man, but he couldn't pick a good girl to save his life. Last fall he'd met a crazy witch who'd tried to kill him and me. Her coven of evil witches were the ones I had to thank for motivating me to take my job as an Intern since they kidnapped Bob to sacrifice him for eternal youth.

"Are you serious?" I was choking on my words. I started laughing. "That is definitely an invasion of privacy."

"Do you want another killer coven in town? They're spending the week in Florida."

That was a very sobering thought.

"OK, that's an excellent point. I agree with that one." I couldn't argue the logic. I glanced over at her and she was smiling wildly.

"Isis, go on a date. Be a girl for once. Look at you: you've lost tons of weight. You're shrinking."

I looked down at myself at her comments. I wasn't that small. "It's called training sessions. Did I mention I do lots of running? I did like four miles this morning."

Abuelita was not buying my defense. I had moved to the lettuce and was almost done with those as well. "By the way, have you heard of anything weird happening at Spring Lake Park?"

"Honey, you need to be more specific. All sorts of weird things happen at that park. Have I told you the story of the guys they found in the bathrooms with their things in a hole?" I had no idea what Abuelita was talking about and my eyes were wide open in shock. I shook my head quickly.

"I don't think I want to hear the rest of that story." I was saved from details when the back door opened. Two of my favorite people walked in, Ana and Gabe. More accurately, one person and one angel stepped in. Gabe was our resident angel and he was absolutely gorgeous. He admitted once that he had been the inspiration for many works of art—not hard to guess that one. Ana was a cute brunette in her late twenties.

I met Ana last fall during our witch crisis. Ana and her boyfriend, Joel, were both kidnapped by the coven. At the time, the pair were living on the streets, jumping from one shelter to another. You'd be surprised how an encounter with evil tends to change people's lives. I got them both a job at Abuelita's and Reapers helped cosign for an apartment for them. It was a blessing they were working here since Abuelita's other employees, aka her family, were totally unreliable. Ana stepped up and took over my hours. Joel worked in the restaurant and was learning to cook. He had also taken over Bob's old role of security.

"Hi, beautiful. You're in early." That was my usual greeting for Ana. Ana was beautiful and one of the nicest girls in town.

"Why thank you, Isis. I miss you, too," Gabe responded instead, giving me an angelic grin.

"You are looking amazing as well, Gabe. What are you doing here?" Gabe was a regular client, but generally came in with the evening crowd.

"I'm in charge of the staff meeting tomorrow, so I need to place an order. Last month, Rafael brought Italian from Little Italy in New York. I'm going to show him up." With that statement, he patted my cheeks and walked over to Abuelita. She gave him a huge hug and the two of them started working on the menu. Ana and I looked at them in awe. Did angels have office politics? I needed to ask Gabe more about this later.

"That's a new one. I hope I'm not the one making that delivery," Ana whispered in my ear. The two of us giggled as quietly as possible. "So, what were you two talking about? You looked worried."

"Have you heard of anything weird going on around town?" Ana was no longer homeless, but like Bob, she still had a connection to the underground.

"Downtown is quiet. Nothing unusual is going on, not even any new faces. I can't say the same for the rest of the town." Ana popped a piece of cucumber in her mouth. She walked around me and grabbed her apron. "How many lunches are we making today?"

"Today?" I was so busy whining, I forgot to check the order list Abuelita kept up front.

"You are in your own world today. Let me grab the list." Ana made her way to the kitchen toward the counter/ bar that divided the kitchen and restaurant area. "Hey, Gabe. Any new people around town?" She asked the angel on her way. I stopped to listen.

"More than usual," Gabe told us over his shoulder as he was pointing at items to Abuelita. "The cities and colleges have done a great job promoting the College Bowl. They're expecting five to ten thousand people. So, needless to say, you have a lot of activity in town. Isis, try to stay out of trouble."

"What? Come on, Gabe. That's not fair. What is that supposed to mean?" I was pretty sure angels couldn't read your mind, but Gabe always had a way of figuring me out.

"Isis, if strange things are happening, you have a way of being in the middle of them. Behave this week."

It was hard to get mad at angels when their smiles could melt icebergs.

"I second Gabe. You're a magnet for trouble and car explosions." Ana gave me a little bump on her hip on her way back.

"Hey, you're supposed to be on my side, remember?" I tried to look intimidating, holding the knife at her, but she wasn't buying it. Ana had spent so much time on the streets that she was a tough cookie.

"Always, but we got work now, so focus, Machete." Ana had nicknamed me Machete since I have one strapped to the inside roof of Ladybug. She thought that was the funniest thing she had ever seen. No support from her on that one. I glanced at her list and realized she was right. I had wasted too much time whining and we had at least thirty meals to make for delivery.

Chapter Four

The day had turned out to be beautiful. The temperature had not reached crazy numbers and by five p.m. it was perfect. After finishing at Abuelita's, I went back to Reapers and spent a couple of hours practicing the bass. I had started teaching myself how to play the instrument. Constantine had my room soundproofed last Christmas after several of my compositions kept making Bob and Bartholomew cry. Every Intern channeled Death's gifts differently. My gifts came across as music. Whatever emotions I created, humans would react to it. That meant joining the local symphony was out of the question.

I loved music, but after hours of practicing, I was tired and bored. Before my new career, I was an avid reader. I loved fantasy novels and comic books. Lately, I hated even looking at the covers. My usual distractions now looked too much like real work now. I tried history books, but Constantine explained those were watered down to keep humanity safe from the real truth. Basically, books were out of the equation. Bob suggested meditation as a way to focus my energy. The only thing I accomplished was falling asleep in the lotus position. Bartholomew joked that I even drooled during my sessions.

My newfound financial freedom was slowly killing me. I made over five grand a month without counting my clothing allowance and had nothing to spend it on. The mall was scary and Bartholomew canceled my Amazon account after I bought a flock of plastic pink flamingos for the grass area. Maybe I didn't have a life, but I was not that excited to go on a blind date with some creepy stranger. At least they didn't suggest online dating. Granted, with Bartholomew being a hacker, anything online was out of the question since he would be able to see behind the smoke screen.

During the days I usually volunteered at one of the nonprofits in town. Of course, those were all closed after five except for Randy Sam's, the homeless shelter. Bob refused to let me volunteer at night there. According to him and Ana, the underground committee loved me for helping them out last fall. They were afraid if I ever got attacked there, many would die protecting me. That sounded like a huge exaggeration, but I wasn't going to argue. Fortunately, one of the volunteers I met in my many wanderings recommended golf. I always thought of golf as something old fat guys did, not even a real sport. I swallowed those words quickly. Golf was a precise sport with a specific form, physically demanding on muscles I never used, and calming.

That's how I found myself at five o'clock at the Texarkana Golf Ranch. The golf ranch was an eighteen-hole club on University Avenue, across from Texas A&M University and by Bringle Lake. For such a small town, Texarkana had some impressive locations. Rumors around town claimed the lake had alligators and somebody had let loose a huge snake. Fortunately, I had never seen either one of those. I pulled Ladybug up to the parking lot near the clubhouse. I wasn't surprised to see all the cars in the area. It was a perfect day for golf.

Mini Coopers looked little, but they were deceiving. They could hold a lot of stuff. I pulled my clubs from the back seat and set the alarm. After a few months of my coming here, Constantine decided it would be a good idea to invest in clubs. So, the boys surprised me with a new set of clubs and a membership in the Ranch. It was a blessing. I had no idea how much the set cost or I would never have dared to leave the house with them. If I was amazed by how much money I now made, I couldn't even imagine how much Constantine was worth, being Death's five-thousand-year-old-Guardian. He probably has so much money that he didn't even consider how extravagant it was to purchase a custom-made, five-star set of Honmas. I could buy a house in Texas for what he paid for the set.

Needless to say, I was very protective of my clubs. At least Constantine didn't pick the gold-plated set, thank the Lord. I entered the clubhouse and Pete was at the desk. He was a middle-aged man with a balding spot who knew way too much about golf. Pete was friendly and very helpful. Pete also gave me a weird look, like he was expecting my "sugar-daddy" to show up any minute. I didn't blame him. I had no skills to be carrying around this bag of clubs.

"Good afternoon, Mr. Pete. How are you today?" The military had taught me it was always safer to be extra respectful regardless of the person. That way they could find very little fault with your behavior. I gave Pete my most charming smile and waited patiently.

"I'm doing great, Isis, thank you for asking. Can't wait for the College Bowl to be over."

Maybe it was the small-town custom or I had been here too often, but Pete knew me by name. I wasn't sure what he was staring at, so I looked over toward the door for a possible culprit. Nobody was there. He just had a weird look on his face.

"I didn't know they were having a golf event during the bowl." I needed to pay more attention to this insane event. Everyone in town was going crazy over it.

"They are not, but the kids across the street are going crazy. I'm not sure if they have a marching band or what, but the noise level is insane." For a golfer, the noise was a significant inconvenience.

"Well, good news, at least they're quiet now." Or as quiet as they could be, considering their actual campus was removed from the main road.

"That's a relief. So, what will it be tonight?" Pete took a calming breath and his chipper disposition returned.

"May I have a bucket of balls and a cart? Planning to do the practice range and then hit nine holes." I wasn't in any rush, but sunset was at eight p.m. I doubted I could finish all eighteen holes and enjoy myself.

An older gentleman walked in and Pete quickly finished my transaction. The faster he could get us out of the clubhouse, the faster his clients could hit the green. I learned that golfers speak their own language and most of the time, I was lost. Nobody ever complained and everyone was amicable as long as you obeyed golfing etiquette. I quickly walked the short distance toward the practice area and waved at several gentlemen already practicing. Golf clubs were a little like gyms. Eventually, you started recognizing the regulars. Since I had plenty of time and money, I was here all the time. So, basically, I was familiar with most of the staff and clients.

"Beautiful day, Ms. Isis. I was worried you were going to miss it."

I wasn't sure why Mikey called me miss. Mikey was at least in his late sixties with platinum-white hair and a fabulous Jersey accent. He was Italian to the core and one of the funniest men alive.

Constantine encouraged my golf addiction and it was becoming a full obsession. According to Constantine, most supernatural beings didn't golf and they stuck out too much. He was highly disappointed when he found out most of the people I met were over sixty. He was afraid I was just making friends with our future customers. It wasn't my fault most people my age were busy having a family instead of golfing.

"I had to work this morning, Mr. Mikey. What did I miss?" I took the empty lane to the left of Mikey. Somehow, we all had our designated spots even on the practice range.

"You will never believe it. George hit an eagle on the eighth."

I was warming up and stopped short. That was almost impossible. George was over eighty years old and a worse player than me, probably because he took too many sips of vodka while he played. So, for George to make his shot with two under par was unheard of.

"I'm officially jealous. That was a huge accomplishment. How did he do it?"

"Easy. The poor thing was sitting on a branch and George nailed him." Mikey started laughing furiously at this point. I stared at him in confusion.

"You lost me. What did he hit?" Maybe Mikey was sharing George's flask this week.

"He hit an eagle, except it was a real one." I shook my head in disbelief, which only made him laugh even harder. "Isis, you didn't think George would ever land an eagle? That old fool is so drunk he sees double. But your face was priceless."

At this point, it was all over. Mikey was rolling in laughter. I wasn't sure who to feel sorry for—the eagle or George having Mikey as a friend.

"You're a nut, Mr. Mikey. Let me get started before I hit a bird myself." I took my stand and started my swings. I always felt stiff every time I came out.

"Just remember, we're aiming for birdies."

More laughter from Mikey followed that. I couldn't help but smile. I felt welcome in this group. I warmed up for about twenty minutes then hit the course. Mikey was planning to have dinner at the clubhouse, so I was expecting to see him before I left. Golf days for some of us were an all-day affair.

By the time I started my game, the other golfers were starting the other half. I was sure the solitude and quiet of the course weren't helping me with understanding humanity, but the peace was terrific. It was like being in the flow when you play music. A feeling of belonging and purpose. My first three holes went reasonably smoothly—not great but not terrible. I made it to the tee box for the fourth hole. Nobody was around, so I took my time to stretch. I grabbed my driver and teed off. Out of nowhere, a guy walked onto the green. I had no idea where he came from, but before I could shout, the ball hit him on the head. How was that even possible? He was at least two hundred yards away. Maybe I should have aimed for birds.

I rushed to the golf cart and drove out to check on the guy. Typically, I would have taken off running, but if he were hurt, I had no way to move him. That would mean running back to get the cart. I parked at least ten feet away from the guy. I wasn't so sure how good the brakes were on that thing and didn't want to add insult to injury by running him over. He wasn't moving by the time I ran over to him. I got on my knees and tried to turn him over.

"Hey, sir, are you OK?" I wasn't sure what to say. My experience ranged from talking to and calming the dead, not waking up the living.

"Ugh." He mumbled something I couldn't decipher. For a guy who didn't look that heavy, I was having a hard time turning him over.

He moved on his own and I took a deep breath of relief. I was sure he wasn't dead or Death would have appeared by now. I was hoping he didn't have a concussion. He slowly turned his face toward me and my smile faltered on my face. The eyes that were staring at me did not look human. He looked more like a rabid dog. I tried to back up slowly. Instead, I landed on my butt. The guy was now moving toward me. I didn't care what Constantine said, we had zombies in Texarkana, and this one wanted to eat me. I scrambled to my feet and took off for the cart. Before I could get in, he grabbed my hair. Of all the days for me to have my hair down, why today?

Last year, if anybody had tried this, I would have ended down and beaten up. But after eight months of intense boxing and martial arts training, my reflexes took over. Instead of pulling away, I leaned back and head-butted my zombie assailant. That was enough to distract him and he released my hair. Our training had never covered zombies, so I was hoping a swift kick to the solar plexus would knock the wind out of him. The zombie staggered back and I took off for the cart.

I rushed back to the clubhouse, trying to get to Ladybug as quickly as possible. I needed to get to Reapers now. I pulled the cart toward the parking area in a hurry and scared the hell out of everyone nearby. Mikey was talking to Pete when I tried to rush by with my clubs.

"Hey, Isis, what's wrong? You look like you've seen a ghost." Mikey was halfway in my direction before I could stop.

"I need to get home. I just got attacked..." I wasn't thinking clearly.

"Attacked? Here? No way. Guys, we need help." Mikey cut me off before I could finish. At a speed I didn't think was possible, he arranged a search party.

"Mikey, no. Wait. This guy is dangerous and out of his mind. You guys could get hurt." I had no idea how powerful zombies were, but I have seen enough of them in movies and they looked scary. It was probably a bad idea to base my strategy on Hollywood's folklore, but that was all I had.

"Isis, we got this. Pete, keep an eye on her. Give her something to calm her down." Mikey was taking off with at least ten other golfers, looking like the mob in Frankenstein. All they needed were pitchforks and they made a perfect picture. I tried to stop them, but Pete grabbed my arm and clubs and brought me to the clubhouse.

"Isis, can you remember what he looked like?"

For the first time, Pete's voice was calm and soothing. I was sure it wasn't good for business to have a woman assaulted on the grounds. Too bad I couldn't explain he had no way of controlling zombie attacks.

"Not really. Average height, black hair, and maybe in his early twenties. I hit him on the head with a ball, but when I went to check on him..." I wasn't sure how to finish that sentence. "He went crazy."

Pete was looking at me, worried. I was visibly shaken up.

"Let me get you some tea. Please stay right here." He told me before taking off.

I wanted to head home and come back with Bob and some firepower, but I nodded. I didn't need Pete calling the police in a panic.

Twenty minutes later, Mikey and his mob walked into the clubhouse. I jumped to my feet and rushed over. I took a quick inventory and they all looked well. I was hoping they hadn't run into the guy. In Texas, over eighty percent of the population carried a gun and most legally. The last thing we needed was panicking men shooting all over the place.

"Is everyone OK?" I was praying nobody was hurt.

"Everyone is fine. We didn't find anyone in the first nine holes." Mickey answered. "What we found was a bloody shirt and some dead animals torn apart. Maybe a wild animal was loose." he looked at his peers, as if making sure he didn't leave out anything. "I'll call animal control and get it checked out. Maybe the guy was bitten by a wild animal and had rabies."

Mickey was reaching for straws with that explanation. We all looked at him a bit skeptically.

"I'm just glad everyone is OK. I'm going to head home now."

"Let me walk you out, just in case. We'll search the place again tomorrow morning during daylight. But whoever he was, I'm afraid he's gone."

Sometimes, Mikey came across as one of those classic mobsters. I was sure if he ever found the guy, or a potential guy, he would make them pay.

"Thank you, Mikey. That would be great." There was no point fighting him. He was worried, and his Jersey accent was becoming more pronounced. He walked me over to Ladybug and stayed till I drove off. I waved several times before gunning it. This was getting too weird for my taste.

Chapter Five

The first floor of Reapers was deserted. The lights in the loft were on though, so I was hoping all the boys were home. I took the steps two at a time. I burst through the door out of breath and was stopped abruptly. I needed baby-cams in the house. I had no clue what my roommates did when I was gone. Bob was sitting at the kitchen table playing an intense game of solitaire. Constantine, on the other hand, was in the command center. That was odd enough since normally that was Bartholomew's area, but Bart was nowhere to be found.

The shocking part was that Constantine was doing Rap God. On top of his incredible memory for pop culture, Constantine was able to recite almost every song with an excellent imitation of the artist. I had not witnessed his rendition of Rap God before, but I was afraid to admit Eminem had met his match. As I was staring at Constantine's insane performance, Bob looked up from his game. He took the pair of earbuds from his ears and smiled at me.

"Don't mind him." He leaned back in his chair and eyed Constantine casually. "He was challenged to duel and he couldn't back down. Are you OK?"

"People keep asking me that a lot lately. I'm not sure." I was still staring at Constantine when Bob cleared the cards from the table. He pulled a chair out for me and got up. Bob was always a gentleman. He headed toward the fridge and started pulling stuff from the shelves.

"Have a seat and tell me what's going on. I baked you a quiche." I was sure I had a look of pure bewilderment on my face because Bob started laughing at me. "Don't be surprised, child. It's a simple recipe. I made two—one with meat and one without."

Did he make two quiches? Bob had too much time on his hands lately.

"Take a seat while I heat you up a slice."

"How often does Constantine do duels online?" I was still wondering about the little scene to my right.

"That I'm not sure. What I do know is his human YouTube channel is tied to the TaylorSwiftVEVO. His ultimate goal is to take the throne from that PewDiePie guy." Bob shook his head, appearing as confused as I was with all this YouTube stuff.

"He actually has fans?" Who in their right mind followed a talking cat?

"He has millions. Based on what Bartholomew told me, Constantine was running a campaign for president, and Death made him stop it." Bob stared at Constantine.

"Constantine for president. The world is not ready for that." Who was I kidding? I wasn't ready for that.

In less than two minutes, Bob had placed a plate of quiche in front of me that was out of this world. The quiche had the whole place smelling fantastic. I was sure it was the smell that grabbed Constantine's attention.

"Take that, Butterfly-Twenty-Three-Twenty-Seven. I'm out." Constantine had finished Rap God and that was the first real sentence he said. I turned around just in time to see Constantine hit a key on the keyboard.

"Please tell me you were not having a duel with a seven-year-old girl." With that nickname, it had to be a kid.

"She's twelve and age is nothing but a number." Constantine was strutting across the room, looking proud.

"Says the five-thousand-year-old-cat." I loved to point that out to him.

"Don't be hating on the skills now. So, why were you so upset earlier, anyway?" Constantine jumped on the table and Bob put a plate in front of him.

"You were listening?" I tried to speak with my mouth full.

"I can multi-task. Besides, I have incredible hearing." He took a bite of the quiche and I was sure he was grinning.

"Bob, this is delicious. I thought you were only going to make gluten-free stuff." According to Bob, Bartholomew's diet was his inspiration for cooking. I enjoyed cooking, but I was never too creative in that area. Bob made it his life passion.

"Oh, it is. Experiment number twelve, but I finally found a good combination for a good flaky crust." Bob smiled like a proud dad. It was crazy the things that made my boys happy.

"Congrats. And I hate to burst this amazing moment of cheering, but a zombie attacked me." With food in my belly, it was a lot easier to deliver bad news.

"I thought we agreed not to use the Z word." Constantine was trying to talk and swallow at the same time.

"We can call it whatever you want, but something crazy is going on." I was not dropping the issue.

"Was it the same one?" At least Bob had practical questions.

"I'm pretty sure it wasn't. They were dressed differently." I told them, questioning myself a little.

"Was he dead?" Constantine threw me off with that one. It was hard for me to tell the living from the dead. Only if I touched a departed soul was I able to say the dead were cold to the touch. Bartholomew had designed a pair of glasses for me to help me identify the living and the dead by heat signatures, since souls don't have any. Unfortunately, most of the time I forgot to wear them.

"I don't know. I never touched him with my hand and I kicked him. I wasn't expecting to be attacked at the golf course, so I didn't bring my glasses with me." I answered Constantine, sure the guy at the course was a zombie.

"So, technically, we can't be sure if it was a walking-dead, a crazy guy, or a demented soul?" Constantine had a point.

"Does that mean we just ignore the whole thing?" I did not like the sound of this conversation.

"Of course not. I didn't get to be this age for not taking precautions. We just need to do a little research. Bob, give Bartholomew a call. Isis, check with Eric for anything unusual. I'll finish my quiche."

I was amused to see Constantine's priorities had not been changed by a potential zombie attack.

Bob grabbed his phone and walked over to the kitchen to called Bartholomew. I wondered where he was that Bob needed to call him.

"Where is Bart?"

"Where do you think? In his shop, working on his robot. I'll be so happy when that silly contest is over." Constantine never bothered to look up when he spoke.

I got up and walked over to the computer area. I needed a quiet space to make my call. I pulled my phone from my pocket and dialed Eric. At least I had remembered to grab it from my golf bag where I usually left it while I played.

"Isis, this better be an emergency." Wow, that was fast. I didn't think the phone rang once.

"Oh, I'm sorry. Are you busy?" I was sure he was just by the way he answered the phone, but it never hurt to confirm.

"Yes, on a date," Eric replied, but got cut off by a female voice that said, "Honey, is everything OK?" I couldn't hear what Eric replied. I guess he put me on mute. A few seconds later he was back. "Make it fast, Isis."

"Sorry, didn't mean to interrupt." Unlike what the boys popularly believed, I didn't have a crush on Eric. OK, maybe a little one, but I was happy for him. At least somebody had a real life. So, I did feel slightly uncomfortable interrupting his date. "Constantine wanted me to check with you and see if you noticed anything unusual lately." I was trying to sound formal and businesslike since I was sure I drove Eric insane with all my questions. I was probably his worst student when it came to martial arts and at times, he acted as if he wanted to kill me.

"More than usual? Besides the hotels getting packed with people for the College Bowl, you might need to be more specific." I was pretty sure he wasn't paying attention to anything I was saying.

"You haven't noticed any walking-dead around town?" Constantine was glaring, but at least I didn't say the Z word.

"What, zombies?" It was the strangest thing he was trying to whisper and shout all at the same time.

"I'm not supposed to say the Z word, but yeah. Have you seen any?" I was aiming for casual as if this kind of stuff happened every day.

"Isis, if this is a joke, it's not funny."

I could tell Eric was moving on his side of the line. I guessed the hot blonde didn't have full access to all his secrets. "I'm sure if something like that were happening, we would have noticed." There was another short pause when I was sure Eric put me on mute again. "I don't have time for this right now. We can discuss tomorrow during training."

"We're training tomorrow? Really?" Oh no, Eric's training sessions were hell on good days. When he was upset, they were straight damnation.

"Obviously Constantine didn't brief you on tomorrow's activities. Have him fill you in. See you at six. Goodbye."

Eric hung up before I could even reply. Tomorrow's session was going to be horrible.

"Well, any news?" Constantine was done with his quiche and was cleaning his face with his paw as he spoke. Moments like this, he looked like a very typical cat. Minus the talking, of course.

"Besides the warning that I'll pay for interrupting, no, he hasn't noticed anything unusual." I walked over to the table and sat down again. "What are we doing tomorrow morning at six?" I was afraid to ask, but I might as well be ready.

"Cross-country training. We're going to train at Ferguson Park. Should help everyone get focused again." I hated when Constantine looked so happy about training. "Back to our small issue. The good news is if Eric hasn't heard anything, it means most people in Texarkana haven't noticed either. Great for damage control."

"I'm glad there is an up to things." I was not very optimistic at all.

The door to the kitchen slammed open and Bartholomew walked in looking angry and covered in more grease. Even his curly brown hair looked matted with the stuff. He was wearing some weird lab coat that had all sorts of wires sticking out of its pockets.

"What could be so serious that you all needed to disturb me?"

Well, I guessed it was the night for me to inconvenience people. I looked at him in utter disbelief. What had happened to my sweet, little Bartholomew?

"Oh nothing, really. Isis got attacked by a zombie and almost died. Just wondering if you would care to help figure out who it was." Constantine was spewing sarcasm left and right. He even said the Z word, which most likely did the trick, since Bartholomew's face turned pale. Not an easy thing to do since he is pretty pale to begin with.

"Zombies? Are you OK?" Bartholomew rushed to my side looking more like his usual self, a concerned little brother. Bartholomew's hazel eyes were huge with worry. Constantine, on the other hand, gave me his most cunning smile. He was evil at times because he knew every button to push.

"I'm fine. One attacked me at the golf course." For only being twelve years old, Bartholomew genuinely cared for people—at least the ones he liked. He had a strange phobia for crowds and strangers.

"What type of zombie was it? Old school slow and sloppy or the new kind, like in Zombieland, fast and agile?"

I had no idea why I was surprised that Bartholomew knew this stuff. I had to blink a couple of times to focus. How could one person switch his attention so quickly from one area to the other?

"I guess fast and agile." At least the one that pulled my hair could move.

"Not good. This could be trouble." Bartholomew sounded like Captain Obvious. Now that he was focused on actual work, I didn't want to ruin his parade. "So, what's our plan?"

"Step one, we need you to track down all necromancers in North America. We need to know if any have made trips in our area."

I had no idea what that meant, so I was glad Constantine was in charge. Bartholomew discarded his lab coat and headed for his command center.

"I'll make us some hot chocolate. We might have a long night." Bob made his way back to the fridge.

"Constantine it sounds like it's time you call Death." I couldn't call her directly but Constantine could. If a group of her nemeses was in town, I wanted Death fully briefed before all hell broke loose.

"Not till we have confirmation. We don't need any false alarms." Constantine finished his sentence by making himself comfortable on the table. I guessed the only thing left to do was wait patiently.

Chapter Six

In the military, I considered myself a morning person. I loved getting up and doing physical fitness with my company. Ever since taking this job, Constantine's work-out program was my least favorite part of the day. His training program felt more like torture sessions. The Army's physical fitness program was a cakewalk compared to Constantine's. I tried to explain to myself why our workout sessions were so painful to me and today was entirely clear. I dragged myself out of my comfy bed at five a.m. to be at this goofy park at five forty-five a.m. after pulling an all-night research session. Constantine had to be a soldier at some point in his long life because he always wanted to be at least fifteen minutes early to everything.

To make Constantine happy, we were standing in an empty parking lot at Bobby Ferguson Park on the Arkansas side of Texarkana before the sun was up. This was crazy; I was staring at stars. This was the first time Constantine and Eric had picked this specific park for training. Most of our sessions were usually inside. Due to the new threat, or Constantine's desire to punish us, we were going to practice cross-country defense maneuvers. From what Bob tried to explain, this would consist of running, jumping, squatting, and dodging things around the mile-

and-a-half trail. I looked around the place and it seemed spooky. The park bordered the Four States Fairground and the campus of the University of Arkansas Community College.

The Fairgrounds was the home for the local fair that took place each year. They also hosted some events including some professional wrestling. I missed the year that John Cena was in town. I'd been to the Fairgrounds a few times, but I'd never been to the park. To be honest, I didn't realize it was an entity. I needed to start paying more attention to the different locations in Texarkana. From what I remembered of the area, there was a lake with a fountain in the middle, a gazebo, and some picnic space. Now that I thought about it, Texarkana—Arkansas and Texas—had a thing for parks with fountains. I leaned against The Camaro, trying to stretch. We all rode out together. No need to draw extra attention to us.

"Why am I even here? I could be expanding our search for those necromancers," Bartholomew complained as he finally stepped out of The Camaro. Constantine had dragged Bartholomew with us. Usually, Constantine gave Bartholomew a pass on physical fitness since he was our computer genius, underage, and never out in the field. But with his increased moodiness, Constantine decided a little fresh air would help his spirit. I doubted he needed air this fresh.

"Bart, sunshine is good for you. Besides, nobody is here yet." If that was Bob's best attempt at cheering him up, he failed miserably. I turned around to contain my laughter as Bartholomew glared at Bob.

"It's not even daylight. I could break my ankles." I had to admit Bartholomew had a point.

"Stop your whining, Bartholomew. You'll be fine." Constantine climbed up on the hood of his car and stretched. "Besides, there are no necromancers within fifteen hundred miles of here. I'm pretty sure they didn't migrate overnight."

I hated that fact. After hours of searching, Bartholomew had found nothing. We had no strange movements from any of Constantine's usual suspects.

"I don't know how he's going to handle the College Bowl when he hates the outside world and people so much," Bob said softly to me. He had walked over to my side of the car while pretending to be stretching.

"I'm thinking tunnel vision. Bartholomew is good at blocking things out when he focuses. Besides, did you notice how competitive he has become?" I replied as we both took a careful glance at Bartholomew.

"I didn't think he had it in him."

I had to agree with Bob. This was a new version of Bartholomew.

"Where is Eric, anyway? It's not like him to be late." Bartholomew was not going to stop complaining any time soon. On the other hand, he was right. I guessed Eric's date kept him up late as well. Ugh, I could puke.

"Calm down, big guy. He's just pulling in. He probably went to the gazebo area instead of this side." As Bob tried to calm Bartholomew down, I noticed the place was pretty extensive. I wondered who was in charge of coordinating the location. We were parked near the entrance closest to I-30.

Eric parked his Ford F-150 right next to The Camaro. I never asked Eric if he named his vehicles, but he looked too serious for those kinds of things. I had no idea how he did it, but Eric looked terrific this morning. His brown hair was tousled and he even looked taller than his six feet.

"Sorry, everyone. I left the vests in my place and had to run back to get them." Eric was running over to open his tailgate as he spoke. Bob gave me a wicked smile. I just shrugged my shoulders. Luckily Bartholomew was in no mood to ask clarifying questions.

"Eric, that's great. I was worried you might forget them," Constantine replied, like that statement made any sense to him.

"OK, everyone, there are three vests in the back. Shouldn't be too hard to figure out which one is yours. Just look for your size." Eric walked over to the driver's side of his truck and pulled out his flak vest. I began to worry that those vests were armor-plated.

Bob, Bartholomew, and I went over to the truck and found our designated vests. My fears were confirmed. The vests had armor plates in them. They weighed at least twenty pounds.

"Oh God, what is in this thing? How much does this thing weigh?" Bartholomew didn't wait long to express his feelings on the matter.

"Ever since you had your birthday, you've become an irate young man," Eric, with a lot of humor in his voice, told Bartholomew. "I'm afraid to see how the teenage years hit you." Bartholomew was a valentine baby. Eric was right. In the last three months, Bartholomew had become angrier. I blamed Constantine for encouraging him to sign up for the College Bowl. Now we were all paying for it.

"I'm not irate. I'm just inquisitive."

"You're whiny. Suck it up and get a move on."

I guessed Constantine was sleep-deprived as well. He usually only chastised me, never Bartholomew. Bartholomew put his head down and grabbed his vest.

It took us a few minutes to get into our vests and get moving. Bob had to help Bartholomew with his. My body went into muscle memory and I was able to lock mine without even looking. I wasn't sure where Eric got them from, but they were military issue.

"OK, everyone, the goal is to work in coordination as well as endurance. I'll take point. The rest of you follow me and do as I do. This is going to be a challenging course."

I had no idea why Eric sounded so cheerful—unless he'd had a great night. Bob gave me a huge smile. I walked up to Bartholomew and just rolled my eyes at the whole scene.

"Ready to die in a new and creative way, Bart?" I gave my voice the most positive sound. That made Bartholomew laugh.

"Great day to try," Bartholomew replied with a huge smile and I winked at him. He was starting to look more like his old self. Maybe Bob and Constantine were right. He needed to get out of the house more.

Coordination and endurance were understatements for our workout. By the time we had made it from our end of the park to the other side, where that stupid gazebo was, sweat drenched my clothes. My thighs were burning, not to mention my shoulders. According to Eric, each vest had plates to mirror our weight and give us a challenge. Unless the challenge was ways to avoid dying, the vests were winning. I thought I was joking when I told Bartholomew about our new creative way to die. But no, this was real. We did lunges across the terrain, followed by ski jumpers, then some weird version of mountain climbers. Maybe Eric had created a super protein shake for himself with extra magic ingredients. Whatever the reason, the boy was possessed.

"I think I'm starting to feel it." Bob was another one of those people that loved torture. So, for him to say he was feeling it—this was brutal.

Constantine was following along at his leisure. With Eric's insane moves, we were not advancing very quickly across the terrain. Constantine had time to chase squirrels around, swat a few butterflies, and even jump over some puddles. In other words, he was having the time of his life. I wanted to choke the hell out of him. When we finally made it to the other side of the gazebo, Eric gave us a five-minute break to march in place. The sun was already out and I was missing my cool stars.

"OK, everyone, make sure you're stretching your legs. We're going to do some sprints on our way back." Eric was still perky. I glared at him.

"Is that guy drinking from that stream?" Bartholomew pointed as he spoke. We all turned around to look at some guy leaning into the water. He did look like he was drinking—or trying to.

Before any of us could reply, the guy fell into the water. Eric took off after him, his cop training probably kicking in. Bob followed shortly behind. Bartholomew and I were too tired to move. So, we slowly walked over, trailed by Constantine, who really couldn't care less what most humans did at times. By the time Bartholomew and I were within fifteen feet of the little stream, Eric was pulling the guy out of the water. I had no idea how Eric managed to make that look so easy with his flak vest on.

"Hey, Bob, give me a hand. Let's see if we can lean him against that tree so I can call an ambulance. He might be hurt or drunk."

Bob didn't get to reach Eric. The guy pulled himself out of Eric's grasp and went berserk.

"Oh, not again." That was all I was able to say.

"Zombie!" Bartholomew screamed from my left side.

"Thanks, Bart. We noticed." I pulled Bartholomew behind me and looked for a weapon. Bob was moving quickly to help Eric.

Our new zombie friend charged at Eric at full speed, drooling like a rabid dog. I had to give it to Eric—he didn't look afraid. Eric dodged the zombie, who started swinging his fist. He didn't have much coordination, but he was relentless and kept on coming. Eric managed to land a punch. His martial arts training took over because he quickly followed the blow with a kick to the chin and a roundhouse to the chest. The zombie went flying. His momentum carried him straight to the tree Eric had wanted to lean him against. The zombie landed with a loud thump that I was sure broke his neck. Constantine was hissing by my right side, looking like he was trying to protect us. Eric and Bob were slowly walking toward the body, but zombie-boy wasn't moving.

"So, when do we call Death?" I asked Constantine. He looked back at me.

I didn't need to turn around to know our fearless leader was now behind me. Everything got very still and even Eric looked pale at seeing Death. "Now would be a great time," replied Death.

"Hi, Boss." Bob gave Death a big wave.

"Death, we can explain." Constantine stepped in, looking rather calm for the situation.

"We can?" I asked him in shock. I hoped he could because I was lost.

"I am curious to hear that explanation." Death made her way toward the zombie. Eric was still standing over the body. "Do you mind if I take a look, Eric?"

"Not at all, sir...Please be my guest." Eric was struggling to make complete sentences. He jumped out of the way and almost ran into Bob. That was interesting; Eric saw Death as a male. I wondered what he was looking at that had him so spooked. Before I could continue pondering, Death turned back around.

"Meet me at Reapers," she said. Death's voice was cold and short. Her demeanor changed and the hairs on my arms stood. I felt a chill run down my back. Before any of us could reply she was gone with the zombie.

"Oh, my Lord, that was scary." Eric was shaking all over.

"Thank you. I've been trying to tell Constantine that those zombies were spooky." For a moment I felt validated.

"Not the zombie. I meant Death. How do you guys handle that every day?"

Great, Eric was talking about Death. I shook my head in disappointment.

Constantine spoke in a low voice. “This is not a normal case. Something is wrong. We’ve got to go. Training is over.” We all looked at him, suddenly concerned.

“Constantine, what about the body? We need to file a report.” Eric recovered quickly and was back in cop mode.

“We’ll take care of it. We need to head back and we’ll fill you in later.” Constantine took off the way we had come. The rest of us followed in silence.

Chapter Seven

Our ride from Bobby Ferguson Park was quick and uneventful. We were all lost in thought. Not even Constantine spoke during the whole drive and he was notorious for his ongoing commentaries. We looked like a funeral procession when we entered the loft. Death was by the glass windows, staring at the first floor—or at least I thought she was. I never considered how far in distance or time Death was able to penetrate. Those thoughts were too spooky for me to ponder. The odd thing was, she was holding a mug.

"I hope you don't mind that I finished your coffee, Bob. You have a fabulous blend." I had no idea Bob had his own blend of coffee. I was a tea and hot chocolate drinker, so I never asked.

"Not at all, boss lady. I'll make some more." Bob rushed to the fridge to grab his blend. I wasn't sure why Bob kept his coffee in the refrigerator.

"How bad is it?" Constantine was not wasting time beating around the bush. He jumped on the dining table and got comfortable. Bartholomew and I looked at each other and then followed suit. We each took a chair on the far side of the table so that we could see everyone better.

"If it's any consolation, he wasn't a walking dead." Death took one more sip of her coffee and placed the mug on the kitchen island. She turned to face the rest of us, waiting for the information to register.

"Does that mean we don't have a zombie problem? That's a good thing, right?" Bartholomew was optimistic, but by the look on Death's face, we were in trouble.

"My dear, it's worse. He wasn't dead, but he wasn't human. Whatever happened to him somehow fragmented his consciousness." Death had turned back around to face the glass again.

"Death, what happened to his soul?" Constantine said the words very softly, almost afraid to ask.

"It's gone."

"Gone? Not again. Is someone stealing souls again? How is that possible if he was moving around?" I wasn't in the mood for more angry witches.

"Not really stolen. More like not truly connected." Death turned around. "Let me explain. This might be an oversimplification, so bear with me. When a human being dies, the mind and the soul forge into one and they transcend the body. They become part of the higher consciousness. The mind grounds the soul to this world while the soul waits for nirvana. Hence the reason we can transport them to their next stage. In the case of this boy, his mind was gone. There was nothing there to direct the soul in the process so the soul just vanished from existence."

"Is that what happens to people who are in a vegetable state?" Bob asked from the kitchen counter as he poured Death more coffee. He handed Death her mug.

"Thank you, Bob. Not really. In a vegetable state, the soul and mind are still fully conscious while the body is the one not reacting. The process is still the same. In this case, something had altered the process and created an abnormal condition I can't explain."

The fact that Death couldn't explain it was scarier than anything else.

"Just to confirm, you don't have the soul?" Constantine asked.

Death shook her head. That was the reason she was upset. A soul was lost and there was no way for us to find it. We were in serious trouble.

"How many more are there?" She was looking out the window again as she spoke.

"He was the third one I've seen, but the only one that died." I volunteered the information since nobody else was going to.

"Complicated. They are vicious and dangerous, but if you kill them, their souls end up in limbo. We need to figure out what causes this and reverse it. In the meantime, find a way to contain the victims and not kill them." Death looked at us expectantly. "Unfortunately, Isis, your gifts will not work on them since their consciousness is gone."

Oh, this was getting better and better.

"That's all. For a moment, I thought this would be hard. You wouldn't happen to know who exactly is causing this, by any chance?" Constantine was dripping with sarcasm that, apparently, Death ignored since she smiled.

"I can only think of one being capable of causing these results. Bartholomew, dear, do you mind connecting me to my sister, Pestilence, please?"

Bartholomew jumped from his seat and headed for his command center.

"Big screen?" he asked as he approached the desk.

"Of course, nothing small for her," Death answered as she walked behind him.

"Sister. Death has a sister?" I asked Constantine in the most urgent tone I could find while keeping my voice low.

"Of course. She is the oldest of four, duh," Constantine replied like I was supposed to know this.

"Wait, what? Death has two more siblings?" I was dumbfounded. When did this happen?

Constantine walked over to me and slapped me on the head. "Ouch!" I yelled, not because it hurt, but for the principle of the matter. Thank God his claws were not out.

"Seriously, girl, aren't you Catholic or something? Doesn't Father Francis have Sunday school classes for adults?"

He was looking serious. I was Catholic, but probably not a very good one by the looks of it.

"I'm so lost, Constantine, just tell me." I wasn't too proud to ask.

"You've heard of the book of Revelation, last one in the bible? Ring a bell?" Constantine was looking at me, focused as he spoke, so I just nodded. I was afraid to open my mouth and sound even dumber. "That's a blessing. The four horsemen of the apocalypse are Death and the rest of the siblings."

"Oh, God. Is judgment day coming? Is this the apocalypse?" My voice cracked, and I was on the verge of a panic attack. How did I miss this? If I worked for Death that meant the other three horsemen were also real. I was going to faint.

"Isis, calm the hell down and shut up. There is no apocalypse happening. That only happens when all four horsemen get together and this hardly warrants a family reunion. By the way, that piece of information was in your manual. When are you planning to read the darn thing?"

Constantine had a way of stopping my rambling hysterics with facts. I was going to burn that manual.

"Well, ahhh..." I wasn't sure how to reply.

"Yes? Spit it out." Constantine did not wait patiently at all.

"I thought it only covered the fringe benefits and Bartholomew explained those. I didn't think you would explain world destruction in an employee manual. Anyway, what is Pestilence like?" I wanted to change the subject as quickly as possible.

“I prefer zombies over that crazy hag.” Constantine looked like he wanted to cough up a hairball. I looked over toward the screen area where Bartholomew had finally connected to someone. I was planning to get up and go over for a better view.

“Don’t even think about it. This is a family discussion. Bartholomew, get over here, now!” Constantine yelled the last part to make sure Bartholomew heard him. “You both stay out of the range of the camera. You can see her but don’t let her see you.”

Bartholomew ran back to the table and retook his seat. I had forgotten all about Bob until he placed two cups of hot chocolate on the table. One for me and the other for Bartholomew. He also brought Constantine a bowl of coffee. Constantine drank coffee? I learned something new each day. On the screen, we could see a large conference room with a table, but nobody was around.

Bartholomew filled Constantine and me in on the current situation. “I finally got some guy named Eugene to pick up my call and then the conference call. He said he was going to find his mistress and would be right back.”

“Mistress? They call her that?” I couldn’t believe it. Bartholomew just shrugged.

I was sure we were waiting for at least ten minutes when finally, a woman appeared. Constantine kept telling us she was doing it on purpose to annoy Death. If she was annoyed, Death never showed it. She was just drinking her coffee. I finally got to appreciate Death’s outfit and it was stunning. She was wearing a white Michael Kors sheath dress with bell-cuff bateau-neck from his Neiman Marcus collection. Too much free time had me spending time online researching Death’s outfits, and lately, she was into Neiman Marcus. I couldn’t blame her. Even if she weren’t Death, she could stop traffic.

While Death looked like a Greek goddess with that long, silky, brown hair, her sister, on the other hand, was a live version of Barbie. Pestilence's hair was so blonde it looked like it was made of gold threads. She had the big boobs with that tiny waist that wasn't possible for any human to ever achieve and bright-blue eyes. Death's white dress was in direct contrast to Pestilence's black pantsuit. If I didn't know any better, I would have put money that Pestilence had a new suit on.

"Pestilence, dear, so nice of you to take my call." Death was overly sweet with her sister.

"Like I had a choice. Last time I didn't answer your summoning, you just appeared. So, to what do I owe the pleasure of this call or did you just miss me?" Pestilence was a royal queen B. No wonder that poor boy called her mistress. That chick was nuts. Constantine looked like he was playing dead on the table. He didn't like her.

"Dear, we had a deal. You wouldn't make any more zombies and I'd stop sending Constantine to inspect your labs. What happened?" That explained Constantine's dislike. Death took another sip of her coffee as she waited. She could make a great poker player.

"Nothing happened. We haven't made any zombies. We had one little outbreak years ago and you went ballistic. You and your soul thing." How old was Pestilence? She was acting like a spoiled brat; she even rolled her eyes at Death. I was shocked at her attitude.

"That's interesting. I just found one in Texarkana." Death looked at her sister and waited for a comeback.

"Why is it every time something weird happens, I get blamed? Have you ever considered it wasn't me or that I was being framed?" Pestilence crossed her arms over her perfect chest and stared back at Death. This was sibling rivalry at its worst. I was so happy I was an only child.

"Easy, Pestilence. This kind of work could never be created by a human alone. So, if you didn't do it, are you sure one of your Interns didn't create one by accident?" By the way Death said 'accident,' I was sure she didn't believe that part.

"Of course, we didn't." Pestilence was not budging.

"And you have nothing missing that could be altered in any way?" It seems Death was not budging either.

"Who do you take me for, an amateur? I have centuries running a lab, remember?" Pestilence was so offended she didn't look at the screen. I wasn't sure how Death was handling this so well. If I ever talked back to my godmother, she would have slapped the smirk off of my face. The funny part, my godmother wasn't even a violent person, but she believed in respect.

"Of course, I know you're good at your job. That's why I'm calling. Nobody else has the talent and skills to pull this off. So, do you mind checking, just once? Please, for me?"

Bartholomew and I exchanged wary glances.

Constantine supplied the missing information for us as he continued his dying cockroach pose. "Yes, she is that vain that she will fall for that. She can't resist Death praising and begging her. I'm going to be sick."

I shook my head and turned back to the conversation on the screen. It seemed Constantine was right because Pestilence had stopped pouting.

"I know this is going to be a waste of time, but fine. We conduct a monthly inventory of all our supplies, so it will be simple to find any discrepancies. Rookie, I need you to compare the last two inventories you conducted."

Pestilence was looking off-screen to whoever Rookie was. There was a pause and the rest of us couldn't hear Rookie's response.

"What!"

OK, that was not good. Whatever the guy said agitated Pestilence. "It seems I have a small problem, hold on." She stepped off camera.

Death took a deep breath and walked over toward Bob, who was holding the coffee pot. He refilled Death's mug and she just smiled at him. They were so comfortable in that routine I had a feeling Death drank lots of coffee with Bob. Death slowly walked back to the monitors in time to see Pestilence storming back.

"How bad is it?" Death asked before Pestilence could even get started.

"Why does it have to be bad?" Pestilence was trying to look as pleasant as possible.

"Because the vein on your temple is pulsating and that only happens when it's bad. So, what happened?" Death just stared at her sister.

"It's probably nothing, but it seems we haven't conducted an inventory since Halloween. It's not Rookie's fault. He's still new, and it was flu season, anyway." The way Pestilence said it wasn't Rookie's fault, you knew he did it.

"You have no way of quickly knowing if anything is missing?" Death was not giving up.

"It might take us a little while, but we can figure it out." Pestilence did not look happy at all.

"That might be the case, but I don't have a while. I'm sending my team over to help you." Pestilence's face mirrored my reaction of shock. I was hoping Death was joking.

"You can't be serious?" It seems Pestilence was hoping for the same.

"My dear, Pestilence, they will be there today. So, have your rookie send the directions to Constantine now. Not a negotiation." Death's tone became hard and final.

"Fine, but I have my staff meeting. They can be here at one. Goodbye." Without waiting for a reply, she disconnected the signal.

"That was pleasant," Bob added cheerfully.

"Here we go again. This is going to be a giant mess," Constantine whined from his position. Somehow, he managed to still have his head hanging from the table.

"Am I going to meet your sister?" I knew that if Constantine was worried, I should be, too.

"Not just you. Take Bob and Bartholomew as well. Pestilence doesn't deal well with women." Death gave me a wink and a smile. Oh, this trip was going to be great. "Constantine, you know the drill. Call me if you need help." Death put her mug on the counter and walked out the door. That was probably for our benefit since she can disappear at will.

Bartholomew checked his phone and figured out where her crazy lab was located. He jumped from his chair, ready to do something.

"That's interesting. According to this address her lab is only in Hope, Arkansas. That's less than an hour from us," Bartholomew informed us.

"Of course, it is. Pestilence always has to be close by. That crazy hag." Constantine pulled himself together and was sitting back up in his Sphinx pose. "Good news. At least, Isis, you still have time for your spa day."

"You're kidding. With everything going on and you still want me to get my nails done." I was sure too much blood had rushed to Constantine's brain while he was lying with his head over the table.

"Isis, your nails are atrocious." Constantine was looking at my hands like they were a dangerous science experiment. I instinctively made a fist to hide my nails.

"I'm a musician; it comes with the territory." I kept breaking my nails setting the strings lately.

"Girl, I knew Prince and his hands were marvelous. Not an excuse. Newsflash, you are a girl, not an infantry soldier. You are going. The appointment is at nine a.m. You have plenty of time. Now, you all go shower, you all stink."

With that last remark, he jumped from the table and headed toward his room.

"This really sucks." I was gloomy now.

"Relax, Isis. Ms. Patty is amazing. Besides, you might like it."

That was the last thing Bob said before he headed out the door to his room. I didn't want to know how Bob knew of Ms. Patty's skills.

"Isis, you handled witches and ghosts. You can handle a manicurist," Bartholomew said on his way to his room.

I was not winning this battle. There was a part of me that wanted to rebel. Unfortunately, the part that was still a soldier had a hard time disobeying a direct order. I figured by now that part would have disappeared. It seemed marines were not the only ones that were always marines. Once a soldier, always a soldier. I took my hot chocolate with me and headed to my room to shower. Constantine was right. I did stink.

Chapter Eight

Who goes to a hair and nail salon at nine in the morning on a Tuesday? It was sad, but I had never been to a nail place in my life. The only time my nails were painted, it was by my godmother. In the military, I never had to worry about nails since having color on your nails was against regulations. So, at twenty-six, I was terrified to enter a beauty salon. That was so depressing. Maybe this was another of Constantine's punishments. I took a deep breath and got out of Ladybug. I practiced breathing exercises when I was nervous or stressing. That was probably the only part I mastered from my meditation classes—how to slow down my heart rate and relax.

Constantine had given me directions to Patty's place. According to Constantine, Patty rented a couple of booths in the beauty salon with hairdressers. Not sure what that meant. I was under the impression you could get your nails done at the same place they did hair. I guessed that was not always the case. Based on the little bit of data Bartholomew gave me, before running off to work on his robot, Texarkana had over thirty nail salons. It probably helped that the city had a couple of cosmetology schools.

I looked around the area, stalling for time. Pleasant Grove, or PG as most people called it, was not my part of town. The salon was located on North Summerhill Road next to a small cemetery. The location was odd since the area looked more residential than business. Somehow, they had created one of those little plazas with several businesses in the same building. From the front, the building didn't look very impressive. I slowly walked toward the door. A hospice occupied the space to the left of the salon. I wasn't sure if it was an actual residence or just a place for the staff to work. I was praying for the second. I usually ran into a lot of souls at hospices and I had a tough time telling the living and the dead apart.

I opened the door and a bell attached to the handle announced my arrival. Great, now they knew I was there. I took another deep breath, debating if I should bolt out. This was such a horrible idea. The central area of the salon had a small waiting area with a couch facing the front door and a chair to the right. A large TV stood to the left of the door and I was grateful it was off. That space was too small for that TV. I was sure people would go blind sitting right next to it. Past the couch was a large room with a window that opened onto the waiting area. The room had a couple of those strange chairs you only see in hair salons. Thank God for TV. At least I knew what I was looking at. The room was empty which validated my theory that nobody goes to hair salons on Tuesday mornings.

"You must be Isis."

I was lost in my thoughts when a tall lady with spiky, reddish-black hair surprised me.

"Hi, yes, I'm..." I was at a loss for words. How do you introduce yourself to strangers who knew your name?

"Constantine said to look for the little girl with the scared-to-death look. You fit the description."

She smiled kindly. Thank God because I wanted to crawl into a hole and then strangle Constantine. "I'm Patty." Patty stretched out her hand. Her handshake was firm but gentle. She had black glasses with rhinestones on both sides. She wore purple scrubs like the ones you see at doctors' offices. Patty was probably at least six feet tall and full-figured. I was surprised. Most ladies in Texarkana were short. Somehow, I managed to find all the tall people in town. I had to smile. At least around them I fit in.

"Thank you for seeing me," I finally said after an awkward pause. She smiled brightly. I was pretty sure she was waiting to see if I was going to bolt out the door.

"Are you ready?" Patty asked me very gently like I was a spooked wild animal. I was afraid my voice would crack so I just nodded. I needed to get a grip here; it wasn't like I was going to an interrogation chamber. "Good. We're going to start with a facial and back massage. Follow me."

Patty was good at her job because she led me down the hall holding my arm. It was probably a good thing because I was ready to turn around. Constantine never mentioned anything about a back massage. We went down to the last room on the left. The place was designed so that the hall ended in front of a sink, with a bathroom on the right and a strange small space I couldn't see on the left.

"Isis, this is Valentina. She is going to do your facial and back massage."

A woman with fabulous blown hair came out of the room. She was in great shape with beautiful black eyes. While Patty radiated warm vibes, Valentina looked like an older, cool sister. It was weird since they were both probably around the same age, mid-to-late forties.

"Hi, how are you?" Valentina took my hand and smiled. She had an accent, maybe German or Russian. How did she end up in Texarkana?

"Hi, nice to meet you." I shook hands with Valentina who was beaming with joy. Was every person in the beauty industry this excited to see people?

"OK, sweetie, you're heading in that room with the closed door." Patty was pointing at the room right next to hers. It was also the only room that had a door. "When you're done, come and see me back here. I'll be finished with Ms. Smith by the time you get back."

I smiled at Patty and realized a little lady with gray hair was waving at me. That was probably Ms. Smith. She had one hand soaking in some strange contraption and looked like she was having a ball. I was afraid to move, but then Valentina led me into her room. The space was dimly lit with only a small lamp on one side. Soft jazz was playing and I was grateful for the music. It was the only thing familiar to me. A weird table with a hole in one side stood in the middle of the room.

"OK, dear, please take your shoes off and undress from the waist up, unless you'll be more comfortable without your pants. If you are, please make sure to keep your undergarments on." Valentina delivered her speech like it was the most normal thing in the world.

"You want me to do what?" Maybe this was a torture chamber and I didn't know it. Valentina was looking at me with a smile on her face and a faint sparkle of amusement in her eyes.

"Is this your first massage?" she asked very softly. My mouth was dry, and I wasn't sure if the fear was showing on my face. I nodded again. "That's a good thing. Listen, most people don't know all the health properties of massages. I do a combination of the Swedish and deep-tissue massages. They are therapeutic and help to relax the muscles and joints, promote better circulation, and helps release toxins from the body." Valentina sounded like a college professor. She took great pride in her work. "My goal is to make sure you're comfortable and that your body gets the care it deserves. Your job is to relax and not get any tenser than you already are. Now I'm going to step out and let you get undressed. When you're done, lie on the table face-up, under the sheets. Trust me; you'll be OK."

Maybe it was the tone of her voice or the look of reassurance on Valentina's face, but I believed her. I nodded again and she stepped outside. I wasn't familiar with massages, but I heard some were pretty expensive. I took a few more deep breaths and settled myself. I had been through war and even survived witches' attacks. I could handle a little massage. I took off my shoes, my top, and bra. I was not ready for my pants. Looking around the room, I slowly climbed on the table and covered myself as much as possible with the sheet. I was surprised how comfortable it was. I started to work on my breathing exercises. A few minutes later, there was a soft knock on the door.

"Are you ready?" Valentina was saying from the outside.

"Yes." I was as ready as I ever could be. She walked in and smiled.

"Good. All I want you to do is relax. Close your eyes and just let go. I'm going to hold your space, which means I will be silent while I work. If you need anything, please just let me know. I'll let you know when it's time to turn around. You ready?" She gave me one of those smiles you give lost little kids. I nodded back afraid to say a word.

Trying to relax was hard, but I closed my eyes and slowly breathed in and out. I wasn't sure how I was going to relax since I was more stressed just coming in. I focused my attention on the music. Valentina placed her hands on my scalp and her touch was firm but soothing. I could feel the tension on my skull as she worked her magic. Valentina massaged my face, worked on my arms and legs before having me flip over. I didn't how she did it, but I felt the pressure in my body melt slowly.

"OK, sweetie, I'm going to step outside and let you get dressed. Take your time getting off the table."

Valentina's voice sounded far away. Did I fall asleep? How long was I out? I slowly moved around. I couldn't describe it, but my body felt light and more limber. I rubbed my shoulders. I didn't realize how much tension I was carrying till it was gone. No wonder people did this all the time. It was amazing. I'd dreaded coming, but now I didn't want to get up. A clock by a table on the far end of the room told me I had been there thirty minutes. I needed to get moving.

When I stepped outside the room, Valentina was waiting with a large glass of water. Constantine explained that everything was paid for, but I still needed to leave a tip. I wasn't sure how much of a tip to leave, so I left a twenty on the table.

"How do you feel?" Valentina was looking at me with concern in her eyes.

"That was amazing. Thank you so much." I truly meant it. Valentina rushed at me and gave me a huge hug.

"I'm so happy. Here, make sure to drink plenty of water. You'll need it to flush all the impurities we moved in your body. I hope next time we will do a full body. Patty said you do lots of running. A massage will be great for your legs." Valentina looked like a kid in a candy store, way too excited.

"That sounds good. I think I can handle that." Honestly, I probably could get used to massages. If she could work my leg muscles the same way, I would seriously pay money for that. Lately, I was always feeling tight and tense. Except now I was ready for a nap.

"Look at you. You look radiant." Patty was coming out of her room, smiling at me. "Are you ready for your nails?" After the massage, nails looked like a breeze.

"Sure, let's go."

"Bye, Isis. See you next time," Valentina said.

I followed Patty to her room. Across the hall, two older ladies were sitting at a hair-washing station. The hair portion of the salon was set up with the sinks in the back that all the stylists shared. The two older ladies had their heads wrapped in some plastic caps. I had no idea what was underneath them, but it looked scary. I took a seat in front of Patty with my back toward the older ladies, but I could still hear them.

"What color do you want your nails?" Patty was asking me as she looked at her extensive collection. I hadn't even thought about that.

"Oh, wow. I have no idea." How do people choose? Is the nail color supposed to match my clothes? This was really hard.

"What's your favorite color?" Patty asked, looking at me.

"Blue." Are people allowed to wear blue nail polish?

"Yes, I've got just the thing for you." Patty walked over with a couple of bottles and started pulling instruments from her table drawer. They looked sharp and scary. I had no idea what was going to happen, so I concentrated on something else.

"Honey, let me tell you what happened. Janice's husband went crazy." The older ladies were talking to one another and I focused on them. "One day he had the flu. The next day he woke up like he was possessed. He started screaming and hitting her. She said he even tried to bite her."

"You're kidding me. What did she do? Is she OK?" I heard the other lady reply.

"Honey, you know Janice is a tough cookie. She took one of her iron skillets and nailed him in the head. She went straight Madea on him." The two ladies started laughing. "She had that poor boy committed and they're running a test on him. Bless his heart."

Ouch. I'd been in the South long enough to know that "bless his heart" was not a nice thing to say.

"Don't pay too much attention to those two. They're notorious for exaggerating," Patty said. "Sorry about that. It just seems a lot of weird stuff is happening lately." My cheeks were heating up and I knew I was blushing.

"Honey, a lot of weird stuff is going on. A couple of my clients who are nurses said there's an increase of strange cases at the ER. They're afraid a new drug might be going around." Patty was busy cleaning my nails and trimming the cuticles.

"We don't need any of that around here," I replied softly. I wasn't sure what to think, but I was impressed by Patty's skills. She started filing my nails and giving them some shape. I was mesmerized by it. We fell into a comfortable chitchat as she did her work.

Chapter Nine

Have you ever wondered if you were privileged—or even spoiled? For the first time in my life, I had to ask myself that. Unfortunately, the answer was yes. How did I know I was both spoiled and privileged? After spending fifteen minutes arguing about which car to take on our little Pestilence field trip, the thought became clear. I really wanted to drive, but both Bartholomew and Bob believed I was a menace behind the wheel. Bob refused to ride in Ladybug, and Bartholomew didn't want to ride in the Beast, due to the lack of space. I had to agree with him on that one. With all the equipment he was taking that couldn't be exposed to the elements, the Beast was out.

Constantine was still pissed about Pestilence in general, so the argument put him over the edge. He sent us in The Camaro just to get rid of us. He also refused to go with us. Every time someone mentioned Pestilence, he started coughing up hairballs. Trust me, it was pretty disgusting. It took us another ten minutes to load up all of Bartholomew's gear before we were ready to go. I wasn't sure what Constantine was planning to do while we were gone. He said he had calls to make and people to set up. The cat had more people than the pope.

Bartholomew had programmed the address into The Camaro's GPS. He was in the back seat, working on his computer and pouting. I was not very familiar with twelve-year-old boys, but if Bartholomew was any indication, they were moody. Bartholomew was still upset that he had to leave his creation. At the same time, he was asked personally to check out the site. He sat in the back and ignored us. I was ready for this season to pass.

Bob was in his driving mode, which translated into absolute focus and silence. He was ultra-vigilant for strange anomalies on the road. On several occasions, his paranoia had saved us from wild shooters in other missions. I had to give it to him. He made the job look good. That left me to stare into space. We were driving east on I-30, heading toward Hope, Arkansas. For some strange reason, this was one of my favorite routes. The Interstate was clean, the trees always changed colors during the fall, and most of the time drivers were respectful. I preferred going east on I-30 rather than west. That drive was dull and boring. Today, I was in no mood to admire the beauty around me. I felt edgy and nervous.

"This is weird. According to the GPS, the directions they gave us are the same ones as the chicken plant in Hope." Those were the first words Bartholomew had said in the last fifteen minutes. The lab was only forty-two miles away, so in 'Texas driving' was less than forty minutes.

"Are you sure?" Bob asked Bartholomew, without taking his eyes off the road.

"There is a chicken plant in Hope?" Unlike Bob, I had the freedom to turn around to talk to Bartholomew.

"Yeah, and it's the largest employer in the area, with over five hundred employees." I always wondered where Bartholomew found his information and how he managed to know it would be important.

"OK, how many people live in Hope?" I probably needed to do my research, but why bother when you have a human encyclopedia with you?

"Over ten thousand people. I'm surprised. I figured it was as small as Wake Village or Nash." At least he was still capable of being surprised.

"Wasn't President Clinton born in Hope? I passed a signed around there all the time." That sounded like an important thing to know, but it was a little before my time. I didn't know many kids who cared about politics. I was one of them. My godmother didn't help. She never followed politics or the news. "I think they have a museum for him. We should go check it out."

"Nah, we're good. It's probably not that great, anyway." Bartholomew never turned down a trip to a museum.

"Are you feeling OK?" I had to ask. He couldn't be this stressed about the competition.

"Of course. It just seems such a long drive just for a house."

Long drive? The boy made me drive to Dallas to check out the Perot Museum. There was something shady here. "OK, back to the chicken plant. According to these coordinates, Pestilence's lab is right underneath the chicken plant." He was changing the topic. I bit my lip and let it go. I would find out eventually. I needed to get back to work.

"Bart, how is that possible? I'm sure the city wouldn't authorize two businesses on top of each other." I have seen some crazy zoning issues around these parts, but even that one would raise red flags.

"I don't think the city or the workers in the plants know about it." Bartholomew's voice got soft as he spoke. I turned around more in my seat so I could have a better view of him.

"Please explain and stop leaving us in suspense." I wanted to know what was going on before we got to the lab.

"Yes, Bartholomew, please clarify. In English and slowly. No 'genius' talk today."

At last, the Jedi master decided to join the conversation. Thankfully, he was focused on the road and not trying to watch Bartholomew.

"That's the amazing part. The lab is underneath the plant. According to the directions, we must enter through the side door across the street."

Sometimes, dealing with a supernatural being will make your head hurt. My head was pounding with information overload right about now.

"Great, so we have a secret underground lab just around the corner from us. I'm not feeling cozy here." Pestilence gave me the creeps. Having her this close didn't feel like a coincidence.

"Don't go over-analyzing things, Isis. We need your focus on the here and now and not conspiracy theories." That was a joke. The chief conspirator on the planet was giving me advice.

"Fine, but I don't have to like it." I turned around and crossed my arms. I could do pouty as well as any preteen boy.

"We're being followed." Bob's voice was grave. "Isis, are you ready?" Bob gave me a quick glance as he cautiously maneuvered through the traffic. I reached under my seat and pulled out a Smith & Wesson from the holster attached to the bottom of the seat.

While most schools and federal installations practice emergency drills, our family practices in-case-of-being-followed drills. I had never killed anyone (besides Trek) and I wanted to avoid the experience as much as possible. At the same time, I had no problems laying down suppressive fire. I just prayed that nobody on the other side walked in front of the bullets. I checked my gun and clicked the safety off.

"Bart, are you ready back there?" Everyone had a part to make sure we were all prepared. Bob was the driver and, if I was in the vehicle, I was the gunner. Bartholomew and

Constantine were supposed to lie down in the back seat and avoid getting killed. I liked their jobs better.

"In position." I glanced quickly over and he was indeed lying in the back seat with his computer on his chest.

"Well," he said. "That answers Death's question if Pestilence's lab was bugged."

"You talked to Death?" I had missed the follow-up meetings. I sucked at my job at times.

"Yeah, while you were getting your nails done. Death had several things she wanted me to look for while we were there." Bartholomew was a persistent, little man. He was still typing in the most bizarre position.

"Bob, are you sure they're following us?" I was hoping he was wrong. Unfortunately, a white car suddenly pulled up to us on my right. Before I could speak, the driver was firing at us.

"Holy Jesus Christ!" I screamed as I ducked down. Not sure why I yelled. Probably out of habit. The Camaro, like all the vehicles in Reapers, had bulletproof windows and armored sides.

At such a close distance, the driver was able to put a few cracks in my window, but nothing dangerous. The driver was a redheaded woman with huge sunglasses and a weird, straw hat. Unfortunately, it didn't take her long to figure out the windows were bulletproof and turn her assault elsewhere. Bob had hit the brakes to let the white vehicle pass us. He wasn't fast enough. Our speed-racer friend hit both of the tires on my side. Once I was out of her line of fire, I lowered my window and fired a few shots her way. At least she had the common sense not to do a U-turn.

"Oh God, Constantine is going to kill us," Bartholomew was saying from the back seat. "How bad is it?"

I didn't want to know. I knew Bartholomew was right, and Constantine was going to be livid.

"Is everyone OK?" That was part of the drill—checking for injuries and shock victims. Not sure why, since Bob could tell we were OK. He pulled over to the side of the road. Traffic was light and I was praying nobody was paying us that much attention.

"We're good, but not the tires." I was Captain Obvious today. I was pretty sure Bob knew precisely what the damages were.

"I only have one spare with me," Bob said, like he was disappointed with himself. Like anybody else carries more than one spare. I had a feeling that from now on all of our vehicles would carry at least two extra tires each.

"I need to call this in." He shook his head and pulled out his phone. "Let me see how bad the damage is and I'll call the boss."

Bob was a brave man. Bartholomew and I watched him climb out of The Camaro. He took a couple of pictures and then proceeded to make the call. I was so happy I was inside the vehicle. In this situation, I was more afraid of Constantine than the shooter. That girl had just signed her death sentence. The Camaro was family.

"How many contracts do you think Constantine will put out on that girl?" Bartholomew asked me from the back seat.

"Enough to make sure there's nothing left of her but fertilizer." It was sad, but Constantine did not know the meaning of overkill. That girl was doomed.

"You are so right." Bartholomew laughed softly. "Whatever is going on at Pestilence's lab, this shooter is involved. I'm sure of it." I glanced over so I could better see Bartholomew.

"How can you be so sure?" I had plenty of people that tried to kill me on a daily basis. This could be any one of them.

"Nobody knew we were coming unless they were listening in to our call. Our system is clean. I check daily.

We're less than ten miles from the lab with an easy exit right behind us. Anybody who knows enough about Pestilence probably knows about Death. We're driving The Camaro, a very distinct car. Not very hard to guess where we're going. We told them the time. All they had to do was wait for us to pass."

I leaned my head against the headrest. He was right and this made things worse. Whoever this person was, she was armed and dangerous. They were smart enough to plan this little show and had no issues killing us.

"This means whatever is going on in that lab is worse than we expect if they don't want us there," I told Bartholomew. Between zombies running loose in Texarkana and killer drivers, this week was turning out to be full of excitement. I was ready for boring times. Bob got back in the car, his face a little pale.

"Do we want to know?" I didn't, but figured I should at least check.

"No, no you don't. He's sending Reggie over. I feel bad when he finds that girl."

I had to agree with Bob. I didn't want to get killed, but I feared the wrath of Constantine more "Bartholomew, please call Pestilence and let them know we're running late."

He leaned his head against his door and started scanning around. "Isis, I'll watch the front. Keep an eye on the rear. Shoot anything suspicious."

I turned completely around in my seat, sitting in the lotus position and facing back. If Constantine needed Reggie, Reggie would drop anything for him. Reggie was the number one towing service for all the supernatural community in the four-state area. The wait was going to be short. Still, we were not taking any chances being sitting ducks again. Being late was going to make a horrible first impression.

Chapter Ten

It took less than ten minutes to reach the plant after Reggie was done. I had never been to a chicken plant. To be honest, I have never been around live chickens. I had no idea what to expect so I wasn't prepared. From the outside, the plant looked like any typical business except it was huge. It was at least the length of a football field. The place was massive. The plant was the only building for acres. On the opposite side of the street was a large parking lot for all the employees. Next to the parking lot stood a pretty decent-size pond. It looked out of place.

It wasn't the building that took my breath away, but the smell. 'Chicken plant' was a very politically correct way to say 'slaughterhouse.' As soon as we reached the first building, it hit us. It was the most wretched smell I had experienced in my life. That was saying a lot since I'd been around soldiers after days of training with no shower. Those boys smelled like roses compared to this. Bartholomew stated gagging and Bob was looking ill. I was taking shallow breaths, trying to avoid puking or passing out. The Camaro was bulletproof, but not smell proof.

Bob drove as quickly as possible past the plant without drawing too much attention. Fortunately, on the far end, the air was breathable again. The GPS said to take a left at the end of the road, which was weird because the road curved right.

"Bartholomew, is this correct?" Bob asked before turning to the dirt path.

"Yeah, you're supposed to head toward that old building. I'm texting them our codes now and they'll let us in." Bartholomew barely looked up as he spoke.

"I know that's not her lab. How do we get in? Cause it's not the chicken plant." It better be around here somewhere or I was going to be mad. It would suck to get shot-up for nothing.

"Regardless where it is, this is a great location for a testing site. Nobody is ever going to complain about suspicious smells." Bob was right. With that plant there, nobody would ever question anything weird.

"In that case, I'm glad we're not chemists. I'd hate to work here," Bartholomew added from the back. "Bob, go straight through the doors. They're expecting us."

Right on cue, the doors to the odd-looking shack opened up. It looked like an old, abandoned barn. As Bob pulled in, we realized we were descending a long tunnel. The doors closed behind us and fluorescent lights came on.

"Underground lab. I told you it was amazing." Bartholomew's voice reached a new high. He was so excited. We pulled up to a very bright area. It looked like a landing zone of some kind.

"OK, this is impressive. How far down are we?" I was looking around the place, probably not as excited as Bartholomew. Underground sites were a little intimidating for me. I feared the dirt above me would one day come crashing down.

"At least seventy-five to a hundred feet, based on the height of those walls. Not to mention it will need separation from the plant and lake above." Bob was giving the place a clinical analysis. I was ready to be out of there. The three of us slowly climbed out of The Camaro.

I felt small in the broad area, especially knowing it was all underground. A group of ten men, all wearing white lab coats, were waiting by a door on the side of a large hallway. Bartholomew and I exchanged looks and slowly made our way in their direction. Bartholomew looked as concerned as I felt. Bob was back to his paranoid self. He had his hands behind his back as he walked. For any bystander, he looked casual, but I knew that pose was for easy access to his guns. By the time we reached the men, one was talking into what looked like a walkie-talkie. A large pair of double doors burst open and the men moved out of the way. They looked like a receiving line, waiting to shake hands and kiss babies.

"Well, it's about time you finally showed up. Do you think I have all day?" Pestilence was yelling at us even before she entered the room. In less than ten steps she had reached us.

"Sorry, ma'am, we had some car issues getting here." I wasn't sure why I was explaining.

"Excuse me! Do I look old enough to be a 'ma'am' to you? Besides, I was talking to the Intern." She didn't even look at me when she spoke. She turned her back on me and looked at Bob, waiting for an answer.

"Sorry, Ms. Pestilence," Bob told her in his calmer voice. "I'm not the Intern. Isis is. I'm just the driver."

Thank you, Bob. I was afraid if I spoke, I was going to say something I would regret. Besides, the look on Pestilence's face was priceless. Pure shock and horror all at once. It was beautiful.

"You are the Intern?" The way she said it, I was pretty sure I was supposed to be offended.

Pestilence was beautiful. The kind of woman that made the Victoria Secret models look like washed-out rags. Unfortunately, she was also arrogant and condescending. It took away from her beauty.

"Yep, that would be me." I gave her my most charming smile. Pestilence had the nerve to walk around me, inspecting me. No wonder Constantine couldn't stand her; she was vile.

"Well, this is a surprise. I guess my dear sister always has a new trick up her sleeve." She finished her inspections and just stared at me, revolted by something. "Let's get this done. I don't have all day."

Pestilence did a perfect about-face and walked right back where she came from. She passed her receiving line and snapped her fingers. The men fell in right behind her, all in step with one another. At least if they ever retired, they could start a marching band.

"Oh, she's pleasant," Bob whispered to Bartholomew and me.

"Like an executioner. I'm sure she was in charge of the guillotines in France," I replied. That woman was nuts.

The three of us followed slowly behind. We entered a large conference room. The walls were white with a white marble table and white leather chairs. A wall of flat-screen TVs was adjacent to the entrance door. Pestilence walked to the head of the table at the opposite side of the room. The wall behind her was glass, overlooking the most significant lab I had ever seen. The view almost felt like Reapers.

"Feels familiar," Bartholomew whispered.

"I was thinking the same thing," I replied.

To the right of Pestilence sat all of the men. They all faced straight ahead, looking focused. I led the way toward the front of the room on the left-hand side. As the Intern, I was the one responsible for talking. By the expressions on Bartholomew and Bob's faces, they were not planning to sit near Pestilence if they could avoid it. So, I was the sacrificial lamb here.

"As you can see, this is a waste of time. This is a secure facility and nobody has ever broken in." Pestilence was pretty sure of herself.

"This facility has always been here?"

I was grateful Bartholomew asked. I was curious as well.

"No, we just moved about six months ago. It's good to move around, keep the humans on their toes." As Pestilence finished, Bartholomew and I looked at each other. This was suspicious. "So, I don't see the need of you guys being here. I think we all can agree this facility is very safe and call it a day."

"We wish we could do that, but Death is expecting a full report. She wants Bartholomew to run a quick scan of your inventory as well as check for wiretaps on your phone and electronics."

Pestilence was making a weird pucker-face as I spoke.

"Of course, she does. Why wouldn't she?" She ran perfectly manicured fingernails down her hair. After my day with Patty, I could tell who spent money to get their nails done. "Fine, let's get this over with. The Rookie will be your contact here." She pointed to the far end of the table.

A young black man probably in his early twenties waved at me. I waved back. He was cute for a chemist. He had a military haircut, high and tight, and a sweet smile. For some strange reason, he looked out of place among the rest of the guys.

"Next to him is First generation, followed by Second, and so on, and so on. You get the point." The gentlemen waved back at us. Bob, Bartholomew, and I waved a bit slower. Why didn't her people have names? "I've got things to do, so make this quick."

Before any of us could speak, she got up from her chair and headed toward a door on the left-hand side of the room. The two older men next to her, Eighth and Ninth generation, got up and followed her out.

"OK, you heard the mistress, let's get moving," a tall guy in the middle said. If I was counting correctly, he was Fifth generation. Why was he giving us orders? "Rookie is going to give you a tour and then you can be on your way."

"As exciting as your plans sounds, unfortunately, Bart, here, needs to check your system. So, would you mind showing him your computer area?" I didn't want to be here anymore than they wanted us, but we had a job to do. I smiled brightly and waited for Fifth to process my demands. It was weird, but from Second to Seventh generation they all looked the same. They were all different ages. They got older with their names. They were different races, but they all still had the same weird aura about them. I was tempted to open my third eye and check, but I had no idea what nasty tricks Pestilence had here.

"This is most irregular, but if it will get you out of here faster..."

He folded his arms in front of his body and stared down at me. I didn't know how to break the news to him, but he was not intimidating. I was pretty sure I could break him in half. We stared at each other for about thirty seconds before he finally realized I wasn't backing down. "First, please accompany this child to our stations and make it quick."

First got up and headed around the table. Bartholomew looked at me questioningly. I winked at him and nodded. He got up from the table and followed the eerie guy out. At least that one seemed semi-human.

"Thank you. We appreciate it." I could be cordial even if people were rude toward us.

"Yes, of course." Wow, he was just as arrogant as his "mistress." That title was so not appropriate. "Rookie will guide you on your tour. The rest of us have work to do."

With that, they all headed out the main door.

"You guys are with me. Please follow me this way." We followed the young man out of the conference room.

"Your name is Rookie?" Bob asked, as casually as possible.

"Oh no, my name is Eugene. Rookie is my Intern name, since I'm the youngest here," Eugene replied with a smile.

"Wait. Youngest? You mean all those men are Interns?" I was in shock. Did I miss that memo?

"Of course. Every ten years Pestilence hires a new Intern and everyone else gets promoted up. I'm entering my second year. The rookies get all the low jobs and duties."

For being at the bottom of the food chain, Eugene did not sound upset. He led us a down the hallway past The Camaro. It seemed the weird ramp just kept going down.

"Here we are. Floor entrance to the lab."

Eugene pulled out a square card and placed it next to the door. It looked like the security system they had at hotels. The door clicked open and we went in. The lab was even bigger inside. This whole facility was surprisingly deceiving. The place was almost the same size as the plant above us. We passed the first table filled with beakers and things boiling in little pots.

"Is this stuff safe?" Bob asked, staring at a purple liquid bubbling in the corner.

"Oh, don't be worried, we're all immune to everything. Gift for working for Pestilence," Eugene replied very proudly.

"That's great, but we don't have your gifts. Don't you have some hazmat suites we can use?" I replied, looking around, just as worried as Bob. I did not want to die of the black plague here.

"Oh wow. I forgot. Follow me."

We rushed back toward the door area.

"You should be fine; you haven't been here too long." He looked around the lab, concerned. "Civilians on site, lock it up!" Eugene yelled as loudly as possible. Three other Interns ran inside and started covering things on tables. Great, we were going to die from contamination from our distant cousins. He turned back around and handed Bob and me each a set of chemical suits—the kind you see in movies that come with a mask and everything.

"Thanks," I told Eugene. I turned my suit over to find the zipper and found a large hole in the shape of a heart in the back. "I think this one is defective." I handed him the suit. Eugene looked at it, entirely shocked.

"What the...? This is most irregular." He turned it over a few more times and finally gave up. He handed me another suit and tried to find someplace to put the bad one. "Aren't you guys immune to death, being Death's Interns?" He was looking at me very seriously.

"I'm just the driver and Bartholomew is the computer genius. Isis is the North America Intern," Bob informed him again.

"And no, we are not immune. For me to get the job, the other Intern had to die," I told him as I struggled into my new plastic suit.

"So weird, Pestilence has never had a female Intern," Eugene said almost to himself. That explained a lot.

"That lady has a mirror on-the-wall complex," Bob whispered to me. Luckily, Eugene was busy watching his peers locking things up. I had a feeling Bob was right. Pestilence did not like to share the center stage.

"Is it me or is the chemistry here scarier than our supernatural community?" I was feeling out of place with all the chemicals and crazy white walls.

"Amen to that. I'll take a trip to Jake anytime." It was terrible when Bob would rather see the devil than the chemist. Bob was terrified of Jake.

"Let's get this party started. You all look pretty secured. Everything looks safe now. Let's go."

I wasn't sure if the suit was going to work since I could hear Eugene perfectly well through it. I looked at Bob, who shrugged his shoulders. I did the same and followed our very happy guide.

Chapter Eleven

Two hours later, we finally returned to the conference room. I had never been so happy to be out of the labs. Eugene had us walking up and down tables full of strange concoctions ranging from toe fungus to smallpox. I was grateful the Army had given me a vaccine for smallpox, but I was still paranoid. Sweat was running down my body, but I refused to take the plastic suit off. I wasn't sure how much protection it was providing, but I wasn't taking any chances. I felt itchy and nasty all over. I wanted a hot shower to scrub the potential contamination off. Even Bob was looking a little pale. Chasing ghosts was looking better and better. I was glad my job did not include exterminating the human race.

When we entered the conference room, Pestilence was already there. She was on another conference call with Death. I could tell from the video feed that Death was at Reapers. Constantine was sitting on Bartholomew's computer desk with his head dangling down. I guessed he was still boycotting having to communicate with Pestilence. Pestilence had changed outfits and was now wearing a navy-blue mermaid dress. I learned that from following Sofia Vergara on Instagram. Yeah, I had too much time on my hands, but Sofia was fabulous.

"The boss looks great in the suit." I had been staring at Pestilence and it wasn't till Bob spoke that I noticed Death had a different suit on.

"Wow, you're right." Death was wearing a blood-red suit that made her hair and eyes shine. I was wondering if Bob and I had similar visions of Death right now.

"Are you kidding? He's scary." I forgot Eugene was right behind us. I turned to answer his question. He was pale and his eyes looked like they were going to pop out of his head.

"Breath, Eugene, before you pass out." I waved my hands in front of his face, hoping to give him extra air. I doubted it would help, but it made me feel useful.

"Oh good, your little Intern is back."

I felt more than saw all eyes on me. I slowly turned around to face Pestilence, who had so kindly introduced me. That woman did not like me. I waved casually at them.

"How was the tour?" Pestilence asked in the fakest tone I had ever heard.

"Impressive. You run an amazing facility." I could give credit to where credit was due. I didn't have to like the fact that their job was to wipe out humanity. I could respect the science as long as I was far away.

"Did you find anything unusual?" Death's voice was neutral. I wasn't sure what she was expecting. Constantine stopped trying to decapitate himself with the table and started paying attention.

"Besides a vandalized hazmat suit, the lab was immaculate. What did you think, Bob?" I asked. Bob was great at finding the smallest clue. I think Death chose the wrong Intern.

"Isis is right; everything looked very organized and clean." I notice Bob was staring at the screen and not making eye contact with Pestilence. That was very interesting.

"What do you mean by vandalized hazmat suit?" Constantine asked from the back. I could always count on Constantine to ask pertinent questions.

"One of the suits had a large heart cut out from it." Bob was not letting that go. The whole idea of somebody tampering with a safety suit was very troubling for him.

"Now that's interesting." Constantine looked amused. His next comments were cut off by Bartholomew walking into the room.

"Hi, Death!" Bartholomew yelled from the door. Bartholomew loved Death. He beamed when she was in the room. Looking over at the screen, I could see she was also smiling at him.

"Hi, dear. Did you find anything?" I was pretty sure Bartholomew could do no wrong in Death's eyes. Bartholomew walked over to be directly in front of the screen. He was carrying one of his tablets with him.

"You were right; the place was bugged. We found microphones in all the major rooms. I'm leaving some of my equipment here for First and Second to complete their sweep of the place." Bartholomew was talking to Death, so he didn't get to see the look on Pestilence's face. It was a mixture of shock, horror, and absolute disgust. This was going great.

"Pestilence should be very pleased to know her lab will be back to normal soon."

I couldn't tell if Death was being serious or just messing with her sister.

"Of course. Thank you, darling," Pestilence replied and I couldn't tell if she was serious or not.

"Anything else, Bartholomew?" Death brought the conversation back to business.

"Yeah. They have two crates of some experimental virus that are missing." Bartholomew was reading from his notes as he spoke.

"What?" Pestilence screamed. She had a very high-pitched scream. My ears were ringing. "Impossible!"

Fifth stepped up to take the blame. "Mistress, this is completely my fault. I told Rookie to focus his efforts on the deployment of the new stomach and flu virus. We got busy researching killer bees and their potential for carrying the plague."

First stepped up right next to Fifth. "Mistress, it's my fault. I was responsible for inspecting Rookie's work. I was distracted developing another acne cream."

"You guys made something good for humanity?" I asked Eugene.

"Not at all. The cream is to promote acne. Pimple creams sell like hot cakes around here," Eugene whispered back in my ear.

Ninth stepped up with his hands behind his back. "Mistress, I approved the change in duty. It is my fault. As the senior ranking here, I take full responsibilities. Punish me."

I turned around to stare at the Interns. They were all standing in a straight line behind us.

I was amazed. In a lot of workplaces, the employees were backstabbing one another to move up the corporate ladder. I had never seen such a unified front. Eugene was the rookie around here, but he was not alone. He walked back to join his peers and take his punishment.

"Fine, I got it." Pestilence waved her hands to calm her Interns. She was outnumbered and they looked like they were going to die for this. I had to give it to Pestilence—her nails were amazing. "Since everyone is personally responsible for this, I expect it to be corrected. Little man, did you find anything else?"

Bartholomew rolled his eyes at her and turned to address Death. At least his attitude problem was paying off for something.

"Not bad. He's not backing down," Bob whispered in my direction. I smiled in reply.

"According to the note the thief left, she plans to prove she is the better Intern than all the guys."

The room was speechless.

"Wait. The thief left a note? Did she sign it?" I was walking up to Bartholomew to look closer at what he was holding.

Bartholomew read from some note on his tablet. "Yeah. From the personnel records, her name is Emma and she was an accountant here. She quit back in December."

Pestilence was outraged. She had her hands on her hips and was tapping her foot. "She quit because I was getting ready to fire her. She was acting irrational, playing loud music in her cubicle, and talking to herself. She couldn't get along with her supervisor and he is a saint."

Bartholomew and I stepped slowly away from her.

"Did she leave any other clues?" I wanted to get out soon, so I was going to focus everyone on the facts.

"Something about 'keep an eye out for Fla...'" The note was ripped and we couldn't find the rest of it. She left it on the empty pallets, so who knows what happened in five months." Bartholomew looked over at me expectantly.

"That is not helpful at all," I said.

"Maybe it's Flakka, the new drug that's out," Bob suggested.

"There's a drug called Flakka?" I wasn't sure why I was so surprised. It wasn't like I kept up with the drug scene. "What are the symptoms?"

"According to reports, it creates hallucinations and victims appear to be possessed and almost zombie-like," Bob filled in for the rest of us. This information would have been useful when I was attacked at the golf club.

"That's the problem; the note ripped off there," Bartholomew replied sadly.

"Of course, it did because having all the details in a full confession was asking for a miracle." I shook my head as I spoke. Bartholomew and Bob were trying to hide their smiles.

"What exactly was in the pallets?" Death's questions were a lot more valuable than mine.

"They were some kind of mind-controlling substance that affected the brain and other systems," Bartholomew replied

Eugene answered from the back. "That batch is harmless. Unfortunately, we were never able to get it to do anything besides give people headaches. It was stored for destruction at a later date."

"Besides, she's an accountant. How much harm can she possibly cause?" Famous last words by Pestilence. She was completely dismissing the situation. I wouldn't discount an accountant. I had seen a few movies when I was in the military with accountants who were insanely dangerous.

"That might not be completely true. According to her personnel file, she had a master's degree in chemistry from Harvard. She has a pretty impressive background." Bartholomew was helping to make Pestilence even more annoyed.

"Yeah, whatever." I could tell Pestilence was losing patience with us. "We need this fixed and our supplies returned. Rookie, you will go with them and assist in this search. How is that for inter-agency cooperation?" Pestilence winked at Death. She was a little too cocky for my taste.

"I'm impressed, Pestilence. I like your initiative." Death was praising her sister while Constantine coughed up an imaginary hairball in the back. "Anything else we need to know about our little accountant?"

"She worked for us for almost thirteen years. She was passed over for the Intern position twice," Eugene answered us from behind. He truly looked troubled by the identity of the accountant.

"Fifth, since you have taken personal responsibility for this, I want to know the possibility that our virus can be mutated. Rookie, you are on the ground, gathering intel. And you...?" She stopped her order distribution long enough to stare at me.

"We're good. Constantine issues our assignments." That was the perfect thing to say; she looked physically ill. Guess the horrible feelings were mutual between Pestilence and Constantine.

"Fine. I'm sure it has a plan for you." Pestilence refused to say Constantine's name. That was classic. "Let's just get this done. I'm sure my stuff is sitting in the poor girl's house, harmless.

"Let's hope you're right, Pestilence." Death replied dryly to her sister. "Isis, make sure to bring Eugene back with you and make sure he has at least an overnight bag. This could take a while."

Death was not sharing Pestilence's optimism by the looks of things.

"Yes, Death." That was all I said and Pestilence gave me the worst look ever. Death terminated the conversation and Pestilence turned her full hate on me.

"As soon as Eugene and Bart collect their stuff, we'll be out of your hair," I told Pestilence, giving her my best smile. She was not interested in it at all.

"Rookie, hurry up and get packed. I would hate to keep my sister waiting." With that, she made her exit from the room.

"Make yourselves comfortable; I'll go help Rookie," Ninth told us very softly. For a guy who looked like he was over ninety, he moved fairly quickly when he wanted to. Bob, Bartholomew, and I made ourselves comfortable by the table in the leather chairs.

Chapter Twelve

Our drive back from Hope was uneventful. We didn't encounter any angry accountants waiting for us. That was probably a blessing for her since Bob had moved the flamethrower to the front. Honestly, the boys did not know the meaning of overkill. Eugene sat in the back with Bartholomew. They spent the whole drive discussing the security breaches Bartholomew had found at the lab. Bartholomew had worked with First and Second to implement some immediate changes to secure their location. They gave him access to their system. Bartholomew was going to patch in from Reapers and do his magic.

It was almost seven by the time we made it to Texarkana and we were all starving. I was sure Constantine was probably hungry as well. That cat refused to eat those weird cat nibbles or cat food in cans. I didn't blame him. That stuff smelled disgusting. Fortunately, for all of us, he was in the same food cycle as the rest of us, making it easy on everyone. The one thing he did very catlike was his water bowl. He drank plenty of water all day and had a cold bowl of water by the kitchen sink.

A new gas station had opened a year ago on the Nash exit to I-30. It was a gas station with sit-down restaurants attached to it, whose menus ranged from fried chicken and BBQ to donuts and burgers. I had no idea how they managed to have all four restaurants next to one another, but the layout flowed very well. We did a quick stop so that everyone could grab some food. Bob ordered Constantine brisket and chicken. No sides required for that one. He was a real carnivore.

When we pulled into Reapers, Constantine was waiting for us on the first floor. I wasn't expecting anything less. His beloved The Camaro was hurt. He looked larger than ever and he was glaring. We slowly dismounted the vehicle, afraid of his reaction. Constantine walked around the car, inspecting the damage. Eugene was looking at him, concerned. Bartholomew gave him a hand signal not to say anything. After his lap around The Camaro, he stopped in front of the passenger front door. He stood on his hind legs to get a better look at the bullet holes. We all waited in silence.

"Boss, we got dinner." Bob was a brave man.

"I want her head on a platter." He hissed the words out.

"OK, Salome. Do you want her spiked as well?" The words left my mouth before I could think. I was hoping Constantine did not get the comparison to John the Baptist.

"Burn the body. Don't leave any evidence of her. Trust me; she will not be hanging out in heaven with John when all this is done." He was serious. That accountant was in trouble if Constantine found her.

"Holy hell! He does speak," Eugene said from behind Bob. I had forgotten he was there; he was so quiet.

"You saw him talk on the conference call, remember?" Did I imagine that he was in the room?

"I thought that was a magic trick Death was doing to confuse us. You know, the horsemen are quirky that way." Eugene was turning pale as Constantine slowly made his way over to him.

"You must be the rookie." He looked Eugene up and down and took a few steps back. "Are you going to be OK? You're looking ill." Constantine was right, Eugene looked like he was going to puke. "Bob, grab the rookie and take him upstairs before he faints on us. Give him some water. He's going into shock."

Bob grabbed Eugene by the arm and led him up the stairs. Eugene kept looking around in a daze. I felt terrible for him. I had a feeling this was his first experience with the supernatural world. At least his third eye wasn't opened. If that ever happened, Eugene would probably have a heart attack.

"Is he going to be OK?" Bartholomew asked as he watched Eugene make his way up the stairs, shaking.

"Yeah, he'll be fine. Isis, get him a shake. It'll calm him down. I'll give him a few minutes to process everything before going up. Bartholomew, help Isis take the food up." Constantine was shaking his head as he spoke. "That's the problem with the other horsemen. They don't prepare their Interns to face the real world. They keep them sheltered in their little human bubble."

That was a different way to see things.

"Should we take his clothes upstairs?" I hadn't considered where Eugene would be sleeping once we got home.

"Not necessary. He'll be staying with Bob in the spare bedroom," Constantine replied.

I was confused. Since when did Bob have a spare bedroom?

"Bob did some work in his place while you were in Canada in February. We opened the place up and added another room." Bartholomew was getting good at reading my facial expressions. I was so grateful that he filled in the blanks for me.

"Well, in that case, we'll see you upstairs."

Constantine went back to contemplating The Camaro. I followed Bartholomew upstairs. I wasn't sure how to help Eugene. When I was having my panic attack, I went to Constantine for help. When Constantine was the one that scared you to death, I wasn't sure what could be done to help you. Bartholomew was hungry, so he climbed the stairs two at a time.

When I opened the door, Bartholomew was busy taking out the food containers from his bags. Bob had Eugene sitting at the kitchen table drinking what I hoped was water. I handed my bags to Bartholomew and walked over to the kitchen. Eric's shakes were a staple at our place. Nobody knew what they were made of and we didn't ask. The results were the same. Within less than twenty-four hours, soreness disappeared, aches vanished, and you almost felt normal.

"Here, drink this." I handed Eugene the bottle. He took it with trembling fingers.

"How do you handle this?" There was a faint shiver in his voice.

"I had to stop trying to make sense of everything with my mind and just go with the flow. It sounds a bit odd." Eugene was looking at me like he had never seen me before. "My mind couldn't process everything I was seeing and experiencing, so I learned to let go. Our minds have limitations set by our upbringing to protect us. It gets easier to handle. Your mind expands and you go on." After eight months at this job, I was sure my mind wanted to go on strike and stop expanding.

Eugene took a sip from his shake. "What is this?"

Bob and I looked at each other before answering.

"A tonic to help you heal. You don't want to know what's in it," Bob answered him. He walked over to help Bartholomew.

"I have no idea what's actually in it," I said. "A wizard makes it and makes healing faster. Drink it and relax.

Constantine will be back soon." By the look on his face, I did not make him feel better at all, but he continued sipping his shake. Outside of his element, Eugene seemed so young and sweet.

I left Eugene to his drink and helped Bartholomew and Bob get all the food ready for dinner. If possible, we tried to eat on real plates and not take-out containers. Constantine felt uncivilized when we used paper plates.

"OK, people, fill me in. What have you learned?" Constantine had walked in through his kitty-door. Usually, he would step in and start talking when he arrived at the table. I think he was trying to prepare Eugene for his arrival.

"The accountant's name is Emma and, based on her personnel file, she has family in Texarkana. Her mailing address is her parents, here in town," Bartholomew told Constantine.

Constantine joined us at the table as Bob passed everyone their own plate of food. Eugene was looking better by the minute.

"She was passed over for the intern position twice," Eugene added from his chair, looking down. "She was always really nice to me, asking questions and checking on me. I didn't realize she was that angry at us. She never said anything."

"It sounds like she was pumping you for information. Did she know about your virus?" Bob asked Eugene after he settled himself in his chair. The food smelled amazing.

"I guess. She was always really curious what I was working on. I really shouldn't have talked to her about it, but she worked there. I had no clue how she felt." Eugene looked so sad and hurt about the whole thing.

"Don't beat yourself up. It's not your fault. Pestilence has horrible hiring practices. That alone is chemistry for disaster." Constantine was right. How could a woman be sexist toward other women? "Did she say what she wanted?"

"To prove she is the better Intern," Bartholomew said, chewing his food.

"That's not good," Constantine replied. He had stopped eating and was staring at Eugene.

"Constantine, do you know what that means?" I wasn't in the mood to play twenty questions today.

"What do Pestilence's Interns do?" Constantine asked. We all stared at him.

"We make plagues, bacteria, and viruses. Anything to eliminate people." Eugene's answer was a little too soft for my taste. But at least he was talking to the talking cat. That was a huge start.

"How would you prove you're the best Intern?" This time Constantine did not wait for a reply. "By creating the biggest plague that would take out the most number of humans in the shortest amount of time."

"That's impossible. To do that with those crates, she would have to re-engineer the virus and mutate it. She's only an accountant."

Eugene sounded like Pestilence. Why was it so hard to believe that an accountant could do those things? And why did they all disregard her master's in chemistry from Harvard?

"She did it and now we're finding zombies all over Texarkana. If she has two crates of that stuff, who knows how many people she could infect and how she is doing that?" Constantine went back to eating, as if the zombie apocalypse was not upon us.

"Guys, not to sound like a broken record, but the College Bowl is this weekend. There will be an additional ten thousand people in Texarkana that could be infected or become carriers." Bartholomew just had to add numbers to an already grim situation. Just what we all needed.

"We don't have a lot of time. We need to figure out what she did." Constantine sounded very calm.

"If I had a sample, I could run some tests," Eugene said.

"You're in luck. We have a fresh body in the lab downstairs ready for you," Constantine answered with a smile.

"We have a lab?" What lab was he talking about?

"Yes, we have one. Death converted our firing range into a lab. It was easier than going to the morgue." In less than ten hours I had lost my range. Constantine gave me a sad look.

"I could start now." Eugene looked ready to do something. I wondered if he felt guilty for losing the crates.

"That would be great. Bob, would you show him the way?" Constantine said.

"Sure thing, boss." Bob smiled at Eugene. "Bring your dinner with you. I'll show you your room while we're down there." They both left in a hurry.

"I'm going to run some checks and see if I can find anything else on our accountant," Bartholomew said, getting up from the table. He headed to his computer station to start his search.

"What do you want me to do?" Everyone seemed to have a job and purpose except me.

"Get some rest, Isis. You're going to have a packed week coming up." Constantine looked at me very sternly.

"It's either feast or famine for me." I felt out of place now.

"Oh, that's another horseman's job." Constantine smiled. He had a point. "You have a package on the kitchen counter. Get some rest. You'll need it."

"Thanks, Constantine."

He winked at me. I got up and took the rest of my beans and potato salad with me.

I had figured it was another gift from another Intern. I grabbed the package and headed toward my room. I walked over to my stereo system and blasted the music. I was grateful for the soundproof walls. I sat on my bed and read the address on the box. It was a gift from my godmother. I ripped the box open and found a smaller box. Inside the little box she had placed a silver half-moon pendant with a necklace. She included a note in her fancy handwriting,

"I love you and miss you, baby girl. This is for your protection." I read the note aloud. I needed to see her soon. I missed her. I had never been superstitious, but after working with Death, I stopped taking chances. I put the necklace on and went to the mirror to look at it. It was lovely. That small token made my day better. I grabbed my guitar and decided to play along with the music. It was a good day to play.

Chapter Thirteen

I wasn't sure when it happened, but in the last six months, I had developed an obsession with running. In the military, running wasn't my favorite form of exercise. Now that nobody was forcing me to run, and I could take as many detours as I wanted, running was fun. It was the one thing I could do without needing hours of training and getting beaten-up. I enjoyed target practice at the range, but I had to concentrate there. Running outside by myself was relaxing and all thoughts disappeared. The only thing to focus on was the road.

I shouldn't have been surprised when I was wide-awake by five-thirty in the morning and full of energy. I crashed so early that my body was able to get its required eight hours of sleep and then some. I had no idea what time everyone else went down. The bad thing about a soundproof room is that you can't hear anything else outside your door. By the time I stepped out of my room to go running, the loft was dark. That was a blessing as it meant they were in bed. Normally, Bartholomew would be playing Warframe when I headed out for my runs. It was a blessing he was a genius because with his schedule he would never have made it in a regular school.

I usually ran three to five miles depending on the weather and my schedule. This morning I had plenty of time and nothing to do. I decided to make it a long run and do ten miles. Lately, I was doing long runs every three weeks. I was due for one since I'd missed the one I scheduled the previous week.

The goal was simple. Ten miles and get it done in eighty minutes. That would translate to an eight-minute mile. I, eventually, wanted to do my long run in seventy minutes. The good news with running, there was no rush. I had the rest of my life to achieve my goal. Unless somebody killed me first. And with my job, that was a huge possibility. I did a few stretches and took off. I had a road vest on since it was still pretty dark and I didn't want to get run over by the commuters heading to the Army depot.

It was almost seven-thirty by the time I made it back to Reapers. It took me longer than eighty minutes, but I found a new little trail past the railroad tracks that was a lot of fun. I made my way through the Reapers security system to find the practice area packed. I guessed I had missed the memo we were having a meeting this morning. Constantine was sitting on top of a bench. Bob was leaning against the weights. Poor Eugene was holding on to the inverted ab bench. I was pretty sure he had no clue what the bench was for. Eric was in as well, looking fabulous in his workout pants. He did have a very sexy butt. The only one missing was Bartholomew.

"How was your run?" Constantine had a strange habit of never saying good morning. He just started talking.

"Pretty good. Found a new route." I spoke to him as I joined the group. Bob threw me a towel, and I started drying my face and hair. I knew I probably stunk, so I stayed a few feet away from the group. "What did I miss?"

"Eric just finished telling us our dead friend in the lab has not been reported missing." Constantine made it sound like we had a new visitor, not a corpse.

"With all the new people in town it's hard to say, but I don't think he was local." Eric sounded disturbed. I wondered if he had ever killed anyone or if this was his first one.

"Eugene, did you have any luck with our guest?" Hey, I had no issues calling him a guest. It was better than "the dead guy."

"Constantine was right," Eugene began, and I knew that was a bad way to start a sentence. Constantine's ego would go through the roof. "I found traces of my virus. But that guy had so much other stuff in his system it was impossible to test properly. I tried all night, but couldn't find a clean specimen."

That explained why Eugene looked like hell. Well, now that I noticed, he was wearing the same clothes he had on yesterday.

"Have you slept, Eugene?" I felt guilty. I was feeling all refreshed, and everyone else looked like hell. OK, everyone except Eric and Constantine. Constantine didn't count since he never seemed bad after an all-nighter. I wondered if he had other superpowers I didn't know about. Eugene tried to cover a yawn.

"Sorry. I thought it was going to be easy. Pull some blood, take a few hair samples—the usual. Nope, not even close. This was awful and disgusting. This is the reason I work with chemicals, not people. People are messy." Eugene was rambling because he was tired.

"What do you need?" Besides lots of sleep and a nice meal, that was what I wanted to ask him.

"We need a live subject. Can you find us one?"

I didn't like it when everyone looked at me with expectation. Eugene was serious.

"Hey, I keep running into them. I'll grab you one next time." It was pretty sad, but I meant that.

"That's a great plan. Isis, keep an eye out for the Z people." Constantine was doing his Sphinx pose. "Unfortunately, Bartholomew had the same luck as Eugene. He checked all the available systems, but somehow our little accountant doesn't have a digital footprint."

"What does that mean, boss?" Bob asked Constantine, a little worried.

"Nothing good. Either she changed her identity or she has a partner. Either way, she's covering her tracks well. Bartholomew did find the real address for her parents. The one on file was a fake. You will need to visit them, Isis."

I wasn't sure how to feel after Constantine's news. If she was that good, we were almost chasing a ghost. Unfortunately, I didn't have the advantage of being able to see her.

"I can do that right after I've showered." I needed a shower now.

"We have another lead we want you to follow before your date this morning. Bob knows a guy." Constantine looked at Bob to continue the introduction.

"You still want me to go on a date with everything that's going on?" I asked him. Was this crazy cat serious?

"Isis is going on a date?" Eric made that sentence sound so incredulous.

"You're meeting for lunch, so you can have a date and eat at the same time. That way at least you're eating something." Constantine was not helping.

"Who is the date with?" Eric was not dropping this, even with Constantine ignoring him.

"A very nice guy. Very respectful, single, no kids, stable job, pays his bills on time, great credit score."

I was so grateful I wasn't the only one staring at Bob after that last comment. Eric and Eugene were also speechless.

"How do you know all that?" Eugene was the first one to recover.

"Simple, we ran a background check on him. We can't have Isis going on a date with some psycho. What kind of family do you think we are?"

Disconcertingly, I was touched by Bob's sentiment and scared. With this process, I was never going to have a real date.

"Is that legal?" It took Eugene a minute to recover before he could speak.

"Not at all. So, let's pretend I didn't hear that." Eric's cop-mode kicked in. Well, at least I had confirmation that Abuelita was right, and the boys had done their homework.

"Ignoring the source of information, he sounds pretty normal. How did you guys meet?" Eugene sounded like he was on a dating show.

"It's a blind date. Isis hasn't met him yet. He's our mailman. He's harmless." Constantine had to add that part of the story.

"Uh, those are awful. Good luck, Isis." Eugene was genuinely concerned for me. He got tons of points in my book. "Make sure to take my number with you. If he turns out to be a freak, text me, and I'll call you back. Give you a reason to leave early."

I liked that idea. This guy sounded too good to be true; there was something wrong with him.

"Thanks, that's a great idea." I liked Eugene. He would make a great wingman.

"Isis, please don't kill him. He's a civilian."

I rolled my eyes at Eric. His moral support was amazing.

"Great meeting everyone. Eugene, go to bed before you fall on your face." Constantine was back in his evil dictator mode.

"Yes, sir," Eugene replied as he tried to stand up straight. He stumbled a little and Bob quickly grabbed him. I shook my head in panic.

"Let me help you out, Eugene. Just in case you see the floor coming and you forget to brace yourself." Bob was guiding Eugene to his place, as Eugene gave him many thanks.

"It's a good thing he's staying on the first floor. He wouldn't make it upstairs on the stage," I told Constantine as I watched Bob now dragging Eugene to his apartment.

"If I remember correctly, Pestilence's curfew is eight at night with lights out at nine. That poor child is not used to being up all night. He might die this week." I feared Constantine was right. Eugene looked awful. Another reason I was glad I work for Death.

"I'll be running off. I'll give you a call if I find anything. Isis, don't kill your date." Without waiting for a reply, Eric took off.

"I'm not that bad." I was pouting again and I didn't care.

"You're not, but weird things do happen when you're around," Constantine said.

"Thanks, Constantine. So, who is this guy I'm meeting?" I was ready to focus on work now. My dating life, or lack of it, was not something I enjoyed talking about with everybody.

"Glad you asked after Eric left," Constantine quickly replied. I had no idea why Constantine was so happy Eric was gone for this conversation.

"Eugene did find traces of drugs in the guy's system. Based on how he was dressed, Bob thinks he is probably well off. Bob believes this guy he knows might be the potential dealer," Constantine told me very calmly. I was going to question a drug dealer? Was he kidding?

"Our theory is the virus is in a drug?" I needed to process all this a little slower.

"The accountant needs to distribute the virus somehow. Adding it to drugs wouldn't be too hard. How else would she spread this stuff quickly? My money is on recreational drugs." That was Constantine's theory.

"Makes sense in a horrible way." The chemist was moving quickly up my list of most dangerous people.

"Bob is going to text you his address and pertinent details. Hope you've rested, Isis. You're up." Constantine jumped off the bench and headed upstairs. I slowly followed Constantine. I needed a shower.

Chapter Fourteen

Be careful what you wish for because you just might get it. I knew exactly the meaning of those words. For the last two days, I felt useless and without a purpose. Now that I had a mission, I realized I had the worst part of the job. The boys' jobs were the behind-the-scenes stuff. I got face-to-face with all the crazy people of the world. I wasn't sure how I felt having to interview one of the resident drug dealers in town. This was not the time for whining. On the plus side, maybe this would take a long time and I would miss my date. I prayed for a silver lining.

According to Bob, the guy he knew lived in the Links. I had never been to the Links. When I first moved to town, the Links were entirely out of my price range. According to their marketing campaign, the Links were luxury apartments on a nine-hole, executive golf course. At the time, that meant nothing to me. The complex, a better description of the place, had a swimming pool as well as basketball and tennis courts for its residents to enjoy. Now that I was playing golf, I wouldn't mind paying the money to live next to a golf course.

Fortunately, the Links was right off I-30 on the Arkansas side and next to the new water park. Beside the location, all I knew about my mystery man was that he drove a red Jeep. Was Bob serious about that? What kind of description was that? I was pretty sure he wasn't the only person driving a red Jeep in town. For the love of God, we had a Jeep dealership in town. I took a few deep breaths before I really got mad. I hated being lost and, in my book, driving around in circles qualified as being lost.

Thank you, God! I didn't have to drive around the complex too long before I found a red Jeep. The Jeep was in front of the apartments on the right-hand side of the reception building. If you had children, that side was perfect since they were closer to the water park. I hadn't noticed but the water park was attached to the new Holiday Inn. Abuelita had told me that in the last five years Texarkana had seen an explosion of hotels on both the Texas and Arkansas side. Some believed it was due to the Army depot employing lots of civilians. I had no clue, but one thing was true—Texarkana had an insane number of hotels and two convention centers.

I pulled Ladybug into the space next to the red Jeep. I had never been on a stakeout, but I'd learned that the easiest way to blend in was to act normal. Act as if you belong there and nobody ever notices. Driving around in circles and asking for directions was the first sign of being an outsider. I got out of Ladybug and quickly looked around. From the outside, the Links looked like any of the other apartment complexes in town. The main difference —the golf course in between the apartment buildings.

Apartments here were not like the ones up north. I was used to tall, boxy, run-down buildings—nothing impressive to look at. In Texarkana, the apartments were two-story houses with porches on both floors and usually two to four apartments in each house. Most complexes had a pool, laundry center, playground, and great landscaping. Even the low-end ones were in better condition than most of the apartments in New York City. They were also much bigger. I had cheaper rent and more space in my old apartment in Texarkana than I'd had growing up.

If this was a luxury complex, I wasn't sure I was ready to go inside. I was finally getting comfortable at Reapers. Bob said I had to be at the Links at least by nine since his boy started his rounds around nine-thirty. He played a round of golf every morning before leaving unless he was playing with a client. I walked around the Jeep and looked inside. The Jeep was immaculate both inside and out. He took care of his vehicle, if this was indeed his. A golf bag sat in the trunk space. Maybe this was the right guy. Granted, I was next to a golf course. Those could belong to anyone.

My stomach made a rumbling noise. I forgot I had missed breakfast. Bob had left me a lunch bag on the kitchen island and I'd never had time to inspect it. Between Bartholomew and Bob, they made sure to pack my lunches. I was always moved by those small gestures; most people were too busy with their own problems to remember those around them. I grabbed the bag I had thrown in the back seat and opened it up. I was amused. After a lunch fiasco one day, where everyone had grabbed the wrong bag, Bob had decided to take action. He'd brought us all monogrammed lunch bags in our favorite colors. Mine was midnight blue.

I pulled a veggie burrito with extra cheese from my bag. Bob was extremely obsessive-compulsive when it came to food. He'd started labeling everything, including heating instructions, if he left the meal for the house. We all thought it was pretty funny. He had added grapes, string cheese, chocolate milk, and an oatmeal cookie. My lunch date was scheduled for noon. This was more food than I needed to hold me over for three hours. I took the burrito and milk and leaned on Ladybug, facing the Jeep.

"Are you lost, miss?"

I barely had taken a bite of my burrito when I heard the voice. I swallowed quickly.

"Depends who's asking," I replied with a smile on my face. I wanted to come across as harmless.

"Considering you are staring at my Jeep with a murderous look, I just want to make sure if I should be worried."

Well, I'd failed at the harmless look. He unlocked his Jeep with his keys and walked over toward his passenger door. If he was the drug dealer, he was nothing like I expected. I wasn't sure what I expected, but this tall, sandy-blond-haired, very well-dressed man was not it. He was handsome with blue eyes and dressed in khakis and a polo. Put him in a suit and change the backpack for a briefcase and he could be in the corporate world easily. He looked American apple-pie wholesome.

"OK, you're giving me that look now. Can I help you?"

"Oh, I'm sorry. I'm probably at the wrong place." I was going to kill Bob, sending me on this crazy mission.

"What are you looking for?" He even had a great voice—strong, confident, and very masculine.

"Hard to explain. I was looking to buy some stuff."

His whole demeanor changed at my words. His face became guarded and hard.

"Sorry, miss, this is an apartment complex, not Walmart. Good luck with that." He turned around to walk away. Could he be the drug dealer?

"James, my man, what's going on?" I recognized that voice immediately without having to turn around. My favorite informant and Bob's best friend, Shorty, strolled next to me. "Boss lady, what are you doing here?" He gave me the most surprised look in the world. Shorty's nickname fit him perfectly. He was a tiny man, around five-four, and maybe 120 pounds fully clothed. When I first met him, he had a crazy look to him. Those witches' arrivals last fall changed everyone, including Shorty. He was still a little off, but now he looked healthy and a bit more sober.

"Bob sent me on an errand, but I think he gave me the wrong address." I was ready to leave. I was feeling foolish here.

"Shorty, you know her?" James was eyeing us suspiciously from his side of the Jeep.

"Of course, this is Miss Isis. Big Bob works for her," Shorty said.

"Bob doesn't work for me. He works with me. We have the same employer, remember?" I wanted to clarify.

"Whatever you say, boss lady. So, what are you looking for?" Shorty did not believe me, but I didn't feel like explaining that in front of Mr. James.

"Nothing. I was trying to find a supplier." I was embarrassed to say 'dealer' and 'supplier' sounded a little better, but not by much.

"Well, you're in the right place." Shorty stopped and looked at me carefully, up and down. "I didn't think you were into that stuff, boss lady." He was looking very disappointed.

"I work for Constantine. Do you honestly think he would let me?" I glared back at Shorty.

"You do have a point." Shorty broke into a huge smile. If I didn't know any better, I would have thought Shorty was concerned for my well-being. "What are you looking for?"

"I need information. I need to know if anyone has been trying to sell any new kind of drugs around town." That was probably the safest way to explain our dilemma.

"James, my man, hook her up. She is good people, I promise." I was staring at Shorty and James. Shorty was my connection to the underground whenever Bob was missing. He was still living on the streets, but at least now he didn't look like he was dying. Shorty was still shady, so the fact that he and Constantine were my constant references didn't say much for my character. Maybe I needed new friends. James looked at us for a while.

"OK, if Shorty says you're good, I'll believe him. What exactly are you looking for?" He was still looking at me suspiciously, but at least he was talking.

"Has anyone come to you offering you a new product or anything like that?" I wasn't sure what I needed.

"I have a very exclusive clientele and distribution network. I only meet with appointments and from very respected referrals. I'm not trying to get any of my clients killed. Just help them cope with their daily hell. I don't do anything stronger than weed."

Was James trying to convince himself or me that he was a respectable businessman? I had fairly easy facial expressions to read and I was sure I was giving him a suspicious look because he kept talking. "Don't get me wrong now; I'm not a good guy. Don't let the clothes fool you. But I'm a businessman. So, no I haven't seen or heard of anyone new trying to cut into my market."

He waited for my answer. I believed him. Great, he wasn't it.

"Thank you, that helps. By the way, nice clubs." I pointed toward the back of his Jeep with my head. James gave me a half smile.

"You play?" he asked.

"Just started." I was still really new.

"If you ever want to play, give me a call. Shorty has my number. Hopefully, you won't be on business and look like a cop."

So, that's what made him so nervous.

"We'll see. Thanks again." I waved at him as he climbed into his Jeep. I looked over at Shorty, who was smiling wildly. "Shorty, what are you doing here?" Shorty walked all over Texarkana, but this was a little too much of a coincidence.

"Bob said you were here and I have some info for you." Now that made a lot more sense. "By the way, James is a cool guy. You should take his offer." Shorty was waving at James as he pulled out. Why did everyone want to play Cupid for me?

"Shorty, focus. What do you have for me?"

"I heard rumors there's a new guy in town. Tough guy with a huge crew. Might be your guy." How did Shorty know all that already? Wait, why was I questioning Shorty's method? That was insane on my part.

"Do you have an address?"

"Will have it soon. Just checking to see if you want it." Shorty smiled very proudly.

I looked at my watch. It wasn't even ten and I had plenty of time before my crazy date. I decided to head to the library. I hadn't been there for a few days and I still wanted to find new things to read.

"Yes, that would be great. The sooner the better. By the way, I'm heading downtown. Do you need a ride?" With Shorty, it was hard to figure out where he was heading, but I could always drop him off.

"Hell, yeah." He was climbing in before he finished talking. "Boss lady, are you going to finish your cookie?" By the time I got in, Shorty was inspecting my lunch bag.

"Nope. I'm supposed to have lunch in a little bit. Would you like the rest of my burrito and milk? I didn't open the milk."

I had a bottle of water with me so I could survive. Shorty took the burrito and milk and emptied the content of the bag on his lap. He knew the lunch bag was a gift from Bob, so he would never ask to take it.

"Thanks, boss lady." He was used to riding with me, so he put his seat belt on without being told. Now that Bob had his place, Shorty took regular showers, so he always smelled fruity now.

"Shorty, I have a question. You know who I work for. You've even met Constantine. How come it doesn't bother you?"

Shorty was the first real human who knew about us and he never changed. Shorty got serious for a moment.

"Miss Isis." He never called me that directly, so now I was nervous. "I met a lot of people in my life. When things took a wrong turn for me, all my so-called friends left me. Your boss and Constantine have never judged me. They see a man full of potential, not a drunk on the streets. Nowadays, when I find genuine people, I hold on to them. Even if they come in the shape of a cat. You know what I mean."

The last part wasn't a question but a statement. I knew exactly what he meant. It was hard to be accepted, especially if we had a messy past.

"I know. It's hard to find people like that." I smiled at Shorty as I spoke. I was wondering what had happened to him. What was his story?

"OK now, boss lady, let's not get emotional. We got work to do and not a lot of time." Shorty was back to his smiling self. He and Constantine had that devious little smile that made you wonder what were they up to.

"So true, Shorty." I glanced at him one more time before putting Ladybug in reverse. He was eating his cookie with milk. He looked like a happy seven-year-old.

Chapter Fifteen

I loved libraries and bookstores. There was something about books that was comforting. After dropping Shorty at the Jeep dealership, I headed to the library downtown. The dealership had moved to Walton Drive around the corner from Walmart. Shorty said he was meeting a guy there for business. I had learned it was safer not to ask too many questions when it came to Shorty's business. I did not want to be accessorized with any unnecessary information. The dealership was nowhere near where I was going, but it wasn't like I was walking. So, taking him was not a problem. The ride was not boring; I got to hear his theories on the alien takeover. Even Shorty had crazy conspiracy theories; I hope they were just crazy theories.

My reading selection had drastically changed, something that was driving me nuts. I couldn't find a new genre that was fun and didn't make me think of work. Even the mystery cat books that were my regular easy read were hard to follow after living with Constantine. I stumbled into the arts and craft area and decided to pick up a hobby. Photography sounded like fun and they had tons of books on how to take and develop black-and-white photos. It appeared I had found a new area and something to do. It was a win-win.

I was still pretty cheerful when I pulled into PetSmart's parking lot. The boys' mystery man sent me a text to meet him in front of this chain store at twelve thirty. Who meets at PetSmart? Maybe we were going to the restaurant next to it, the Catch. Then again, if we were going there, why didn't he just say that? I was super nervous and today, I hated my obsession with being early. I didn't want to get out of Ladybug so it was precisely twelve-thirty when I walked over. It was adoption day at PetSmart so there were groups outside with the cutest puppies. I wondered how bad Constantine would take it if I brought a dog home.

"Isis, is that you?" A nasally voice called me from behind. I turned around a little worried.

"Yes, can I help you?" I asked.

"It's me, William. Didn't Bob give you my picture? He sent me a copy of yours."

William was my date and true to his word he was holding a smiling picture of me on his phone.

"No, he didn't. He probably forgot as we've been so busy." Sure thing, he forgot. He didn't show me a picture because I would have never ever shown up. William was different—a weird combination of Sheldon and Steve Urkel with a pair of BCGs on and red hair. BCG stood for Birth Control Glasses as the soldiers called that style. He was skinny, maybe five feet seven inches, and he looked fragile. I probably could break him in half.

Now he was smiling like crazy at me. "Well, I'm glad he sent me yours. This could have been awkward. Nice to meet you."

He extended his hand. His grip was like a wet fish, totally limp. Oh, I was going to kill the boys.

"Nice to meet you." I wanted to wipe my hands on my pants, but that would have been rude. "So, Bob said we were having lunch. Do you have a place in mind?" How was I going to get out of this?

"Yes, we're going to my favorite place, Cici's, across the street. I hope you didn't mind meeting here. I needed to pick up a few things for my cats and didn't want to forget."

I was speechless. We were going on a date to Cici's, the buffet pizza place? Was he kidding?

"Oh, no, not at all." I finally noticed the two bags he was carrying in his left hand. He had some strange string toy sticking out of one of them. "How many cats do you have?" He did say cats, right?

"Not many. Just six. They are all pure-breed Siamese."

Oh lord, what was I doing here? I have heard of cat ladies, but was there such a thing as a cat-gentleman or cat-man? No wonder Constantine liked him. He was a cat magnet.

"That's...That's impressive." I was hoping a car would drive by so I could jump in front of it. I looked around and the street in front of the store was deserted. Just my luck. "So, William, do you want to drop that off in your car so you won't lose it?" I was terrified to see his car.

"That's a great idea." He crossed the street and headed toward a gray Ford Focus. I followed a few feet behind him. He was a single guy, who according to his background check made really good money. Why was he driving a family car? This had to be a joke. I was looking for the cameras to show up any minute. "OK, I'm ready." We walked across the parking lot to Cici's.

"So Cici's. Was Chuck E. Cheese packed this time of day?" I knew I was nervous because I was cracking jokes. I wasn't expecting his reaction. He stopped in the middle of the parking lot to look at me.

"No offense, but Chuck E. Cheese is not for first dates. You have to build to that." He shook his head and started walking again. It took me a minute to process all that. He was serious. I was in the twilight zone. I needed to find a fast-moving vehicle soon and put myself out of this misery.

We made it to the restaurant and he opened the door for me. That was a small blessing. I smiled, but I wasn't sure how to act. I've never been to an all-you-can-eat pizza place for a date.

"I hope you didn't mind that I opened the door for you. Bob mentioned you were a very progressive kind of girl. So, I figured we would go Dutch, so I wouldn't insult your liberal ways."

It was a blessing I got paid well or I would make Constantine and Bob reimburse me for this disaster.

"Sure thing." We headed to the register to pay.

"Hi, Mr. William, welcome back," the very cheery teenage girl behind the register told my quirky date. "Your regular booth is open."

"Thanks, Margaret." He gave her a huge smile which was a little creepy for my taste. "I got connections here," he whispered to me.

I was hoping he left them a great tip. Margaret was not nearly as friendly to me.

I followed Mr. Charisma to his favorite booth and was amazed how everyone knew him. I was wondering if this was how I looked when I went to Big Jake's. I was praying it wasn't so. The place was pretty packed for a weekday. It seemed like all the stay-at-home moms were here with their kids. Every once in a while, a new lady waved at William and he gave them a casual nod of acknowledgment. I guess if you were the only man in a group of women with kids, you got it going on. Maybe that was why he liked this place. I, on the other hand, felt old and out of place.

"So, how do you like your job? Cause I love mine. I got to meet all sorts of interesting people and see cool places. One time..."

I blanked William out. I made all the appropriate sounds like I was listening. Instead, I started paying attention to all the other patrons. There was no need to hear what he said. Every question he asked, he answered it himself. This was going to be the longest lunch of my life.

"William, are you OK?" I asked him after twenty minutes of his nonstop talking. He was sweating profusely. His skin had taken on a weird yellowish color—almost jaundiced.

"Yeah, I'm fine. I went to the doctor four days ago. I think I have the flu again. I was feeling achy, shivering, runny nose. I tested negative for the flu. Today, I feel better, that's why I didn't cancel. Now I just have a bit of a headache. Nothing major."

William was starting to shake. If this was nothing major, I didn't want to see him when something significant happened.

"Maybe we should go. You're not looking too well." And I didn't want to catch whatever he was carrying.

"I am..."

William never finished his statement. He was looking at me one moment and the next one, his head hit the table. It sounded painful.

"Ouch. William, are you OK?" I touched his shoulder, hoping he wasn't passed out. That was my big mistake. William raised his head slightly. And the guy looking at me wasn't William.

"Holy cow!" He was going straight zombie on me. I needed to do something. "Sorry, William," I whispered. When I thought nobody was looking, I slammed his head on the table hard. This was the worst first date ever. I jumped from my side of the booth to William's side before anyone could notice. "Oh, William, you look awful, let's take you home." I made sure everyone heard me.

"Is he OK?" asked one of William's admirers.

I smiled at her as sweetly as I could. "Oh, he just has the flu. He can't keep anything down, but he wanted some pizza. I need to take him back." I was pulling William out of the booth as I spoke. I was giving God thanks that I was so much stronger than him. I left a twenty on the table and rushed him out the door with the excuse that he needed to puke.

I made it to the end of the block without drawing too much attention. I did not want to take this semi-zombie in Ladybug. If he woke up, he'd kill us both in a traffic accident. And I didn't have enough trunk space to stick him there. Maybe I could put him in the trunk of his Focus. Those things could fit a couple of bodies. I just didn't want anyone to notice. I didn't want to end up in jail for kidnapping.

I was almost dragging him across the parking lot when a Dodge Ram extended cab headed straight for us. Here was a fast-moving vehicle now that I didn't need one. The truck stopped abruptly in front of us.

"Boss lady, do you need a hand?"

Was I seeing things? From the driver's side Shorty jumped down.

"Umm, Shorty. Whose truck is this? Never mind that, why are you driving a truck?" I knew I left him at the dealership, and they sold trucks there, but who would be crazy enough to give a truck to Shorty? I was pretty sure he didn't have a driver's license or even believe in traffic laws.

"The boss man hooked me up." Well, that explained it. Only Constantine would think it was safe to put Shorty behind the wheel. I rolled my eyes in worry.

"I'm your new cleanup crew."

"Cleanup crew? What are we, the Sopranos?" Honestly, my boys had lost their minds.

"Well, I can leave, but how are you planning to carry that guy?" Shorty was eyeing William very suspiciously. I thought about it for a minute and realized Constantine was right. It wasn't like I could go driving around picking up zombies in Ladybug.

"Good point. Help me get him in the back." Shorty ran around and opened the tailgate. Between the two of us, we lifted zombie William into the truck bed. "Don't stop anywhere and get him to Reapers, ASAP. I'll be right behind you. I don't know how long he will last like this."

"Moving out, boss. See you at Reapers."

I barely had time to close the tailgate, and Shorty was already in the driver's seat. Without another look, Shorty took off, driving like the proverbial bat out of hell.

One good thing had come of this mess: I now had another reason not to date. You never knew when the guy might turn out to be a zombie.

Chapter Sixteen

By the time I got to Reapers, Bartholomew and Bob were dragging William from the back of the truck. I was surprised I had caught up with Shorty. He was an absolute menace in that truck. I prayed Constantine had added extra insurance to the policy. We were probably going to need it. I pulled up next to Shorty's truck, ready to jump out and help. I had my window down by the time I stopped.

"Isis, we got this. Meet us inside." Bob was right. Between him and Bartholomew, they had everything under control. Then again, William was tiny, so even Bartholomew could move him alone.

"OK, see you guys inside," I told Bob. "Thank you, Shorty."

Shorty was already in the driver's seat, ready to take off. He rolled down his passenger window. "Going to make some rounds and see what else I find. It's going to be a busy week."

I was afraid Shorty was right. I waved at him and drove around to the back of Reapers to the vehicle's entrance.

After Ladybug and I had cleared all the securities, we slowly pulled up to our spot. Bartholomew and Bob had dragged William to the practice area and laid him on a bench. He looked like a rag doll, lying around all limp. Constantine was sitting on the opposite side of the bench, looking down on the poor man. I jumped out and walked over to the boys. As I made my way over, Eugene was coming out of Bob's apartment. He was wearing jeans and a Beatles T-shirt. He looked so young in his casual clothes.

"What's going on? Who's the guy?" Eugene asked as he got near. I was staring at zombie William, who was looking worse by the minute.

"Isis's date," Bartholomew immediately replied, being the kind of twelve-year-old that he was.

I glared at him.

"You went on a date with that guy?" Eugene was staring down at William. I glared back at Eugene as well.

"It was a blind date, thanks to those two." I pointed at Constantine and Bob for extra effect.

"Hey, he looked normal in uniform," Bob replied.

"Besides, his resume, background check, and credit report were excellent," Constantine added.

"Newsflash, gentlemen. Everyone looks great on paper. But in case you both missed it, it was a date, not a job application. I wasn't looking for a secretary." For such a wise group of men, when it came to dating, they were worse than me.

"We might need better interview questions," Constantine told Bob.

"You guys interviewed him?" Why was I asking? I didn't want to know. "You know what? Never mind. Don't tell me."

Eugene was inspecting William very closely. "What happened to his face? That bruise looks fresh."

"I slammed his head on the table," I replied almost to myself. Unfortunately, they all heard it, and they were staring at me.

"Really? Was it that bad of a date?" Eugene was the first to recover.

"Well, he did take me to Cici's and we went Dutch. Really, how cheap can you be? But that wasn't why. He started turning into a zombie."

All the boys took a step back from William. Even Constantine took a backward step on the bench.

"I thought you said his drug test was negative," Bob asked Bartholomew. They were not kidding when they said they conducted a background check.

"He looks a little too nerdy to do drugs. Besides, he said he wasn't feeling too good and thought he had flu symptoms three to four days ago." Eugene was back to examining him.

"Hey, you have your live specimen now," I told Eugene.

"I'm impressed you thought about it." Eugene looked amazed. "If my date had turned zombie on me, I doubt taking her for testing would have crossed my mind."

I had to smile. "You'll be surprised the things you think about on this job," I answered.

"Well, let's not waste any time. Based on your date's info, this thing might have an incubation period and not a very long one at that," Eugene said to nobody specifically.

"While you figure out what's going on, we need a way to knock these guys out without fighting." I had no idea how to pull that off if my powers did not work on the zombies. Constantine was staring at Eugene.

"Why are you looking at me like that?" Eugene asked a bit worried. I didn't blame him. Constantine's ideas could be dangerous to your health.

"Considering you are the only mad-scientist here, it seems this is your area of expertise." Constantine was right. Eugene was our resident chemist. Bob and Bartholomew both nodded in agreement.

"What, me? You want me to come up with something? I don't even have any supplies here." It seems Eugene was not used to being the top Intern in charge.

"Come on, Eugene. According to your file, you graduated at the top of your class at MIT. How hard could this be?" Bartholomew dropped that piece of information like it was nothing. Now it was my turn to be impressed. "I can order you anything you want." That part was a fact. Bartholomew was the best supply sergeant I ever saw.

"Unfortunately, Bart, we might not have twenty-four hours. We need this now before more people keep turning. I can't afford to kick somebody and take them out like Eric. Death would probably kill us." I hated to be the bringer of bad news, but we needed to move fast.

"I can pick up most of the stuff I need from Walmart. I just need to get there," Eugene told us very calmly. Now I was worried. If Eugene could pick up all his supplies at Walmart that meant everyone else could do so as well.

"Please tell me you're kidding?" I shook my head quickly. "Unfortunately, I can't take you. According to Shorty, we got a new drug dealer in town. Some tough guy and he might be moving quickly, so I have to go soon." This was going to be the week for drug dealers and zombies—great combination.

"You shouldn't go alone. I'll go with you. If Shorty says he's bad news, this guy could be a straight sociopath. Shorty underplays people's insanities."

Why hadn't Bob mentioned that part before? How bad could this guy honestly be?

"Are you sure you're not just feeling guilty for setting me up on a blind date with a zombie here?" I was going to milk this little situation for a while.

"It's not a guilt offering. Granted, your date did not turn out how we expected. I know you can handle yourself, but there's no need to take chances." Bob was so sincere, I felt sorry for picking on him.

"I can go alone; I just need some wheels. Can I take that one over there?" Eugene pointed to the Death Mobile.

"No." The four of us replied in unison. Eugene jumped a little.

"You don't want to drive the Death Mobile unless you want to die a prolonged and horrible death," Constantine told Eugene very serious and drily. Eugene looked almost pale. I wasn't sure if Constantine was kidding.

"Don't listen to him. Unless it's a dire emergency, we don't mess with Death's car. I'll be going with Bob, therefore you can take Ladybug."

Eugene was a little too happy for me.

"That works, but Bartholomew is going with you," Constantine said. "I need you back, so no shopping around the county without supervision." At least it made me feel better that Constantine had no issues.

"That really sucks—" Bartholomew was getting ready to start whining.

"Bartholomew, we got two options. One, either all of us help to stop this or two, we watch everyone in Texarkana die. You wouldn't have to worry about winning because everyone would be dead."

Constantine was looking at Bartholomew as he spoke. I slowly walked away from that conversation. I didn't want to see Bartholomew freak out. He was quiet for a minute.

"You're right. What's the point of having the best robot if everyone is going to be gone? I want a fair chance."

We needed to work on Bartholomew's priorities.

"I like the plan, but what are we going to do with little zombie over there? We can't just leave him there. He'll eventually wake up and try to kill us."

"We can tie him up in the lab," Eugene answered.

"You have stuff in the lab to tie him up with?" I wasn't sure why I was shocked about that.

"You'd be surprised how well stocked your lab is. Anything you need to test and experiment. Not enough to develop concoctions." Eugene smiled brightly.

"In that case, that's perfect." I had no clue what else to say.

"Do you mind giving me a hand, Mr. Bart?" Eugene asked Bartholomew. "This boy is tiny enough we can take him."

Without answering, Bartholomew walked over to William and picked up his right side. Eugene grabbed his left and they dragged him along.

"Let's go get this zombie tied up." Bartholomew sounded a little too happy about that last part.

"If you guys give me a minute, I can help." Bob was looking indecisive, a very un-Bob thing.

"Mr. Bob, I'm pretty sure we got this. Besides you two need to get going."

Eugene was right; we were short on time.

"Old man, listen to the rookie. He has a degree from MIT, so you know he has it going on," Constantine said with a little smirk. I think Eugene was growing on him.

"We have too much to do and not enough people or time," Bob said. "I need to change. Isis, meet you back here in ten?"

Before I had time to reply Bob was gone.

I took a seat next to Constantine on the space William had occupied. I didn't want to go and talk to another drug dealer. I just wanted lunch.

"Why are you making that face?" Constantine said.

"What face?" Was I making faces now?

"That one, like someone beat your puppy." Constantine kept staring, waiting for me to say something.

"I thought that I was hungry. I was trying to be good and skip the gluten. So, I had a few bites of salad." Maybe I pouted when I was hungry. I was very spoiled lately.

"Oh, if that's the whole problem you're in luck. We got you cheese and tomatoes quesadillas, horchata, and flan from Abuelita's. The only thing you'll need is to take it to go, so that you won't be late." Constantine was sitting next to me, doing his Sphinx pose. I was ready to kiss him.

"Yes! That is the best news I got all day. Thank you!" I scratched him under his ear and he slapped my hand. Not very seriously since Constantine was smiling already.

"It is unfortunate, but everyone in this house works for food. We have the greatest technology, best fringe benefits, yet everyone goes crazy for Abuelita's. I'm in the wrong business." Constantine was shaking his head as he spoke.

"Don't even act all offended. You know you're crazy about her cooking, too." I poked his side and he slapped my hand away again.

"Girl, go get changed and get your food. You don't want to keep Bob waiting."

Constantine had a point. When Bob said ten minutes, it was only ten minutes.

"True. Here, give these to those two." I left Ladybug's keys next to Constantine and got up. My keychain had ladybug decorations. Constantine shook his head in disgust. I laughed to myself and ran up the stairs to get ready.

Chapter Seventeen

Quail Brook Estates off South Lake Drive was all the instructions Shorty gave me. Somehow, according to him, I was going to recognize the place. Shorty had high expectations for me because I was pretty sure this was going to be harder than it looked. Considering we had no clue where we were going, Bob and I dressed like respectable home security salespeople. I had seen a few of them around Wake Village. Somehow, people always opened their doors to them. We had slacks, polo shirts, and company clipboards. Since nobody had a clue what Reapers was, we could use our business cards for anything.

I was convinced we were going door-to-door looking for this guy. I didn't want to get the local authorities called on us for looking suspicious. We made sure we had a cover story for being in that area and something to tell people if we knocked on their doors. I had never been on the south side of town so I had no idea what to expect and I wanted to be prepared. We used the GPS to find the address. I was so happy Bob was with me because by the time we saw the road I was lost.

Texarkana had tons of new subdivisions popping up everywhere. Quail Brook Estates was one of them. From the road, it looks like a long street with about twenty houses, ten on each side. Every house looked the same from the outside. The lots were not very big by Texas standards. Some of the homes were fenced off, but for the most part, they all had connecting yards.

Right now, the "estates" were packed with cop cars.

"Is that Eric over there?" Bob asked.

"Eric and half of the Texarkana PD." I was praying they were not here for the same guy.

"This can't be good." By the sound of Bob's voice, he had the same horrible feeling as me. "Well, let's go check in with Eric."

Bob parked a little farther away from Eric's patrol car. The street wasn't blocked off, but we didn't want to get in trouble. I was so happy I was wearing my insurance outfit instead of Rambo clothes. We probably would have ended up in jail if we came in with all of our gear. We got out of the car and sauntered toward the patrol car. Eric saw us from his side mirror and got out of the vehicle.

"Do I want to know what you two are doing here?" Eric crossed his arms over his chest, not looking happy. Eric was spending a lot of time outside and was getting a great tan.

"Not sure if you would believe us if we told you." I was not sure our story made sense to us.

"Try me." Eric was not changing the subject.

"We got a tip from Shorty who knows a guy who moves a lot of stuff. We came to ask him some questions." Well, it didn't sound too crazy when I said it out loud. I was pleased.

"Did Shorty tell you where to find this guy and what he looks like?" By the tone of Eric's voice, it was not a coincidence we were all here.

"You know Shorty; he wasn't very specific."

Bob jumped in to help me, thankfully. "He said the guy was new in town. Some heavy hitter in the drug cartel—

maybe Columbian or Mexican. Not sure what he was doing living here of all places."

I was wondering the same thing.

"Of course, Shorty knows all that. Why do we bother doing work when the underground knows the stuff before we do?" Eric was not happy with Shorty's intel.

"Maybe you should hire Shorty as your informant. He does great work for us." I was trying to make a joke. Unfortunately, judging by the look he gave me, I had failed.

"Yeah, we tried. Unfortunately, the underground doesn't work for cops. They'll never interfere with us, but they won't rat out anybody. Imagine that." Eric looked mad. At the same time, I was feeling pretty special. We had our intelligence network that put the authorities to shame. Point for the Reaper team.

"Sorry about that." I figured I had to say something instead of bragging about our connections.

"No need. Unfortunately, narco boy, here, is not your guy. He's been under surveillance for the past week. He hasn't left the house and no unusual guests have visited." Eric sounded pretty sure about all that.

"I assume all the lines are tapped and you've been monitoring his communication." Bob was pretty familiar with the police's operating procedures.

"Our equipment is not as sophisticated as Bartholomew's, but our people are top-notch. They have been monitoring everything from phone, email, to even the things they watch." Eric was looking over at a white van parked across the street. "We're getting ready to take him out. He's preparing to move a large shipment, but no mention of zombie drugs anywhere."

Great, we drove all the way over here for nothing.

I guessed Shorty was right. We were not going to have any trouble finding the place. I looked over at the house the cops were surrounding. It was the house Bob had parked in front of. Of course, it was. That was our luck for everything. As I watched the house, a short man was sneaking around the back slowly. He was probably less than five foot five with shiny black hair. If he was the infamous narco, we had a small problem. The man was not Latin at all, but Asian, and he wasn't wearing any pants.

"Eric, by any chance is that our guy?" I pointed at him.

"Holy cow, it's him. He hasn't been seen outside since he got here." That was the understatement of the century since they didn't even know his nationality. Great work, Eric and Shorty. "Where are his pants?"

"Who cares about his pants? What is he carrying?" Bob was staring at the little narco very closely. In his left hand, he had what looked like a bottle. I wasn't quite sure because that was his side facing away from us.

"Probably his liquor. He is stumbling around," I said.

"I don't think so unless he takes his vodka flaming."

I couldn't see what Bob was pointing at.

"Die, you pigs!" Little narco screamed. He threw the bottle and it landed on the back of The Beast. We heard the bottle break.

"Look out," Bob yelled and pushed me to the ground. A loud explosion followed. My ears were ringing for over a minute.

"What just happened?" My head was spinning. Bob was helping me get back on my feet.

"Oh, Bob, I'm so sorry, man. He blew up your truck." Eric was looking in the direction of the truck in pure horror. "What did he have in that bottle? I'll be back."

Eric took off running in the direction of the fire.

"I'm pretty sure it wasn't the bottle that made that explosion." Bob looked at his truck and then back at me.

"Bob, do I want to know what you were carrying in The Beast?" I was a little concerned about the well-being of the cops around the truck.

"Let's just say it's a blessing it's in flames. By the time the fire department shows up, there won't be anything left. Let me make some calls." Bob took a few steps away to use the phone.

Bob wasn't lying. The fire was massive. The flames were growing. I walked around to check out what the cops were doing on the other side. They had surrounded the half-naked narco, who was lying on the grass. Some other cops had rushed into the house and were dragging people out. The scene looked like massive chaos. Half of the people they were dragging around were half-naked and looked stoned. If they were genuinely dealing drugs, they were using a lot of their merchandise. Eric was running back in my direction. That boy liked to run.

"What happened?" I asked Eric before he made it to me.

"I have no idea what he was packing, but the explosion knocked him twenty feet in the air against the building. That's what the guys on the roof said. The explosion was so strong it blew out half of the house's windows." Eric was looking at the damaged Beast left behind. "We're lucky Bob warned us. It would have been bad for us."

It was a good thing Eric had no clue what Bob was carrying.

"Poor Bob. He liked his truck." I was hoping to change the topic somehow.

"Isis, no offense."

You know every time somebody starts a sentence that way, you'll be offended. "Sometimes, I think you're a magnet for car explosions and mayhem."

Oh yeah, I was offended. I gave Eric a dirty look.

"You cannot possibly blame that on me. I was standing right next to you." How was this my fault? I didn't tell Bob to be carrying half an armory with him.

"I didn't say it was your fault. But you have to admit, crazy things happen when you're around."

Eric had lost his mind in that explosion if he thought I agreed with that.

"Reggie is on his way. He can give us a ride when he gets here," Bob informed me as he walked back.

"I can give you a ride if you don't mind waiting for a little. They don't need me here anymore," Eric offered.

"That would be great. I'd hate to wait for Reggie to cool the Beast enough to move it. We need to make it back and check on the status of William." Bob sounded calm, but he had wrinkles forming on his forehead. He was not happy at all.

"Who's William?" Eric asked.

Before I could change the topic, Bob answered. "Isis's date."

I was praying the conversation ended there.

"Your date was today? How did it go?" Why was Eric even asking this? My mouth went dry and I couldn't talk.

"He turned into a zombie and Isis knocked him out. Eugene has him at Reapers, running experiments on him." Like I mentioned before, Bob was too helpful at times.

"And you doubted that you were mayhem. I can't believe you knocked the poor guy out. Ruthless!" Eric was laughing. I was never going to live that down.

"I didn't have any choice. I couldn't afford for him to go full zombie in the middle of CiCi's pizza." I was a horrible person, but I didn't feel too bad for hitting him.

"You went on a date to Cici's pizza? Please tell me you're kidding."

I was not finding Eric's laughter amusing at this point. And he just kept laughing even with me glaring at him.

"Hey, I didn't pick the place." I wasn't sure how else to defend myself.

"Sorry, Isis, but you need to admit that is funny." Eric was trying to control his laughter, but it wasn't working.

"So, Eric, did your people find out anything about the drugs inside?" Bob was watching the third group of people being dragged away.

"That's the weird thing. They didn't find anything more than a few bags of weed. If they had anything else, they're not telling us." That calmed him right down.

"If you do find out, please let us know. It could help." I doubted it. That group looked more like lost souls than criminal masterminds. Another dead end, and all in one day. This was becoming a new record for me.

Chapter Eighteen

It was late afternoon by the time we walked into Reapers. Bob and I both smelled like smoke and were looking rough. I didn't realize that when Bob knocked me down, we had landed in mud. I was happy to be in one piece, so I didn't complain. Now I was feeling sticky and dirty. We headed straight upstairs to report. All the lights were on so hopefully, the rest of the boys were in one place. I wasn't looking forward to tracking everyone down in the whole building. When we walked in, Constantine was sitting in his favorite spot on top of the leather couch. He jumped off the back and strolled toward us.

"You two are on a roll," Constantine said. "First bullet holes in The Camaro and now a blown truck. Poor Beast."

"Reggie really should stop broadcasting his frequency." For some strange reason, the entire supernatural community in the four states area followed Reggie. He had more followers than a YouTube channel. It was crazy.

"He tried once and we all found it again. He's better than CNN." Constantine was a little too proud of that fact. I had a feeling he was personally involved in the discovery of the new code. He was nosy like that.

"Bob, I'm so sorry. Poor Beast," Bartholomew said from the doorway. He was coming in from his bedroom. He was carrying a pack of cables and some strange controller. I guessed he was working on his robot.

"Thanks, Bart. At least he went down in style. That explosion knocked the little guy at least twenty feet in the air. Priceless." Bob was proud of his baby. I couldn't say anything. Last year my blue minivan, the Whale, went down in flames as well. We were all a bit crazy with our vehicles.

"Well, I left you a list of potential vehicles on your desk. Let me know which one you like and we'll order it tonight." Bartholomew was always on top of things. "By the way, why are you both so dirty? You weren't in the Beast when it blew up?"

"Thank God we weren't or we'd both be gone," I answered.

Bob provided the rest of the details. "When we hit the dirt for cover, we landed in mud. The smell is from standing next to the Beast." Everyone nodded.

"We got bad news. According to Eric, there haven't been any abnormal activities from the regular pushers in Texarkana. Not to mention no increase in hospital visits from the usual users."

We were running out of suspects here.

"In that case, we can cross out the human dealers." I did not like how Constantine said that.

"Why do I have the feeling there are other dealers I know nothing about?" I was not ready for more insane information, but by the smile on Constantine's face, I knew I didn't have a choice.

"Of course, we have more than human dealers. Those dealers cater to a particular community. They might have a large demand, but they're not the only ones. It might be time to start looking at the supernatural community." Constantine was pleased with himself.

Bartholomew shot me a look that said how much he didn't like that idea. Bob was listening from the kitchen as he opened the freezer.

"Boss, do you have a lead, and when are we heading there?" Bob asked from inside the fridge. I had no idea what he was looking for. I was tired of standing, so I dropped down on one of the dining chairs. Bartholomew followed me, while Constantine made himself comfortable on the kitchen island. I had a feeling he enjoyed looking down on us.

"I know a guy." This was already sounding bad. Constantine smiled wickedly. "He is a powerful dark wizard. It's too dangerous to go at night, so you'll need to wait until morning."

"Every time one of you says 'I know a guy,' it only means trouble. How many people can you all know?" I couldn't help myself from asking. This was a horrible pattern.

"We know a lot. It just happens all might not apply here."

I shook my head. Constantine's answer did not amuse me.

"That's perfect. In that case, I got time to make some banana fosters for us."

We were all looking at Bob in shock. His baby had just got blown up to all heaven and he wanted to make flaming bananas. Bob might need therapy over this.

Constantine was the first to respond. "I want mine with salted caramel ice cream."

"That sounds great. I want one, too." Bartholomew did not waste time putting in his order.

"Isis, the same for you?" Bob asked as he peeled the bananas.

"Why not? Sounds great."

"Good, I'll make them all the same. I hope Eugene doesn't have any allergies."

Bob was always conscious of other people's needs.

"Where is Eugene?" I still wasn't used to the additional member. At times, I forgot he was supposed to be here.

"In the lab, working. He said he needed some privacy. So, I left him with all the supplies. I left your keys on your dresser." Bartholomew was back to playing with his cables as he spoke.

"Thanks, I appreciate it." I did. Bartholomew was probably the most respectful one when it came to taking care of others' property. I figured he was that way since he took great care of his own stuff. "So, what are you working on, Bart? How is the robot?" I was afraid to ask, but Bartholomew did not look like he was ready to kill the world.

"It's going great; I'm almost done. I got a few wiring issues to correct in the controller box, but other than that it's great. I guessed I just needed to step away from it for a while and then the solution appeared." Bartholomew gave me his biggest smile and I was thrilled. Maybe he was ready to come back to normal.

"Wasn't it Einstein that said, the level of the solution will never be found at the same level as the problem?" I loved that saying; I just had a hard time following it. It was hard for me to separate myself from a problem and allow for answers to come naturally to me.

"He was right and I needed just to step away." Bartholomew was smiling as he fiddled with his cables. I stretched in my chair and debated about getting up to shower when Eugene burst through the door.

"I hate that woman." Eugene was almost screaming. No need to ask what woman he was referring to. "She's good. I have been chasing rabbit holes all day, trying to crack her code." That did not sound very encouraging.

"Did you figure it out?"

Eugene's shoulder slumped when I asked. "Not yet, but we're working on it. I'm sending all my findings to the lab. We're working multiple theories at the same time. She is not going to get away with this." Eugene was pacing back and forth. I was pretty sure our dear rogue accountant was not making it easy at all for the boys.

"What happened to your lab coat?" Constantine was inspecting Eugene from his location. Eugene looked embarrassed. His lab coat was covered in all sorts of crazy stains, not to mention the burned marks everywhere.

"I was working on your knockout serum and a couple of beakers exploded. Don't worry, we don't have a fire in the lab and everyone is safe. I did test the formula and it knocked your date, William, right back to sleep." Eugene smiled brightly at the last part. "I'm not sure exactly how you're going to give it to the zombies."

"How did you use it on him?" If Eugene did it with William, maybe we could so the same with the rest.

"I gave him a shot," Eugene replied.

Yeah, that was out of the question.

"Can it be administered topically?" Bartholomew asked, casually looking up at Eugene.

"Umm, that's possible. I can make it happen. I'll need to make it stronger to ensure it takes them out quick." Eugene looked like he was running the formula in his head.

"Great. Can we make bullets out of them?" Bob asked from the stove. He started flaming the bananas and we all stared in silence. The loft was smelling delicious.

"Let's avoid guns; we don't want the impact to actually kill them," Constantine said. That was rare. Constantine was usually the first one that wanted to blow things up. That showed how strongly Death felt about preserving each soul.

"I have a blowgun. Would that work?" I remembered my gift. Maybe those things would come in handy.

"Maybe, but you'll need to be close and have lots of lung capacity."

I frowned when Eugene answered. That was not very helpful.

"By the way, why do you have a blowgun?" He was looking at me, confused.

"It was a present from another one of Death's Interns. Like a welcome-to-the-family gift." I had to smile. It was pretty sweet.

"Wow, so not fair. I got a pocket protector when I joined Pestilence's lab," Eugene said.

"That's a perfect gift for you," Constantine replied. "You'll get a lot more use from that than a blowgun in a research facility. Don't dismiss it. Do you use your pocket protector?"

"Yeah, every day. My lab coats kept getting stained before," Eugene explained. "It just sounds so geeky."

I wanted to go over and hug Eugene as he spoke. He looked so vulnerable.

"Eugene, you are a chemist in the best facility in the world with the smartest people on this planet. Of course, it's geeky. It's not like Pestilence recruits a bunch of jocks. Own it and be the greatest geek in town. Don't dismiss who you are. Nobody can take that away from you, so stand up tall and know you are unstoppable."

I was amazed. Eugene did as Constantine told him, straightening his spine and standing tall. Constantine never looked down at people. Instead, it was almost like he could see their real potential and soul.

"How about paintball guns? I still have all the ones we got for my birthday party," Bartholomew added to the table. He placed his new creation down and smiled brightly. "I'm done. I'm going to dominate tomorrow's competition."

Eugene looked at Bartholomew very confused. I waved at him before he could start asking questions.

"How about paintballs?" I needed to keep this meeting focused.

"We can make that work. I just need to make a whole lot more and package them. The last part will take time."

Eugene was doing that thing where he stared at the ceiling. I was starting to figure out he did that when he was calculating stuff in his head.

"I can help with that. I got plenty of practice from Bart's party. I just need to take a shower and I'll be down there."

"Me, too. I got plenty of time now," Bartholomew chirped.

Oh, thank you, God. My boy was back.

"Nobody is going anywhere before dessert. Isis, grab some plates and the ice cream. Bart, get everyone drinks. Eugene, sit down before you pass out. Let's go, everyone. It's been a long day. Let's eat in memory of the Beast."

Bob did not have to tell us twice. Bart and I were on our feet, following orders. Eugene was looking lost, but at least he did as he was told. Constantine jumped on the table and took his position. The place smelled amazing and I was so grateful to be home. Bob was officially my hero.

Chapter Nineteen

It was Thursday morning and according to my clock it was 6:15 a.m. I had planned on getting up at five to go running but we didn't finish making those knockout paintballs till way past midnight. I had flashes of being deployed and filling sandbags. Every time I thought we were done, more bags appeared. It was like they were multiplying in the back. Those little balls were the same way.

I was pretty sure we had enough ammo to knock out both the Arkansas and Texas side of Texarkana. I was tired and sore from leaning over filling those little balloons. At least we knew that one dose of the serum was good for at least five hours. Eugene had to hit poor William with another dose while we worked. I was afraid to ask Eugene precisely what was in them. He did assure us that they had no harmful side effects. I was praying he was right or Death would be mad at us.

One of the many lights on my phone was flashing. Bartholomew had programmed my new phone and now I got notifications for everything. It drove me nuts. I used my cell for my alarms, the only reason it was still in my room. While the clock on my night table had a lot of fun memories for me, I hated the alarm in it. So, I was stuck with my cell phone and all the weird stuff that came with it.

I pulled the phone closer and checked to see what notification was blowing up my phone now.

Unlike Constantine, who was the social media king of the house, both on the human side and the supernatural, I sucked at it. Constantine was so impressive. Not only did he have two YouTube channels—one for humans and one for supernatural—he also had a twitter account. I had no idea where he found the time. I struggled just to keep up with my text messages and voice mail.

I had a text from Abuelita.

Isis, emergency. I need you at the store at 0700. I'm panicking. Too much to do, not enough people or time. Please help.

I was so happy Abuelita's texts were getting better. For the longest time, I had no clue what she was talking about. Out of habit, I glanced at my clock on the night table for the time instead of the phone I was holding. My brain was still not focusing because it took me a minute to process the information. By the time I processed the text, it finally hit me that I had less than thirty minutes to get up and get ready to head to Abuelita's. I disliked short notices and lately, my whole life was full of them.

I rushed to the restaurant with my hair still wet and messy at five minutes after seven. I wasn't sure what I was expecting, but it was a giant disaster zone. It honestly looked like a hurricane or a tornado had hit the poor place. Abuelita was extremely organized and everything had a place in the kitchen. So, to see this monstrosity was out of character for her.

"Do I want to ask what evil-doer attacked your kitchen?" I was trying to make it a joke. Unfortunately, my voice sounded more like an accusation.

"Thanks to all the stars and the moon, you are here. I wasn't sure what to do." Abuelita rushed at me and gave me a huge hug. What was going on?

"I'm so confused. What's so urgent that I had to drive here so early?" I could always be honest with Abuelita and she never got offended.

"This College Bowl is going to be the death of me." Abuelita had released me from her bear hug but kept a grip on my arm. She was not letting go. Was she afraid that I might run away?

"It's killing you and poor Bartholomew. He has been stressed for over a month." Nothing should be this crazy. "How can I help?" I had no clue what I was supposed to do here.

"I need your organizational skills now. I'm making pastelitos to compete with that crazy fried-pie lady. She is making a killing and stealing my peeps." Abuelita started pacing the kitchen. That was a terrifying sight since space was very cramped.

"Abuelita, you can't be serious that some fried pies are stealing your business. We don't have a dessert menu, remember?" Was I missing something here?

"That's the problem; she is stealing any potential clients we might have. Besides, people are questioning my skills compared to hers." Now it made sense; this crazy thing was about pride.

"Got it. No need to panic. I'll start packing your supplies and labeling things. We'll get you ready to roll for tomorrow." Abuelita rushed to give me another hug. I was afraid if she did, she might crush my windpipe. "Hold it. No more hugs till we at least get semi-packed. Not to mention I'm starving, so I want to hurry so I can eat."

"Are you seriously going to get food somewhere else when you are already here?" Abuelita was looking at me, a little offended.

"No need to get mad, now. I didn't think we had anything to eat or time to make brunch." Abuelita looked like she needed food herself.

"You're in luck; I made breakfast earlier. Start doing your magic over there and I'll get you food."

Maybe Constantine was right and we did work for food. I was so excited I wanted to whistle.

I started organizing boxes with trays, utensils, napkins, and condiments. I labeled and numbered each box. I wanted to make sure there was no mistake or lost time trying to figure out what was in the boxes. Before I could start my second box, Abuelita brought me a plate of huevos rancheros with tons of cheese and refried beans. She had added corn tortillas to my plate as well. My mouth was watering at the smell of the eggs with the sauce. I was surprised when she placed a cup of Mexican hot chocolate in front of me. The hot chocolate was a mixture of rich cocoa and chili powder. I was in heaven. If all I needed to do was fill and label boxes, this was amazing.

"I love this hot chocolate. And the food is delicious." I was trying to chew and talk at the same time. It was not a pretty sight.

"You love them so much because you are not eating enough food, Isis. You are shrinking to death." Abuelita's definition of health was a woman with plenty of meat on her bones.

"I'm healthy. I just run a lot, remember." I gave her my brightest smile. Abuelita was not buying it. Fortunately, I was saved by the bell. We both looked at the back door to see who was coming in.

"Sorry, I'm late." Ana rushed in. She looked awful and I had no idea what had happened to her.

"Girl, have you been crying? You look awful." I gave Abuelita a look at her statement. Ana did look like hell, but Abuelita didn't have to call her out like that.

"I'm sorry. I fought with Joe. He's been acting all sorts of weird." Ana looked like she was going to cry again.

"Weird how?" I was probably paranoid, but I wasn't taking any chances with weird-acting people in Texarkana.

"Angry, moody, and aggressive. It's crazy, cause a couple of days ago I thought he had flu symptoms. The symptoms are gone, but now he's off." Ana was almost ashamed for telling us.

"Ana, I need to ask you a question, but I don't want you to get mad." I wasn't sure how to ask, but I needed to know. "Has Joe been using lately?" Joe had a hard time adjusting to normal life. I was afraid he had fallen off the wagon.

"No, Isis, I swear. We both been clean for months now. It was awful at first, but Abuelita gave us each a tonic and that took some of the withdrawals away. Isis, what is going on?" Ana was becoming even more desperate and I was not helping.

"We're afraid there's a plague loose in Texarkana. What you're describing sounds familiar. Ana, do you trust me?" I wasn't sure if she could handle all of this. She was so attached to Joe; I was afraid she might lose it if he relapsed. "I want to get Joe examined by our friend just to make sure he's OK. Would you mind?"

"Is it going to hurt him?" Ana was scared, but she always put the welfare of Joe before her own.

"I doubt it. But I want to make sure he's in a safe place, just in case he might turn." I wasn't sure if I could explain everything without scaring her to death.

"Turn into what? Isis, please just tell me."

Ana's voice was trembling and I couldn't stand it. I was so worried for both of them. I knew I could trust Ana with anything. After last fall, she knew I worked for Death and was OK with the supernatural world. She wasn't afraid and was still my friend. I bit the inside of my cheek before starting; this was going to scare her.

"He might turn into a zombie and try to kill you."

Ana almost passed out. I had to rush to her side and hold her up. "We're trying to figure out what it is and how it's transmitted. I just want to make sure you're both safe. What do you think?"

"Isis, please don't let him turn into a zombie. Do whatever it takes." Ana was squeezing my arm. It was still amazing to have so much support and faith from her and Joe. I didn't want to let them down, but I also didn't want Joe to hurt her.

"We'll do everything we can. Let me make a call."

She hugged me. This was the day of hugs, it appeared. I walked toward the exit. Ana went over to Abuelita. They started whispering to each other. I dialed Reapers and prayed one of the boys was up. It didn't take long to get someone on the other line.

"Reapers Incorporated, how may I help you?" Bob's voice was professional and soothing all at once. I was impressed.

"Hi, Bob, it's me. I need your help."

"Isis, where are you? Are you OK?"

Bob sounded worried. Maybe my intro was too quick. I needed to slow down now and explain things.

"Sorry, Bob. Yes, I'm good. I'm at Abuelita's. Ana is here and she mentioned that Joe is acting odd." I tried to explain without scaring Ana, who was probably listening.

"Do you think he might be infected?"

"Maybe. Could you have Eugene check him, please? I'll get Shorty to pick him up." I hated waking everyone up, but this could be important.

"Too easy. I'll get him myself. Is Ana coming as well?"

I hadn't even thought if she wanted to join him. Good point on Bob's part.

"Hey, Ana, would you like to go with Joe to get tested?" I asked Ana from across the kitchen. She looked at Abuelita first before replying.

"Child, go take care of your man. We got this here," Abuelita said softly.

"Thank you so much," Ana told Abuelita. She turned toward me. "Yes, I'll head home now."

Ana looked a little too frazzled to drive, but we didn't have that many options.

"Are you OK to drive? Bob can pick you up on his way to your place." I didn't want her in a wreck.

"I'm good, Isis; I'll head out now. Thank you so much." Ana smiled at me and took off.

"Bob, she'll be home when you get there. Thank you." I was so grateful for Bob I didn't have enough words to thank him.

"Anytime. Be careful out there and I'll see you later." Bob hung up before I could reply.

"Well, that's settled," I told Abuelita as I put my phone back in my pocket.

"That's great; now we got tons of work, just for the two of us. So, my little helper, let's get started."

Abuelita was right. I had just sent away our only helper. I took a sip of my hot chocolate and got back to work.

Chapter Twenty

Next time the brilliant idea pops into my head to send away helpers, I will slap myself. With Ana gone, it took Abuelita and me twice the time to get everything done. She was planning to fry the pastelitos and some of her meats on site. This meant everything still had to be prepped, seasoned, and packaged. I was so grateful she was keeping her menu simple. I still felt like I chopped millions of pounds of tomatoes, lettuce, and all sorts of food products. It didn't help that Abuelita was still planning to cook for her customers at the restaurant tonight. For the first time, I was grateful I didn't have to work at Abuelita's this weekend because it was going to be insane.

By the time I got in Ladybug, it was past ten, and I had four missed texts. I couldn't answer anything while I was working. It was getting too crazy. Constantine wanted me to stop by the accountant's parents and see if their prodigal child had stopped by. That was going to be an interesting conversation. Bartholomew had loaded the directions directly to my phone. The technology was awesome.

As I sat in Ladybug trying to stretch my muscles, I had to laugh at myself. I had started the week moping around, feeling left out and almost useless. Now, I was the only one doing work. Constantine was wrong. I was officially the infantry of this team and everyone else was a support element. I was starting to believe the support element had a much easier job than I did. I was the one in the front getting shot at. No wonder Interns didn't last long.

Nothing in Texarkana was very far. According to Bartholomew's directions, the parents lived on Stonegate Drive off Summerhill Road in Pleasant Grove. For a person who was never on this side of town, I was making up for it. Like most things in Pleasant Grove, the houses on Stonegate were beautiful. The parents lived in a charming two-story home. I was used to most of Texarkana being one story tall, so anytime I ran into anything taller, it caught me by surprise. The place was beautiful, but I would hate to have to cut the lawn here. That looked like a lot of work.

I made a quick U-turn and parked facing Summerhill. In case I needed to leave in a hurry, I wanted to be facing in the direction I felt most confident about. I took a quick breath. Even as an adult, talking to other people's parents made me nervous. I always felt that they were judging me. I looked around. The street was deserted. I hope Bartholomew was right and her parents were home. Coming back tonight was out of the question. For some strange reason, this type of cute and sweet neighborhood unnerved me. Way too pretty to be true.

I sprinted up the sidewalk and rang the doorbell. It didn't take long to hear footsteps coming to the door. Thank you, Father. I wanted to be out of there, ASAP. A thin woman maybe in her late sixties opened the door. She looked terrific. Her hair was done very fashionably and her makeup was spotless. She was probably a knockout in her twenties. She still carried that grace of youth about her.

"Hi, I'm sorry to bother you, but I was looking for Ms. Emma. Are you her mother?" I started improvising as quickly as possible.

"Yes, dear. Do I know you?" Emma's mother was looking at me very suspiciously.

"No, sorry. I'm a friend of Emma's from college. I heard she was back in town and decided to stop by." That sounded fairly convincing. I was sure she would know that I wasn't from here.

"You're a long way from Harvard."

Mom was a little too sharp for my taste. I tried to smile and play it off.

"True. I joined the Army when I got out of college and recently, I got a job with the military base here. I remember Emma said she was from Texarkana so I looked her up. I'm still trying to get used to the new location." I was starting to ramble and I was hoping Mom-dearest was buying it.

"Dear, you must be having such a hard time adjusting." She sounded worried about me. I was impressed.

"It gets easier each day. Everyone here is so helpful and understanding." That statement, for the most part, was correct. Most people in Texarkana were nice.

"That is so true. Texarkana is twice as nice." I smiled when she mentioned the popular slogan for both cities. "Unfortunately, dear, my daughter hasn't been around for a while. I think she's embarrassed by us." I looked around, not sure why anyone would be embarrassed by this lady. I guessed we never really know what goes on behind closed doors. She kept talking. "As soon as she graduated, she moved out. She was tired of the small town and left for the big city."

"I'm so sorry to hear that." I had no idea what else to say. "Thank you for your time." I was getting ready to walk away when she grabbed my arm.

"Have you checked with her boyfriend? We haven't seen her, but we know she's back in town. She had sworn she would never move back here. I suspect she's embarrassed to come and tell us." Her mother looked down the street, as if she was expecting her daughter to show up.

"You wouldn't happen to know where he lives?" That was my first real clue and I intended to milk it for all it was worth.

"The boy is a low-life loser." Sweet, little mother almost spat at me. I guess she wasn't a fan of the relationship. "Last time I heard, he was jumping from place to place. He can barely hold down a job. I don't know what my daughter ever saw in him." She looked disgusted.

"How long have they been together?" The accountant has been gone for more than fifteen years. How were they still together? The girl graduated from Harvard; I had no idea how she made that work. I had a new respect for her commitment to things.

"They were high school sweethearts. They have been on again, off again for years. I have no idea why. I'm sorry I couldn't be more helpful." She looked sad. She did miss her daughter.

"Ma'am, you were a huge help. Thank you so much for your time. I appreciate it." That part was true. At least we had a lead now.

"I'm so glad, dear. Have a good day and be careful. People are crazy lately."

If she only knew the truth of that statement.

I made my way to Ladybug. Bartholomew was terrific at programming my schedule as well as the directions on my phone. Sometimes, I wondered if he thought I was that flaky. I sat inside Ladybug trying to decide what to do next when I noticed two joggers. Joggers in town were frequent, but there was something odd about one of them. One was falling behind and looked shaky. His friend turned around when he noticed he wasn't next to him. He ran back just in time to see his friend fall on his knees.

I didn't have time to wonder too long what was going on. One minute, the guy is on the ground, the next, he jumps up and is attacking his friend. I looked around, wondering if anybody was watching. In that short time, the guy had gone full zombie. I looked around Ladybug for a weapon. I had my machete attached to the ceiling, but killing anyone was out of the question. I glanced back and a gym bag was sitting in the back seat. I pulled it over and found a paintball gun, fully loaded. A small note read: Watch your back and happy hunting. Bartholomew had signed the note. He was amazing.

I grabbed the paintball gun and ran at full sprint toward the joggers. The zombie was inflicting severe damage on his friend. I didn't want to take any chances of having him turn on me. When I was about twenty feet away, I took aim and fired. I knew Eugene had increased the dose on his formula, but I wasn't prepared for the results. The zombie dropped like a sack of potatoes as soon as he was hit. My mouth dropped wide open in shock. That was one impressive result.

I ran over to check on the friend. He was lying on the ground, looking like hell. He tried to move but was barely able. I shot him, too. The boy passed out in less than a second. The last thing I needed was a screaming guy drawing more attention to himself. Besides, I didn't feel like explaining what had happened to his friend. I was leaving that part to somebody else. I grabbed my phone and dialed Reapers.

Constantine picked up the call. "Isis, what's wrong?"

"Why does it have to be something wrong?"

"You only call when something goes wrong." Constantine was right about that.

"Good point." I hated when he was right.

"What happened? Did you find the parents?"

"I found the mother, but that's not why I'm calling. I just knocked out two joggers. One went full zombie on his friend. Constantine, this is getting worse," I told him as I looked around the street.

"I'm sending the cleanup crew. Secure the area till he gets there. See you back at Reapers." Constantine hung up before I could reply. Guess I was stuck here guarding the comatose.

The cleanup crew didn't take long to arrive. Probably because Shorty was still driving like a maniac. I wondered if he realized he was driving a truck, not an Indy car. I wasn't sure if he saw me, but I jumped out of the way just in time to watch him hit his brakes. Fortunately, they worked amazingly well. Shorty jumped out of the truck, carrying a large blanket.

"Shorty, you're going to kill somebody someday," I told him as I walked back to his truck.

"Boss lady, the big guy said to hurry. We can't have people finding dead people on the road." I couldn't argue with his reasoning.

"You do know that they are not dead." I wanted to make sure he wasn't dropping off people in a grave now.

"The fact that they are alive is worse. They could wake up and jump off." Shorty had opened the tailgate of his truck. The bed was now covered with some foam material. At least they would be comfortable on their way. We walked over and dragged the zombie first.

"Fair enough. By the way, where are you taking them? I don't think we have that much room at Reapers." I never asked Constantine where they were dropped off.

"The big guy has it covered. Father Francis is taking them in. Converted the basement to a hospital wing. That dude is the bomb."

Two things jumped out. First, my priest had converted the parish hall of the church into a hospital wing for zombies. Second, nobody said 'bomb' nowadays to describe people. Shorty was showing his age.

"Is that safe?" We loaded the beaten-up friend in the bed and closed the tailgate.

"We got this, boss lady. Next time call me directly. It'll save us some time. Be careful now; if you are finding them in the morning, it means trouble." I watched Shorty hop in his truck and take off. I had a feeling we were past the trouble category. We were now in the apocalyptic department.

Chapter Twenty-One

My head was hurting by the time I got to Reapers. The main area on the first floor was empty, so I rushed upstairs. I hoped Eugene had good news for us because I didn't. I walked into the loft and Eugene and Constantine were talking at the dining table. Constantine was sitting on the table while Eugene leaned on a chair. Eugene looked worried and he was holding some papers with him. Constantine did not look too happy either.

"What did I miss?" No need pretending now. I might as well get right to the point.

"We got a problem," Eugene answered.

"If that's all we got, we're doing good. Let me hear it." I walked over and took a seat. I was not in the mood to get lousy news standing up.

"I've been monitoring your date," Eugene stated.

"Can we call him William? I'm not dating that man. That situation was just a horrible mistake." I glared at him to make sure he got the point. Constantine tried to hide the smirk on his face.

"Fine. I've been monitoring William. At the rate this thing is progressing, in about five days, it will start devouring his internal organs." Eugene looked back at his charts to confirm.

"Hold on, what? What do you mean, devouring?" I was hoping his definition of devouring was not the same as mine.

"It will start killing him from the inside. I don't know how she did it, but she mutated it to create maximum damage. She was right; she'd make one hell of an Intern. She's good." Eugene sounded like a teenager with a crush.

"Enough praising over there. Focus. Can you stop it? Make an antidote or something?" This was way outside of my realm. We were in the soul business, not the mutations and killing business.

"You want me to do what? Isis, we don't cure things. We unleash plagues into the world. I can't be making cures."

Eugene was offended. I was speechless

"We're on the brink of a zombie apocalypse due to your boss's horrible hiring practices and you are telling me it's not in your job description to stop it?" Eugene was quite lucky I was sitting across the table from him because I wanted to slap him silly.

"Isis, these are our company's practices. I can't go against them."

I was going to hurt Eugene.

"Eugene, we don't have time for this." Constantine was glaring at him. His claws on his right paw were out and I was pretty sure he had grown at least twice his size. Eugene was smart enough to back away. There was an awkward silence in the room. "So, according to your policies, you cannot develop cures or antidotes." Constantine gave Eugene a moment to ponder. "But can you kill a current strand gone rogue?"

Wow, Constantine was a genius. Eugene thought about it for a minute.

"Um. We're talking about an unauthorized specimen. Seek and destroy is part of my job description." Eugene was smiling broadly. Now that his moral dilemma had been resolved, he looked a lot calmer. Pestilence had her Interns trained to follow instructions.

"Another problem, though," Eugene said, a little softer. "The moment the virus enters the human body it starts mutating. I need a sample to be able to know what I'm looking for."

I leaned my head back. These issues never ended.

"Do we know how she is delivering it? Have you found the drugs she's using? I need to know what I'm looking for to find it."

"I'm waiting for the results from the lab. We dropped off the samples yesterday when we went out to look for supplies. Bob dropped off the ones from your friends this morning."

Eugene didn't seem very worried about the wait.

"How long does it take to get a drug test back?" I had done urine analysis for the military, but I had no idea how long it took for the results to get back.

"You do know this is not TV? It's going to take hours to get the results back. Fifth is taking that task personally." By the sound of Eugene's voice, that was a big deal.

"Can wonder boy get the results faster?" Constantine took the words right out of my mouth.

"Unfortunately, no. Not even Fifth can speed up science. As soon as he has it, he'll let us know." Eugene at least sounded hopeful.

"How are Ana and her boyfriend?" Neither one of them had mentioned them. Eugene looked at his paper very intently. Constantine lowered his head on his paws, looking back to normal.

"Isis, it's not good. He has it, and he's starting to convert. She's also infected, but at an early stage." Eugene couldn't meet my eyes.

"How is that possible? I know they're clean. I can vouch for Ana. I see her all the time." I dropped my head back again. This was horrible. How was I supposed to tell her she was going to die if we didn't find the cause of this?

"If I'm not mistaking, the virus can be transmitted through bodily fluids. If they were intimate recently, he probably passed it to her." I knew Eugene was trying to make me feel better, but I wasn't buying Joe doing drugs again.

"Great, now we have an upgraded AIDS virus." I rolled my eyes at the insanity of it all.

"I wish. At least with that one, I know what I'm looking for." Eugene was staring at his notes when he spoke. I wondered if Pestilence peeps were responsible for that one as well.

"Good to know. Back to bodily fluids. Does that mean if one of those zombies licks me, I'm going to convert?" If that was the case, I wanted to stay far away from them.

"Eew, that's gross. Unless they lick an open wound, licks are safe. If they bite you and break the skin, that could be bad. How much of the virus they have in their system will determine how likely they can pass it to others." Eugene looked happy to be able to clarify that.

"Can you tell how far along each person is in their mutation?" I was hoping Ana and Joe had more time. I didn't want to think Ana was going to die in the next five days.

"Not yet, but I got a few more tests to run." Eugene was persistent, thank the Lord.

"Please do, and let me know as soon as you find out the carrier she's using. We need to narrow this down. I don't want to chase every drug dealer in the four states area." As exciting as those visits were becoming, we were running out of time.

"In that case, I better get back to work." Without a glance back at us, he hurried out the door.

"I like him. He should come and visit us more often." Constantine was watching the door after Eugene.

"Is that before or after you pluck out his eyes?" I eyed Constantine from my side and waited for a reply.

"He just needed some motivation, that's all. As you can see, it worked."

I couldn't help myself. I had to laugh. If that was Constantine's brand of motivation, he should avoid public speaking.

"Changing the subject on you. What is Father Francis going to do with all the zombies?" I did not like the idea of my sweet priest hanging out with crazy zombies.

"Obviously, we needed a place to keep them safe. Reapers does not have enough room to convert everything out. So, I made a few calls and activated all the churches. As soon as one fills up, the others will start taking them. The Staff and volunteers from the Church Under the Bridge agreed to help."

That explained all the calls Constantine had been making lately. I was impressed how quickly he got everything organized.

"Nice job. That's amazing." Constantine was full of surprises.

"Don't be that impressed. Texarkana, fortunately for us, has strong community values. The citizens still believe in taking care of their own. It just took a little coordinating and they're onboard."

The way he described it, it sounded simple enough.

"Changing the topic again, what are we going to do if we fail?" My biggest question was, how was I going to explain to Ana that she might die due to a killer zombie plague? I wasn't sure if I wanted to cry or punch something.

"Failure is not an option here. So, focus on the task at hand. Don't try to figure out how to boil the ocean, just work on getting in it first."

I wish I had the confidence Constantine had. Granted, he was also five thousand years old, so he had plenty of practice facing horrible obstacles.

"What's the next step?" I needed to focus on the present and not the potential what if.

"First things first. You need to get dressed to meet our local dark wizard."

Oh yeah, I had that guy. "What do you wear for such a meeting?" I had never met a dark wizard. Even his title sounded menacing.

"I'd recommend combat gear. Your black, anti-spell fatigues would be perfect. You never know when those tricky wizards will attack." Constantine sounded like he had personal experience with crazy wizards.

"I can do that. What time am I leaving?" Constantine was either nervous or slipping. Typically, he would have given me all the details in one breath. Now I was asking tons of questions.

"You leave in ten. Bob is ready, waiting in his quarters."

"He is that bad that you are sending Bob with me?" I wasn't too upset, just a lot more aware of the potential threat.

"Let's just say, if he's involved, I'm not taking any chances. I want you back in one piece." "Aww, I didn't know you cared. Thank you." I was debating scratching his ear but decided against it.

"Don't get emotional. I just don't want to have to train another Intern so soon."

Now that sounded more like Constantine. I stuck out my tongue at him. He glared back and I laughed. He did care.

"Anything else I need to know?" I started getting up from my chair.

"Yes, one more thing. You're taking The Camaro out. Make sure no more bullet holes appear on him." Constantine gave me his evil glare, like he was holding me personally responsible.

"Yes, sir." I was not going to argue with an angry cat about his car. I gave him one quick salute and took off to my room to change.

Chapter Twenty-Two

A couple of small cities surrounded Texarkana. I had recently learned if you were too close to any city in Texas, people automatically assumed your city was annexed to it. I was pretty sure the residents of those cities did not appreciate it. We were heading to Red Lick, which was on the north side of I-30. We did a quick left turn at the Roadrunner and drove down the long, winding road. It didn't matter how long I lived in Texas, my mind was always blown away when we passed horses and cows in pastures next to houses. I felt like I had traveled back in time to a more peaceful world.

Bob pulled off the road and parked half a block from our destination. I was a little confused. According to Constantine, the dark wizard lived on FM 2148, next to the Red Lick Middle School and across the street from the elementary school. There had to be some mistake. The house we were looking at was a lovely brick home with great landscaping. I felt a little out of place in my black combat gear with a machete strapped to my leg and an M16. I was sure somebody would call the cops on us any minute.

"You know we can't go out like this. If a teacher sees us, we're doomed," I told Bob as I glanced around for the tenth time.

"Oh, good. I was wondering if I was the only one feeling a little out of place here. I vote we leave the rifles and stick with handguns."

"Sounds like a plan. Dark wizard or not, we could still be drawing that much attention in the middle of the day."

We switched weapons. Bartholomew had given me a smaller paint gun to fit in my cargo pockets in case I needed it. That one was coming with me.

Bob and I got out of The Camaro as casually as possible, trying to avoid any extra attention. We made our way to the side door of the nice house. I didn't see any cameras or security devices. I pulled out my Smith & Wesson special and Bob took out his pistol. No matter how hard I tried, Bob's weapons always looked more intimidating than mine. He gave me a nod and kicked in the door. I rushed in with my gun in hand, followed quickly by Bob.

I figured a dark wizard would live in some dark cave with cauldrons boiling, bats hanging from the ceiling, and maybe tarantulas crawling around. The reality was different. The house was just as beautiful on the inside as the outside. Cream-colored walls with soft silk curtains—and they even had ceramic roosters on top of the cabinets. The side door led right into a foyer facing the kitchen. If the house was an immaculate surprise, the man staring at us was a total contradiction.

"Are you David, the dark wizard?"

A tall man with dark hair and gorgeous blue eyes was standing in front of us with an apron and a bowl. He didn't look surprised to see us, but he did roll his eyes at me in disgust.

"Yes, and you are?" He kept mixing whatever he had in his bowl and I was ready for all hell to break loose.

"Isis." I was a little confused how to respond. He raised an eyebrow, a little confused himself.

"Is this a new recruiting campaign? I'm impressed. Unconventional, but I'm not interested."

Bob was staring at him as David spoke. It was my turn to roll my eyes.

"Not the terrorist group." I despise that group for stealing my name. Why couldn't they call themselves Carol or Joe? I was still fuming when David spoke again.

"Well, that was going to be a great conversation topic at the country club. Isis who?" David went to a country club? We had to be at the wrong house.

"Isis Black."

His facial expressions did not change. "Is the name supposed to ring a bell?"

I was shocked. I had finally met someone in the supernatural community who didn't know who I was. I looked at Bob and he just shrugged. I had no idea how to proceed. This was so rare; rule number one came into effect here.

"Can you give me a minute?" I told David. "Bob, keep an eye on him."

Bob turned back to face our deadly wizard, according to Constantine.

We weren't wearing earpieces this time. Constantine was afraid our dark wizard would pick up the signal somehow. I was looking around the house that would have made Martha Stewart proud and wondered what secret powers this boy had. I pulled my cell phone and found out I had perfect reception. I hit the speed dial to Reapers and prayed Constantine was near the phone.

"What happened now? You just got there." Constantine did not sound amused at all.

"He has no idea who I am," I whispered over the phone to Constantine.

"What's your point?" Constantine sounded a bit irritated.

"What do I do now?" I was lost. How was I supposed to introduce myself if I wasn't supposed to tell people I worked for Death?

"Girl, are you seriously calling me about that? You work for Reapers. Ask him the questions. By the way, where are you calling me from?"

I shook my head at my stupidity. I was making this too hard and Constantine was right.

"In his kitchen," I answered, very embarrassed. I could feel the flush creeping up my cheeks.

"Isis, get off the phone and stop looking crazy. Get to work."

Typical of Constantine to hang up before I could reply.

I walked over to the guys who were busy discussing the bowl. Somehow, Bob had put his gun away and was leaning against the wall, just chit-chatting. I didn't put my gun up, but I wasn't pointing it at anybody now. I cleared my throat and both men looked at me.

"Did you check in with Mom? Are we ready now?" David was dripping with sarcasm. I was not amused.

"Yeah, sorry about that. So, I am Isis and this is Bob. We're from Reapers Inc. We want to ask you a few questions." I stared blankly at him. I was not going to squirm.

"Do you normally bust people's doors down to ask questions? Not much of an incentive to help, is it?"

"Were you going to let us in if we knocked?" I was not backing down.

"Guess we'll never know now."

Mr. Dark Wizard David was not intimidated by two people with guns. I was starting to see Constantine's point. I considered opening my third eye to check him out, but if he was as scary as Constantine said, that vision would terrify me forever or I'd go insane.

"Guess not. But you didn't seem that surprised when we busted in." That was bothering me. It was like he was expecting us.

"Child, you set off all my magic wards twenty feet from the house. Considering you were not carrying any spells or magic weapons, I figured you were safe. You weren't planning on shooting me, were you?"

Of course, he would have wards. We had them all around Reapers. I needed to get more info from Constantine before another crazy mission.

"No, we weren't. We just have a few questions. Are you planning to blow us up with your spell?" That bowl was making me nervous.

"Only if you're allergic to chocolate chip cookies." He tilted the bowl so we could see its contents. He was right; it was chocolate chip cookie dough.

"That dough looks great." I had no idea what Bob was talking about, but the house did smell delicious now that I was paying attention to it. "Do I smell chocolate cake?"

"Yes. I just finished a German chocolate cake. I've been baking all morning," David replied, proud of himself.

"You did a whole cake just this morning? I'm impressed," Bob said and I knew I had lost all control of the situation.

"Hey, I made two. Do you want a piece? It's to die for." David offered Bob a slice and I was sure he was going to fly away from the excitement.

"Darn, we quit gluten. Horrible timing." Bob looked devastated.

"Well, that explains why she's so thin." David and Bob both looked at me.

"Nah, she doesn't eat meat." I wasn't sure if that was Bob's idea of defense.

"That is extreme." I was not amused by the pity look David was giving me.

"OK, foodies, can we get back to the business at hand. You can discuss the Food Channel line-up at a later day." That brought them back to reality. I ignored the skinny comment. I was getting tired of always having to defend myself. I might look thin, but I was solid muscle.

"Fine, Ms. Isis-Not-the-Terrorist-Group, how may I help you?" David was very arrogant.

"Has anyone approached you with a potential deal to help them make zombies?" I knew I sounded crazy as soon as the words left my mouth.

"Zombies? Girl, please. What do you think this is, the sixties? Nobody is in that business anymore."

I looked at David closely and realized Bob was doing the same. He didn't look a day over thirty. How was he familiar with the sixties? That was impossible?

"How old are you?" I demanded. David gave me a questioning look. "Never mind. So, you haven't heard of anyone trying to make zombies around here?" I was desperate.

"Nope. They'd be crazy to even think about it—even more, to do it. Necromancers and zombie- making in any capacity is an automatic death sentence by the Order, unless Death finds you first. So, no. Nobody is that crazy anymore."

Great. If David was right, that ruled out most of the supernatural community. Now what?

"Do you have any more questions? If not, I got a dinner I'm catering and you're wasting my time."

He caters. This was insane.

"No, that was all. Thank you for your time and sorry about your door." I was sorry about the door. I wondered if our insurance would replace it.

"I would say it was a pleasure, but let's not do this again. OK?"

Before we could reply, David had pushed us out of his house with some invisible force and slammed the door in our faces.

"Hey, that went well," Bob said, smiling at me. We needed to work on his definitions. Before I could reply, we heard loud screams from across the street. "The elementary school, hurry."

Bob didn't have to tell me twice.

We sprinted across the street to find a scene right out of a nightmare. We both jumped the short fence toward the playground. It appeared three of the kids had gone zombie and were terrorizing everyone. I quickly switched guns, putting my Smith & Wesson on my back holster and pulling out the paintball gun. I had never shot at small moving targets and I found out it was harder than I imagined. I took aim and hit a couple of the victims instead of the little zombies. Bob managed to get one that was getting ready to jump one of my collateral damages.

After five kids were down, I finally got the little redheaded kid. I was sure that kid was not even seven years old, but he moved with a purpose. He could have been a leprechaun for all I knew. From the corner of my eye, I saw a flash of movement. I was too slow to turn and aim. Fortunately, Bob saw the little, round kid moving at me, ready to bite. I was pretty sure if that kid took a bite out of me, I would get infected. The kid went down fast. I felt really bad; these rounds were designed for adults. I had no idea how they were going to affect children.

We had screaming kids everywhere. Some had been bitten; others were scratched. It was a horrible, messy sight. I went over and picked up a little girl. She was pushed on the ground and couldn't get up. I was afraid they had broken her leg. She screamed when she saw the gun and went into panic mode. I felt terrible, but I shot her, too. We didn't need extra screaming kids. Not to mention she wouldn't be in pain till we got her fixed. Bob made his way toward the teachers, who looked terrified. I wasn't sure what he was saying, but he was calming them down. I picked up my phone and call Reapers again.

"Now what?" Constantine hissed at the phone.

"We got serious problems. We just knocked out three zombies, all under the ages of eight," I told Constantine as I examine the area.

"This just got worse. I'm sending the cleanup crew and Father Francis. We're going to need a respected source to move those kids. Secure the perimeter and make sure nobody else turns. Will debrief when you guys get back."

We had such a huge mess now, I didn't even mind when Constantine hung up on me. I put my paintball gun away to avoid scaring more kids. We had no idea how many of these little ones were infected. How could anyone hurt innocent children just to prove they were a better Intern? This was madness.

Chapter Twenty-Three

The loft was empty when Bob and I came in. I was mentally and emotionally exhausted. It took Father Francis over two hours to get everyone calmed down and able to move the children. I had no idea how he handled his job. Kids were crying, parents were panicking, school staff was upset they might get sued, and we still had to get the children to the church. Zombies and zombie-makers were going on my list of least favorite supernatural creatures. They sucked the life out of you. I dropped all my guns on the dining table and collapsed on the couch.

"This is officially my worse week ever," I said aloud, not sure if Bob was listening.

"You said that three weeks ago, after chasing the ghost in Seattle," Bob reminded me from the kitchen.

"That was awful. I smelled like seaweed all week long. Not to mention my hair was all matted and tangled." I was sent to find a poor soul that had drowned in Seattle. The poor guy drowned at sunset and every evening he would appear screaming for help. The entire area was starting to get spooked. Unfortunately, getting him out of the water was a nightmare. Every time I got close enough to catch him, he went under water. It took me three days to finally get to him. I was pretty sure I swallowed enough ocean to fill an aquarium. "This is an omen; we are destined to have horrible weeks. How do people that work in morgues or funeral homes handle it?"

"Easy," Bob said. "They don't talk to the ghost; they just fix the body."

That was a valid point. Bob was good at analyzing situations. I wasn't sure I wanted to work on a dead body.

"I think I'm making cupcakes. I picked this gluten-free cake mix at the Granary yesterday. I think I can make mini pineapple upside-down cakes. What do you think?"

I thought we shouldn't visit any more foodies in town, so Bob didn't get food envy. Naturally, I couldn't tell him that. Instead, I leaned my head over the couch so I could see him better.

"Bob, if anyone can make a gluten-free cake taste like pineapple upside down, it's you. You got my vote." I did my part in moral support for the day. Bob was beaming with joy. After years of seeing the worst in people when he was living on the streets, very little bothered Bob. He empathized with people, but he never took it home with him. I might need to learn that someday.

I started to get comfortable on the couch and was dozing off. For a leather couch, this thing was a sleep magnet. If you were ever tired, the couch would lure you to slumber. I was getting pretty relaxed when I heard the door slam open. I jumped at least two feet in the air from the sound.

"What is going on?" I was pretty sure I shouted it.

"We got a problem; it's not in the drugs." Eugene looked like he'd been hit by lightning. His lab coat was all crumpled up, and he had stains everywhere. That was the fifth coat he'd destroyed in two days. I was starting to wonder what exactly he was doing down there. Ink fights?

"Yup, we figured that out," I yelled from the couch. Sleep was out of the question with Eugene looking all frazzled. I got up and took a seat in a dining chair. At least I could see him better.

"How did you know? It took me hours sorting through lab results to get to that conclusion." Eugene was not happy we had stolen his thunder.

"We got three elementary students attacking the playground, all under seven years old. It was a pretty good guess all three were not in a gang selling dope on the street." I gave him a flat look that managed to calm him down.

"OK, that's an excellent deduction." Eugene took a seat as he spoke. At least he wasn't pacing like a maniac.

"Please tell me you figured out how your plague is getting into their systems." I was adding Pestilence to my list of least favorite supernatural creatures. I didn't care if she was technically family.

"I have been running a test on all our patients. They have no needle marks anywhere. Ana said she and Joe hadn't inhaled anything abnormal." Eugene looked at his notes. Somehow that boy was always carrying notes.

"So...what's your conclusion here, Sherlock?"

"They eat it." Eugene followed that statement with a shoulder shrug, making him look innocent. I wasn't sure what to reply. I looked at him and then at Bob, who was staring at him.

"You do know that's worse than drugs," Bob said to Eugene. Eugene just nodded. "We live in Texas. Do you know how many food places we have in Texarkana alone?"

Bob had a point. If we did something big in town, it was eating. I dropped my head on the table.

"I think so far this is the worst week ever," I told Bob with my head still down. We had no leads, a bunch of zombies, and now tons of possible locations to search. Oh yeah, I almost forgot. Bartholomew's College Bowl was taking place in two days. I wasn't sure if I wanted to scream or cry. Before I could do either, Bob put a huge mug of hot chocolate in front of me. He gave one to Eugene as well. He even added extra marshmallows.

"Thank you, Bob," Eugene and I said at the same time.

"Jinx." We did it again. I started laughing and Bob just shook his head. According to Bob, hunger leads to horrible decision-making, so whenever things were going bad, he fed us. Crazy idea, but I was feeling calmer. Maybe Bob was right.

The kitchen door burst open again. Why was everyone slamming that poor door today? Constantine came into view, followed closely behind by Bartholomew.

"I have info on the boyfriend." Bartholomew was almost yelling with excitement.

"Great. Do you know where he lives?" I was ready for some good news.

"Not exactly. I have a couple of old addresses. Maybe one of the people who currently live there can help us out," Bart replied.

"Cheer up, Bart. It's better than nothing. Let's go."

"Not so fast. We got other pressing matters," Constantine said as he jumped on the kitchen island. Bob put a bowl of hot chocolate in front of him and another mug on the table for Bartholomew. Either Bob was always prepared or he had a sixth sense I knew nothing about.

"More pressing than finding the accountant?" I had no idea what could be more critical.

"We have a customer complaint that you must handle tonight."

I stared at Constantine with my mug in midair.

"You get customers' complaints?" Eugene said, more like a question than a statement.

"I have no idea. This is the first time I've heard of it. What customer is complaining?" I put my mug down and waited for an answer.

"You're not going to like it. Your favorite devil, Mr. Jake." Constantine said it before licking more of his hot chocolate. I slapped my head with my hand. This week was getting worse by the minute.

"When you say favorite devil, what exactly do you mean by that?" I forgot Eugene lived in an underground lab away from the rest of the world. He probably had never met Jake.

"He means Lucifer," Bob said, "Prince of Darkness. The deceiver, the fallen angel. You know, that guy fighting to get your soul."

Bob did not like Jake at all. According to Bob, Jake gave him the creeps and he avoided him pretty much like he avoided the plague. Funny thing, we were hanging out with both in one week.

"You are kidding, right?" Poor Eugene, he was having a hard time catching up here. "Do you have to go and see him?"

"Technically, you're going, too." Constantine dropped that bomb on Eugene like it was nothing. I was pretty sure Eugene just changed colors.

"What?" That was all Eugene could say.

"Why is Eugene coming with me?" I figured I could help my boy out before he gave himself a heart attack.

"It's Latin night at the Cave and only couples are allowed. This is Intern's work and it just happens Eugene is an Intern." Constantine looked at Eugene, waiting for him to pass out. I held my breath, waiting for his reply.

"Latin night? Are we going to a club? I'm in."

That was the quickest change of attitude I had ever seen in my life. Bartholomew had stopped drinking his hot chocolate and was staring at Eugene, confused.

"You're willing to go see the devil as long as it's in a club? That's crazy."

"I took ballroom dancing in college. I haven't been dancing in years." Eugene looked around the room, excited as he continued talking. "Come on now, you've seen where I work." Eugene had an excellent point. I doubted he ever saw people besides those crazy Interns and the few in the support department. After this incident,

I doubt they would ever see any of the support people again.

"You got me there. But can you dance?" Bob was not letting this go. I was surprised he was still following the conversation while he made his cupcakes.

"I was pretty good. I even went to a few competitions. It's been a while, so I might be a little rusty." Eugene was so excited he was beaming.

"In that case, I guess we're going dancing. Cheers." I gave him an air salute with my mug and he returned the cheer.

"Well now that we settled that, Eugene needs some clothes." Constantine was full of surprises today.

"Yeah, dude. You can't go in your lab coat to a club. Even I know that."

"You're in charge of getting Eugene ready," Constantine told Bob, who was putting cupcakes in the oven.

"Too easy, boss. Eugene, my man, are you ready for a make-over?"

Eugene was looking at Bob a little stunned. This was happening to us a lot lately. "Isis, would you watch the cupcakes while I'm gone? Twenty minutes, stick in a toothpick, and if it comes out clean, take them out. Wait at least ten minutes before taking them out of the muffin tin."

"I got it." I gave him a huge nod for added reassurance. With Bob around, we were all designated sous-chef duties. Bob headed out of the kitchen with Eugene rushing behind him.

"So, where is the entrance this time?" I asked Constantine. The Cave was Jake's private club and you were only allowed in by invitation or special card. Entrances to the cave appeared in different locations throughout the world. The site of the Cave also changed depending on Jake's mood.

"At the front of FCI." Constantine said the last part softly.

"What? Are you kidding me? He placed the entrance in front of the Federal Correction Institution?" There was a reason you should never trust the devil.

"I told you he had a complaint. Not a social call, so he's not going to make this easy. I recommend you bring some music to keep the guards and wandering neighbors away."

Constantine had a point. The last thing we needed was to get arrested for trespassing on federal property.

"Guess I have work to do before the boys get back." I looked over at the oven, trying to figure out how to listen to the timer from my soundproofed room. I guessed I needed to set my alarm.

"I got the cupcakes, Isis. I got more research to do on the boyfriend up here."

Bartholomew was a saint. I smiled and winked at him.

"Thanks, Bart. Let me get started." Being Death's Intern came with some perks. Recently we had discovered that I could make my music do more than just knock people out. Depending on my intentions, I could add other subconscious messages to them. One message I was good at sending now was to stay away from an area. I needed a new recording that would blend with the area. I had hard metal, and in Texas, that would draw attention. I guessed today we were playing country. I left the kitchen and headed toward my room to work.

Chapter Twenty-Four

We didn't have a dress code as Interns. What we did have were categories of outfits. For me, I had three main categories: normal standard work clothes, consisting of jeans or cargo pants, T-shirts, and running shoes. That was for regular days to run around town looking for lost souls or just everyday research. We had combat gear, which looked a lot like military-issue fatigues, except all black and made to repel magic spells as well as bullets. The last category—and the strangest one—was what I called costume outfits. Those were the ones you needed when you were trying to blend in at specific locations. My costumes ranged from nurse's uniforms, maids' uniforms, to even Catholic school uniforms. I was pretty sure if my godmother ever looked in my closet she would panic, just jumping to conclusions.

After several occasions of getting kicked out of places and other times getting beat up, I learned to embrace the costumes. If they kept me alive and able to do the job, then my insecurities had to get out of the way. Tonight's trip to the Cave required a costume outfit. I had on a black Latin dress, with a low back, one side longer than the other on the legs, and lots of red sequins. It was the type you would see in Dancing with the Stars. Jake took his club very seriously and the dress code had to match the theme. I learned that the hard way when I showed up wearing jeans and boots to a disco night and couldn't get in.

Eugene and I drove Ladybug down to FCI. I was still appalled Jake had picked the prison for his entrance. He was the one who wanted to see me. Why did I need to get arrested in the process? Eugene looked amazing. He was wearing a black pinstripe suit with a red tie and a pair of Wolf Shepherd closed cap shoes. I had no idea how Bob had pulled it off, but Eugene had the swagger of a Latin guy.

"You clean up well, Eugene." I was hoping to distract him. He was holding on to the door handle for dear life.

"We were aiming for a Pitbull look. Did we pull it off?" He gave me a quick glance, then turned back toward the window.

"You pulled it off. Now if you'd relax a little, it would be even more convincing," I told him with a smile.

"Isis, we're going to see the devil. Aren't you nervous?" His voice was a little shaky.

"Unfortunately, this is not my first time. So, I'm not. You get to test killer bees and find ways to kill humanity; I talk to the devil. That's part of our job descriptions." He did not see the humor in my statements. "OK, Eugene. Here's the trick. Don't make any deals with him. You must remember that whatever he offers, you don't need, and it's not worth your soul. If you get nervous, let me do all the talking and don't say a word. Simple enough?"

He took a deep breath and forced himself to nod.

I smiled back. "Good, 'cause we are here."

"Already?" Eugene looked around, confused. "There's nothing here."

I had to smile at him. "That's the point of the Cave. You can't find it unless you know you're invited. Here, put this on until we get inside." I handed him a pair of earplugs, and he looked at them. "I don't need you running away once I start playing my music."

"Oh right, I forgot." Eugene plugged his ears. When I was sure he was ready, I started the recording. We lowered the windows and left Ladybug running. The music wasn't blaring, but it was loud enough to discourage any humans from wandering near it—at least within a thirty-foot radius.

We stepped out of Ladybug. I made my way around and grabbed Eugene's arm. According to the invitation, we were heading to the first building near the road. I could tell Eugene was still nervous as I led him toward a side door. I squeezed his arm for encouragement.

"You look fabulous, by the way."

I was sure he tried to whisper but failed miserably due to the earplugs. I tossed my hair away from my face so I could see him better.

"Yes, she does. Our little Intern is finally embracing her inner diva."

Eugene jumped out of his skin when Adam first appeared. Adam, as usual, looked breathtakingly handsome. Adam was one of Jake's bodyguards; I was still not sure why the devil needed a bodyguard. This time he had red highlights in his hair, making his complexion glow.

"Thank you, Adam. You are looking as gorgeous as usual," I replied with my most charming smile.

"Flattery is not going to get you out of trouble, but please don't stop." Adam gave Eugene a quick inspection. "Not bad for short notice and he's a pretty sexy, little thing."

I pulled Eugene around before Adam could touch him. I was so grateful for Eugene's earplugs.

"Sorry, Adam, he can't hear you." I pointed at his earplugs and then the music.

"Nice little trick, I love it. You're learning." He gave me a wicked smiled. I had a feeling Adam was used to stopping traffic with it. "I'm doing double duty tonight, so I must check you. You know the drill."

"Of course. Let me go first, so you won't scare my date away." I winked at him. I could play this game. I looked at Eugene and made sure he could see me before I spoke. "Do as I do." He nodded in confirmation.

It took Adam less than a minute to search us both. Weapons were not allowed in the Cave. At least not ones you could bring with you. If you happened to find some inside, those were fair game. Adam gave us one last look-over and led us toward the entrance. Instead of opening the door we were facing, he pulled a pair of velvet curtains aside. Eugene was staring at the magical curtains in awe and not moving. I grabbed Eugene and pulled him along. Typical Cave, we went down a flight of stairs to another set of curtains. I knew better than to enter without Adam. He made his way to us and let us in.

"Welcome. His Highness is on the other side. You must dance your way across. Good luck." He gave me a quick kiss on the cheek and was gone. I felt like Judas had just kissed me.

"How is this possible?" Eugene screamed in my ear.

"Earplugs," I replied, as I pointed to my ears. Eugene got the point and took them off. "Don't lose them; we'll need them when we leave."

He put his earplugs in his coat pocket and stared at the place.

I had to admit, it was impressive. We were at a poolside party under the stars. The huge pool was to our right and packed with gorgeous people in tiny bathing suits drinking who knew what. Palm trees with small colored lights were scattered around the area. The DJ was on the left in a fancy-looking gazebo and right in front of us was a huge dance floor. Couples were moving like it was the finals at the World Dance Council. Yes, I could admit it. I watched those every year. I was grateful I picked this dress, because we fit right in.

"I hope you remember your dance lessons," I told Eugene. I hoped he wasn't freaking out on me.

"Oh, God, it's Mark Anthony and Maluma. I love this song. I got this, girl." I had no idea what took over Eugene. If it wasn't because I could see ghosts, I would have sworn he was possessed. Eugene did a turn, grabbed my hand, and spun me around. "My turn to lead."

We were dancing Salsa. I didn't have time to process Eugene's change completely. Growing up we moved around a lot, but my godmother always made it back to NYC. I grew up dancing Merengue, Bachata, and Salsa with my Dominican and Puerto Rican friends. I was amazed how well Eugene danced; he was a natural. Salsa was an eight-count dance and he was terrific. He owned the floor and he was aware of everything. That was a blessing, since he dipped me just in time as one of Jake's sword-carrying ninjas passed us. I was grateful Eugene made sure I didn't lose my head.

The song mixed right into Bachata and I was hoping Eugene could follow Romeo Santos's sexy beat. "Propuesta Indecente" was one of my favorite Bachata, a little controversial. Unlike the structure dance of Salsa, Bachata had a lot more hip and arm movement. With a primary three-step and a hop, the music made you move. Eugene was comfortable in a Latin club; he moved like a pro.

"Watch out for the sandpits," I told Eugene as I pointed to the new additions to the floor. He danced us across the floor without sending us to hell. Eugene was having too much fun. He was getting ready to start the Merengue when I pulled him off the dance floor.

"Remember, this is a business trip, not pleasure. We got work to do, so focus." I dragged him along. "I'm leading now, so let's go." Eugene looked over at the dance floor with longing.

I was grateful Jake was standing by a tall bar table not too far away. He was wearing a white suit that made his blond hair looked almost platinum. His deep-blue eyes were brilliant. I wasn't sure how he did it, but Jake always looked smoldering hot, no pun intended.

"Well, look who decided to show up and you brought a guest. How nice." Jake's voice was like silk running down your spine. I always pity the people that were lost in his charm. With that thought, I did a quick look at Eugene to make sure he was still in one piece.

"Your entrance was a little out of the way, but we made it. Eugene, meet Jake, the devil. Jake, meet Eugene, Pestilence's Intern." I didn't want to be there, but he was still our client, and I couldn't be rude.

"Wow, I feel honored. How did you manage to get out?" Jake was asking Eugene.

"Special assignment. I got a pass," Eugene replied, a little shy.

"I'm confused. What are you two talking about?" I was not following the conversation at all.

"Come on, sweetie, don't tell me you don't know. Pestilence's Interns are forbidden to leave the lab. They're almost like monks or hermits."

Was that in my manual? Maybe I really should read that thing. Jake gave me a wicked grin. "With those moves, Eugene, I would offer you a lifetime membership, but you'll never come. What a waste. Aren't you glad you work for Death instead, Isis?"

For having a customer's complaint, Jake was in a chatty mood.

"Believe me, I am. But I'm sure we're not here to discuss my work conditions. Constantine said you had a complaint. What is it?" We needed to get out of there soon. Eugene kept looking around like a kid in a candy store. Now that I knew he never left that lab, he might trade his soul to stay here.

"Fine, if you insist. Business, it is." Jake's tone became very serious as he faced me. "You have lost three of my souls, which is not acceptable."

"Three? We only know of one dying." How many others had died that we didn't know about?

"Do you expect everyone to die in front of you?" Jake had a valid point there. "I recommend you fix this as soon as possible or I'll have my pets start recruiting for new candidates a lot harder."

Was that a threat and how did that apply to me?

"You do know we just deliver souls, right? We're not responsible for the actions of the souls." This was getting complicated.

"True. But my souls were not delivered, so I see no problem taking some earlier." Jake said that like it made sense. "I'm sure your favorite angel might get a little disturbed if he finds out his souls were coming to me because you failed to stop a disgruntled employee." Jake was officially mocking me.

"If you know about the accountant, why don't you stop her?" I put my hands on my hips and glared at him.

"Do I look like an Intern to you? Stop losing my souls or else," Jake replied. We were staring each other down when Eugene pulled me over.

"I don't think it's safe that you are yelling at the devil in his house." I followed Eugene's gaze and realized half of the room was staring at us.

"Thanks, Eugene." I needed to calm down if we wanted to get out of here alive. "Is that all you have to tell me?" I asked Jake in a softer voice.

"Pretty much," Jake said, extremely sweetly.

"Why didn't you just tell that to Constantine?" He made me come all the way over here just for this?

"The Guardian does not take complaints. That's an Intern's job. I tried it once and I had scratches on my legs that lasted weeks. Not a good look. Besides, I wanted to see you. It's been forever. You only visit me when you want something."

I wasn't sure if Jake could tell, but I wanted to scratch his eyes out myself. I took a deep breath and shook my head.

"Of course, only Interns take the complaints. Great. Next time send me an email. We're leaving." Damn the devil to hell; he was a pain in my neck.

"Do come by more often, sweetie. By the way, I heard you should avoid sugars; they're more addicting than cocaine." Jake winked at me. I resisted the urge to flip him off; after all, he is still a customer.

"I'll make a note of that. Good night, Jake." I dragged Eugene around the pool away from the dance floor. I feared we would never leave if he stepped on it again.

"Don't we have to dance our way back?" Eugene asked, extremely hopeful.

"No, darling. You only paid to see the prince. Going home is always free if you have enough consciousness left to walk out. Hence the reason we're leaving now. I would hate to carry you." I gave Eugene an evil glare and he stopped staring at the dance floor.

"Thanks, Isis. As terrifying as it was, I had a blast." Eugene took my arm and kissed my cheek. I guessed it was 'kiss-Isis' night. He looked so happy all I could do was smile. I squeezed his arm one more time as we headed toward the curtains.

Chapter Twenty-Five

Time functions differently in the Cave compared to the rest of the world. What felt like twenty minutes turned out to be hours. It was midnight by the time we made it back to Ladybug. Eugene and I were exhausted but hungry. I felt like I had been clubbing all night long. We made a quick stop at Whataburger on our way home. Eugene had a bacon cheeseburger. He almost inhaled the sandwich. Working for Pestilence meant he gave up a lot of the things I took for granted like fast food. I was starting to appreciate my Horseman more every day.

Unfortunately, a late night did not translate into a late morning. Bartholomew woke me up at six-thirty and I was pretty sure he was having a panic attack. He needed to get to A&M by eight to confirm his registration. Bob and Constantine were out inspecting zombie patients and he needed a ride. I had never seen him so nervous, so I dragged myself out of bed. He was smart enough to give me plenty of time to get ready and to wake up slowly. I needed it because my hair was a giant knot and I forgot to take my mascara off the night before. I looked like an electrocuted raccoon.

We were out of Reapers by seven-thirty. Bartholomew made for a great copilot. The child thought of everything. He handed me a protein shake to wake me up. Pulled up the GPS to get us the fastest directions. Not sure why since all we had to do was get on Kings Highway and head north. It was one curvy road that let directly to Richmond Road and then the college. I wasn't going to point it out since he was stressing. I was looking forward to it. I had never actually been inside the campus. I'd been across the street at the Golf Ranch.

"Bart, are you OK?" He hadn't said a word since we turned on Kings Highway and that was very unusual.

"What happens if I lose tomorrow?" he asked without looking at me.

"What do you mean? Nothing is going to happen." I was wondering if I was still asleep because I wasn't following him.

"Isis, I'm a freak." Bartholomew had huge tears in his eyes. My heart broke.

"Bart, honey, what are you talking about? You are not a freak." I wanted to hug him, but I was driving. I pulled into the lot across from the Roadrunner. I needed to focus and not drive.

"You didn't see the way those guys looked at me when I signed up. Like I was a weirdo. I'm the orphan kid. I'm the kid who's homeschooled. I'm afraid of crowds. I can't eat gluten. I don't have any friends." Bartholomew started crying and I cried with him. Oh God, he was in so much pain.

"I'm a freak."

"Bart, you are not a freak." I tried to make him look at me, but he wouldn't. "Bartholomew, look at me." He eventually looked me in the eyes and I could read the fear and self-doubt in them. "The world is made up of lots of lost souls and some of those are dead. There is nothing wrong with you. You are a brilliant, funny, talented, incredible human being. At times, the world will call us names. It's never what they call us that matters but what we answer."

Bartholomew's lips were quivering.

"Have people called you names?" he asked, almost pleading.

"Honey, I was also the orphan kid. For most of my life, I was a loner. We moved too much for me to make real friends. I only felt like I belonged in the Army. There nobody knew my past. I could be whatever I wanted to be each day." I smiled, wondering if I was making a difference. "Then I met you guys and realized families comes in all shapes and styles. I spent years letting people who care very little for me rule a lot of my emotions. No more." I wasn't sure if I was counseling Bartholomew or myself. "You're not alone. You have a family. You are home-schooled because you are a genius and regular school will never be challenging enough. You take college classes, for the love of God."

"But what if I fail and my robot sucks?"

I was starting to hate this contest.

"Bartholomew, your self-worth is not measured by what you do. Who you are is never going to change. How we feel about you is not going to be diminished because of any contest. We're proud you want to do this and take a chance." Thank the Lord his tears were stopping. I wiped his face and smiled at him. "You have unlimited funding and you are twelve. Whatever you make is already going to put people to shame. Stop stressing and have fun. If this is not fun, you should not do it."

He looked at me thoughtfully. Before I could say anything, he hugged me.

"I love you, Isis." Bartholomew squeezed me tighter. Now I was crying again.

"I love you, too, Bartholomew. I couldn't have asked for a better brother."

Death had a sense of humor. Only she could have found two orphans and made them a family, against all the odds.

"Now, can we go and give all those little college students hell?"

I pulled back so I could look into his eyes. He was still shaking, but a little sparkle was returning. He gave me a nod and I winked back.

After our little breakdown, the drive down was pretty smooth. Bartholomew was going over his application forms. According to Death and Constantine, Bartholomew was never allowed to use his real last name. That explained why he was so nervous about turning in the application. That was a simple problem. From now on, he would be Bartholomew Black and I would sign as his legal guardian. Who was going to argue that he wasn't my little brother? Bartholomew was smiling from ear to ear; I felt like I had solved all the problems of the world. Then again, for a twelve-year-old, I had.

We pulled up to the parking lot of the college. The campus was beautiful and I was impressed Texarkana had such excellent facilities. I was always impressed with Texarkana College as well. How was it possible that a community college had a campus that big? If I decided to go back to school, I had great options. We got out and Bartholomew pointed the way. I was not impressed with the long walk from the parking lot to the front of the building. That was a horrible design flaw or maybe they were preventing suicide bombers. Either way, the walk felt like a little hike with the summer heat kicking in.

"Isis, are you sure you want to be my sister?" Bartholomew whispered to me.

"Bartholomew, I am your sister. I don't have to be sure. I learned very early on with my godmother that family is more than blood. Some are forged out of steel and will last lifetimes." Those words finally made sense to me. How right was my godmother? I played with Bartholomew's hair. He put his shoulder back and nodded. I wasn't sure what had happened, but he looked more settled, more grounded.

We made it to the main student building. Of course, it had to be the farthest one of the two. Just to make us walk a bit more. The place was packed. I glanced at Bartholomew, afraid he might bolt. Somehow, I was the one feeling scared of crowds today. He was moving with a holy determination I had never seen. I followed behind, trying to dodge the kids. They all had food containers that smelled delicious. My stomach was grumbling. I needed real food and not just a shake. Fortunately, we made it to the center of the building. The first floor was an open atrium with stairs going up and a reception desk right in front of them. Bartholomew walked directly in that direction.

"Hi. Where is the registration table for the robotics competition?"

I was proud of him; he sounded very professional and calm.

"If you go right behind us in that hall, the registration tables A&M are in charge of are inside." A young lady maybe in her late teens told us. She had spiky, pink hair and her face was painted. She was all about this College Bowl.

"Are there other registrations areas in the city?" Was I missing something?

"Oh yes, TC has half of the events, so they're managing that registration. It was easier to split the work so nobody would get burned out," a young man with blue hair replied over his shoulder. He was helping another group but decided to join in. It was nice to see both schools working together to pull this off.

"Good to know. Thanks." Bartholomew and I waved at the couple and headed toward the registration area. The place was organized chaos. Students were in every corner, directing traffic. Bartholomew found his table quickly and headed straight for it. I wasn't sure if it was his excitement or his height, but he was able to move around the crowd a lot quicker than me. By the time I got to the table, he was almost done.

"This must be your sister." A girl with brown hair said to me. She had an A&M shirt on with a nametag that read Julie. Mercifully, her face and hair were not painted.

"Yes. I don't move as fast as Bart." I smiled back.

She glanced at the crowd and smiled. "It's only going to get worse. I'm happy my shift is only three hours."

I felt sorry for Julie. Three hours in this mess was too long.

"Question, do you have a restaurant around here? The food smells delicious."

"We do, but that's not the cafeteria food you're smelling. Recently, some local vendors have been coming to the dorms and campus, and the food is amazing." Our little friend Julie was probably hungrier than I was, because her face took on a very dreamy look.

"What kind of food?" I couldn't help it; the curiosity was killing me. I wanted to know what could make someone smile like that.

"Well, we have the tamales lady and a local food truck that serves only breakfast food." Julie was almost bouncing with excitement. "And just recently we have a fried pie lady."

Bartholomew and I looked at each other and rolled our eyes. Once you give up gluten, fried pies were a horrible temptation. I wondered if Jake had stock in them. "Oh no, you don't understand. These are not just any fried pies. These babies are flaky and gooey and just addicting. You can't have just one. I'm getting hungry just thinking about it."

"Wow, those sound great." A terrible thought hit me. "Are we done here? We need to get going and get his robot finished." I started pulling Bartholomew away.

"Yes, here are your numbers. Make sure to wear them and good luck. I hope you do great."

I had to admit, Julie was a sweetheart. We waved at her and made it back to the central atrium where the crowd of kids was increasing.

"What's going on? We both know my robot is done." Bartholomew asked me once we stopped outside the doors. I was looking at all the college students with the food containers.

"What's more addicting than cocaine?" I asked without looking at him.

"Heroin," Bartholomew replied in less than half a second.

"Not that one. Sugar," I told him.

"You do know that claim has not been scientifically proven yet."

I almost forgot that Bartholomew was a genius.

"No, that's what Jake said last night." Was that crazy devil trying to help?

"Oh, in that case, that might be true. He is the Prince of Darkness; he should know his deadly substances. But what does that have to do with anything?" Bartholomew looked around.

"Bart, what if the note you found was supposed to say flaky and not Flakka? What if we were supposed to be looking for a fried-pie lady and not a drug dealer?"

"First of all, fried pies are not flaky. If she was planning to leave a note, the least she could do was be accurate. How were we supposed to guess pie? That's crazy." Bartholomew threw his hands in the air in pure disgust.

"Add that one to the lists of complaints we have against her. Right now, we need to find out if I'm right. We need to find TJ. Let's go." I was not planning to lose Bartholomew again, so I grabbed his arm and dragged him away.

Chapter Twenty-Six

"Why exactly are we going to Big Jake's at nine a.m.?" Bartholomew asked me as I parked in front of the door. "Don't get me wrong. I could get BBQ all day long, but I don't think they open till ten."

Everyone at Reapers loved Big Jake's. It was our Friday lunch place, so we knew the schedule by heart.

"The restaurant is not open, but TJ should be smoking the meat." TJ was my favorite on Big Jake's staff and one of the nicest guys in town. He was at least six feet tall with gorgeous hazel eyes, brown hair, and a great mocha complexion He was the poster child for the phrase tall, dark, and handsome. I wasn't sure what he was doing, but he kept getting better looking each day. "We need to talk to him before they open."

Bartholomew and I rushed to the side door facing the road that led to Beverly Park. I looked through the window and the place looked deserted. I was pretty sure TJ was working today. I banged on the glass door, praying somebody would hear us. After several minutes, TJ poked his head from the back room. Bartholomew and I waved and he waved back. He made his way quickly to the door. He had a large key ring hanging from his belt loop. He let us in and then locked the door behind us.

"What a pleasant surprise. You guys are a bit early for lunch," TJ told us with a huge smile. In the time I lived in Texarkana I had never seen TJ angry or upset. "I'm surprised you have time to come and see us little people," TJ said to me.

"I figured you'd be having another hot date at Cracker Barrel!" he said, bursting out in laughter.

I glared at him and at Bartholomew, who was trying to hold it in.

"How do you know about that?" I had my hands on my hip. I was ready to choke the responsible party.

"Who do you think? Shorty, of course." TJ told me, still smiling too much for my taste.

"That boy needs to work for TXK Today or the Gazette at the rate he delivers information. He is faster than Facebook for spreading news." Shorty was on my list of people to hurt. Then again, Shorty was probably on everyone's list.

"So, your Cici's date wasn't memorable?" TJ was still teasing me.

"Oh, it was memorable all right, but not for the right reasons," Bartholomew added from behind me. TJ and Bartholomew shared a look and both shook their heads. I was not happy being left out of the loop.

"Anyway, my crazy dating life is not the reason we're here. We need your help. We're trying to find this pie lady everyone is talking about. If we show you a picture, do you think you'd recognize her?" This plan made a lot more sense in my head than when I said it out loud.

"Of course, I would help. But why didn't you just call me instead?" I probably looked puzzled because TJ kept on talking. "I enjoy the visit, but if you were in a hurry, phone calls and text are usually faster."

I looked down at the floor a bit sheepishly before answering. "I lost your number. I'm sorry."

TJ smiled without getting upset. "That figures. Give me your phone." TJ gave me a stern look and I gave up. I pulled my cell from my back pocket, unlocked it and handed it to him. Not sure why I bothered with passwords when Bartholomew could hack into anything. TJ took the phone and started programming his number to include a photo.

"I'm glad I'm not the only one who needs to program your phone," Bartholomew told me quietly. I rolled my eyes at him. He just laughed.

"Here you go. Who are you looking for?" TJ handed me back my phone.

Bartholomew very quickly gave TJ his phone with the picture of our favorite accountant.

"Have you seen her around?" Bartholomew asked TJ

"Wow, I have. She's stopped by a few times. She was looking better in this picture. She looks a little rough now." A loud alarm went off and TJ looked over his shoulder. "Uh, hold that thought. I'll be right back."

Based on how quickly he moved, that was probably one of his meat timers.

Bartholomew leaned in to whisper to me. "You know, he has potential. Friendly, great personality, has a job, and can cook."

"Don't even think about it. No more playing Cupid," I was telling Bartholomew when I heard footsteps heading our way. I gave him one more glare before turning around.

"Hi, Isis. Hi, Bart. What's going on?" A tall, thin woman in her early forties spoke to us. She had a greasy apron on and rhinestone glasses. The glasses made her look younger than she was, and the pink stripes in her hair gave her a semi-punk look.

"Hi, Big Amy. Sorry to bother you guys. We just had a quick question." Big Amy was the owner of this location and she ran a tight ship. I wasn't sure why they called her Big Amy. The girl was super thin.

"Anything I can help you with?"

Big Amy was always lovely but usually not a big talker. I didn't want to push our luck. Bartholomew gave me a questioning looked and I shrugged.

"We're looking for this lady." He handed her the phone with the picture.

"Hey, I know her," Big Amy told us cheerfully.

"You do? How?" I didn't like coincidences.

"She came by wanting to buy the recipe for our fried pies. She offered me a huge amount of money I couldn't resist. I almost felt bad; she paid me for something everyone knows how to make."

Big Amy looked like the cat that got the mouse, a little too proud of herself.

"You wouldn't happen to know how to find her?" I asked. I was afraid I was pushing her too hard. I didn't want her to stop talking now.

"Unfortunately, she lives with Fred in the apartments across the street from TC." This was the most Big Amy had ever talked to me.

"Thank you so much, Big Amy. This is a huge help." I meant it. Anybody that could provide information in the next two days, I would be their new friend forever.

"His apartment is on the second floor, the last unit. Just be careful." Before we could ask her any questions, Big Amy took off back toward the kitchen area.

"What was that all about?" Bartholomew asked me.

"I have no idea. I plan to start tipping more if this helps us." Not sure how since Big Jake's didn't take tips.

"What did I miss?" TJ asked us.

"Big Amy just told us how to find this girl's boyfriend." I was so happy I wanted to dance.

"Really? Who?" TJ was not as happy as we were.

"Some guy named Fred that lives across the street from TC. We're heading that way now," Bartholomew answered cheerfully.

"I wouldn't recommend just you two going." TJ looked over his shoulder in Big Amy's direction. "Fred is a sociopath. Big Amy used to date him, but he was violent. Don't go there alone."

Well, that explained why Amy didn't feel bad enough not to take the money.

"Is he that bad?"

"He's nuts and he's never alone," TJ said, a little disturbed. The last part helped me make up my mind. I was not about to walk into a group of people that could potentially beat me up.

"Fair enough. I'll take Bob with me," I told TJ, trying to calm him down.

"That's a great idea. I wish I could go with you, but I'm the manager today." For some strange reason, TJ looked sad.

"No big deal. Bob won't mind at all." Bob might be roughing somebody up today.

"Bob is a little scary; you know that, right?"

Bartholomew and I were looking at TJ, surprised.

"You think Bob is scary?" I recovered faster than Bartholomew and asked for the two of us.

"He is extremely scary. He has this crazy intensity that is nuts. To make things even worse, he's built like a brick house. He screams dangerous."

I was pretty sure if Bob heard TJ's description of him, he would be thrilled. Bob spends a lot of hours honing his mean look. I guessed it worked.

"Well, that is good news. Now we just need to drag poor Bob with us and find this Fred guy. Nothing major." As long as Bob was somewhere to be found. I was praying he wasn't working on his new truck.

"Good and be careful." TJ smiled at me. He looked at Bartholomew before talking. "Are you still competing in the College Bowl?"

"Yes. We just finished the registration process." Bartholomew looked his age when he smiled. It pleased me to see he was slowly returning to his cheerful self.

"Great, I'll make sure to stop by and cheer for you," TJ said with a huge smile of his own.

"Speaking of College Bowl," Big Amy said from the cash register. "Your little pie lady is planning to be there. I saw her there last week registering for a booth to sell fried pies. I'm surprised she's doing so well."

Big Amy did look a bit puzzled about the situation. I looked at Bartholomew in horror.

"Oh no. Please do me a favor and do not eat anything she is selling."

"Isis, what's going on?" TJ was looking at me, very concerned.

"We don't have proof yet, but we think her food might be contaminated," I told them.

"Oh, that sucks. Can we at least pass the word to others?"

That was a great idea TJ had.

"Yes, please. That would be a great help. Thank you so much. You guys are busy, so we're going to get going."

Big Amy waved and went back to the back. Bartholomew waved back.

"Try to use your phone more often, Isis, and don't be a stranger," TJ told me with a smile.

"Sounds like a plan." I gave him a mock salute and dragged Bartholomew out the door. "Don't even think about it," I told Bartholomew outside.

"I have no idea what you're talking about," Bartholomew remarked with an innocent smile.

Yeah, right. I knew better than to believe that sneaky little smile of his. "Well, at least we have a valid location for the boyfriend. I wasn't tracking this one."

Chapter Twenty-Seven

This was becoming a stimulating morning. It brought to mind that I was once told that exciting times ended up in war. Maybe I needed dull days to balance the chaos. I parked Ladybug in her designated parking space. Bob's new truck had arrived. He got a Ram 2500 Heavy Duty work truck. Compared to the Beast, this thing was a monster. As massive as the truck was, Bob picked baby blue for the color. If he thought that made it looked less intimidating, Bob was fooling himself. Bartholomew and I did a quick double take and grinned at one another.

We rushed up the stairs, hoping to catch the rest of our peeps. When we entered the loft, Bob and Constantine were at the kitchen table, studying some maps. There was no sign of Eugene. Bartholomew and I joined them.

"What are you two doing?"

They looked a little too focused for my taste. Constantine got this focus when he went into war mode. He was still mad at the accountant over The Camaro.

"Tracking the appearances of the zombies. There is no pattern," Constantine replied, still staring at the map. "Most drug dealers have a base of operations or a hub area. You don't just wander into other people's territory. There's no way she made that many connections and expanded that fast in less than six months." Constantine was beyond himself.

"She didn't," I told him. Bob and Constantine both looked up at me. That much intense attention from the two is a tad intimidating. Maybe TJ was right about Bob being scary. "We've been looking for the wrong drug, if you believe Jake."

"What did the devil tell you this time?" asked Bob as he straightened himself out.

"He hinted at sugar." I needed a quick explanation; we were running out of time.

"Sugar? Is that a code name for something?" Constantine looked at Bob.

"One of his weird riddles, but he was right. Our accountant is using fried pies to spread the plague. This is a plague, right?" I was still not sure if it qualified.

"Damn the devil to hell," Bob muttered under his breath. I couldn't help a quick smirk. Lately, that was our favorite phrase when it came to Jake. We heard it around town and we used it all the time. One time, I let it slip in front of Jake and he glared at me.

"Anything that comes or started with Pestilence is a plague. That woman will be the death of humanity." Constantine was not a happy camper.

"I'm pretty sure that's her goal," Bartholomew added from the fridge. I guessed he was hungry as well. He was pulling covered dishes out. The rest of us looked at him. "Sorry, I'm hungry now. Big Jake's smelled too good, made my tummy grumble. "

"Open the oven instead. I made biscuits and gravy. Your plate and Isis's are in there." Bob said food and I jumped at the word. I was pretty sure all those stupid shakes Eric made were speeding up my metabolism. Honestly, I eat all the time, and the boys were right—I was thinner. Bart pulled the plates out. I had no idea where Bob found a recipe for gluten-free biscuits and gravy, but I didn't care as I was ravenous.

"Before you start devouring your food, explain yourself. Quickly." Constantine stopped me midway toward the kitchen. I turned back and took a seat at the table with them.

"It all fits. In the last couple of weeks, everywhere we go people have this fried-pie obsession. The campus at A&M just picked up a fried-pie lady, randomly. Abuelita has been plotting to take down the fried-pie lady. The parents of those kids in Red Lick did not look like the type to give their kids weed, but I'm sure they gave them fried pies." I looked at Constantine and Bob for a response.

"Now that makes sense," Bob said. "There was a strange lady last month in downtown trying to give fried pies to the underground. Everyone just ignored her."

"Wait, what?" Bartholomew brought our plates to the table. He placed the most incredible plate of biscuits and gravy with scrambled eggs in front of me. I was so happy; Bob made sure my gravy never had meat. Bartholomew's plate was overflowing with bacon, which was the reason his sentence stopped; he was busy chewing. "The underground passed on free food, especially fried pie?"

"Hey, after last fall, nobody is taking any chances. Unless the food is coming from one of the vetted shelters or soup kitchens, nobody is taking things from strangers." I agreed with Bob. The underground could not take any chances.

"That explains why we hadn't seen any zombies in downtown or the underground. That is a blessing," I told the boys in between mouthfuls of food. There was something good that came out of those crazy witches taking people last fall. The underground had developed a new vetting process for shelters and food kitchens.

"We have the how, now we just need to find her. Bartholomew, do you still have the info on the boyfriend?" Constantine asked, as he got comfortable on his side of the table. Bob was walking around supplying drinks to everyone.

"It's a good thing we went to Big Jake's. My research said the boyfriend's last known address was in Ashdown. Big Amy said he lives here in town." Bartholomew tried to talk and destroy his bacon at the same time. I was pretty amused by it.

"TJ said the man is dangerous. That's why we're back. Bob, we need you." I took a sip of my hot chocolate. "By the way, the food is delicious. Thank you."

"Yes, thank you," Bartholomew added.

Bob was beaming and I wasn't sure if it was because of the compliments on his food or the fact that I needed him.

"In that case, we better get changed," Bob said. "By the way, Isis, we're riding Storm. It's her first day. Let's not blow my baby up. Give her at least a week."

"Can't make any promises, but I'll do my best," I replied, trying not to smile. At least Bob was not too attached to things. "Hey, Bob, please tell Eugene to get ready. We might have a sample for him."

"That might be hard. I'll leave him a note." Bob had a devious little smile on his face. "Eugene doesn't handle late nights very well. He looked awful."

I smirked at the mental picture; Bob headed downstairs.

"Isis, you probably are going to need another recording. We don't need any witnesses today." Constantine was right. The last thing we needed was people calling the cops on us.

"What do you think if I take the sleep one and the stay-away-from ones?" I asked Constantine.

"You won't have a lot of time. Keep it simple." Constantine was not the subtle type, so when he was worried, I knew we needed to be careful.

"Let me go change before Bob takes off without me." I walked over to the sink to wash my dish. We hate having a nasty loft. I left the boys and headed to my room with my hot chocolate.

It didn't take me long to get dressed. I had my standard black cargo pants with boots and a black T-shirt. Clothes were simple. My hair, on the other hand, took a little longer. I decided to do a French braid. I loved my hair long, but I hated when people—and ghosts—used it against me. The tighter the braid, the harder the time they would have trying to pull it. TC was located in the center of Texarkana. So, our M16 and rifles were out of the question. I made a mental note to take more ammo for the nine millimeters and the paint guns.

When I walked back into the loft, I found Eric talking to Constantine. It appeared Reapers was the meeting location for people. Eric was staring at Constantine in what seemed to be shock or horror. Or maybe he was just constipated, but I doubted that.

His demeanor quickly changed when he saw me. "I see you're ready for another hot date," he said from across the room.

"Bob and I are going hunting." Just because we were hunting humans, it didn't make it any less real.

"Right." Eric gave me a quick look-over. "Constantine just filled me in on your theory. If you're right, this is going to be a nightmare." Eric was back to looking worried.

"We know she's not distributing the plague in drugs. Eugene checked and found nothing. This makes sense. But you're right; there's no way of knowing how many people ate pies lately." This was going to be painful.

"Isis, the colleges send us a copy of the park layout so we can help with security. According to the plans, there will be two pie stands on opposite sides of the park. Unless we get some proof, I can't just go over there and shut her down."

I rubbed my face. No wondered Eric was worried. This insanity kept getting bigger and bigger.

“Great. More pies easily accessible to the world.” I took a deep breath. My mind wandered to Ana and Joe, who would start dying slowly if we didn’t find a cure. “I’m not sure if I’m glad or not that Pestilence never hired this chick. If she was a full Intern, I’m not sure humanity would survive her experiments.” Pestilence’s mission was going to be the death of us all.

“If she were a full Intern, her actions would at least be regulated and tracked. Major experiments would be contained in secured locations. We would be able to put a stop to it at any moment,” Constantine told us.

That made sense. Pestilence people were scientists and, like most scientists, they liked to collect data and analyze it. This was a total fiasco.

“At least I can blame this apocalypse on Pestilence. We are tired of getting all the heat for the dark ages.”

Before I could ask him to explain about the dark ages, Constantine jumped off the table. “Bob is ready. Don’t be late.” Last words he said as he walked out the door.

“Isis, I know this is hard for you, but please don’t blow up Texarkana.” Eric was looking at me thoughtfully.

“First of all, last time it was not me. That was all Constantine.”

Eric stared at me. “Isis, you’re a magnet for crazy, outrageous things to happen. Try to keep the city in one piece.”

I was not going to convince Eric at all. “Fine, I’ll do my best,” I replied.

I was proud of myself I didn’t roll my eyes while I was talking to him. “Got to go.” I gave him a lazy hand wave and headed out the door. I was pretty sure if I stayed any longer, I was going to say something mean to him. I needed to focus on the mission, not try to convince sexy Eric that I was not a menace to society.

Chapter Twenty-Eight

I never realized the obsession we have as a society to name things. In Texarkana, every apartment complex, regardless how small or run-down a place it was, had a name. The apartment complex across from TX was called the Windsor Place Apartments. The Windsor Place Apartments on North Robison were not very fancy, but they catered to the students in the area. I gave the campus a quick look, noticing a lot of joggers on the trail. Bob made a sharp left and parked at the end of the complex.

There were a lot of people out and about for a Friday morning. Bob and I had dressed in combat gear again and I didn't want to attract unnecessary attention. We lowered the windows in the Storm and I quickly hooked up my recording; the goal was for people to avoid the area and be confused. I was getting good at finding songs that fit the mood I needed. It was impressive the amount of stuff you could find online now. Bob put his earplugs in, just to be on the safe side. Death said anybody working at Reapers should be immune to my music. Unfortunately, we found out that extensive exposure gave the boys horrible headaches.

The music was playing and we were out of the truck. Bartholomew was taking care of any cameras in the area. We decided to bring only handguns and paintball guns.

With all the crazy active shooters running around the country, we were trying to make sure nobody called a SWAT team on us. We dashed to the second floor. The stairwell led up to two units, one on the right and one on the left. The door on of the left was filthy and covered in spider webs.

"What do you think?" I asked Bob.

"I can't believe anyone is staying in that one. Let's aim right." Bob was right. I gave Bob one last nod and he kicked the door open. I had my gun ready and burst through the doorway.

"Ahhh!" screamed a naked girl from the couch.

"Oh God!" screamed a half-naked male boy.

We were prepared for a horrible scene, just not this kind. Two teenagers making out was not on my list of things to find. I felt terrible for the boy; he went limp from fear. This was so embarrassing for everybody. We needed to do a better job at recon from now on.

"OK then, obviously we are in the wrong apartment. Do you know a Fred that lives in this complex?" I lowered my gun, perfectly aware they were not armed, not even with courage. The boy couldn't say any words. He just stuttered.

"Across the walkway." The girl was at least able to speak and point.

"Great, thanks." I was ready to be out.

"Shouldn't you two be in school?" Bob asked the couple. I wasn't sure who was more shocked, them or me.

"Ah."

Well, we were back to one-syllable words from the teenagers, if that was technically a word.

"Answer me." Bob was dangerous and mean. He was glaring at them.

The boy finally spoke. "We skipped school, sir."

I was glad he found some courage, but if Bob kept this up, they were going to have an accident in the middle of the room.

"Is this what you want for your future—no education, babies, being irresponsible, and wasting your lives away? You're too smart for that. Remember this face because I'll be watching you two. You better get straight or I'll be back and it won't be pretty." Bob gave them one long look before heading out the door. The kids looked like they were going to die.

"Trust me; it's for your own good." I pulled my paint gun from my holster and shot them. After Bob's little stunt, I couldn't leave them to call the cops. I left the apartment and closed the door. "Do you know those two?" I asked Bob when I was standing next to him.

"Nope. But I will now." He gave the apartment another look.

"Are you planning to go around scaring kids straight in Texarkana? What are you, the Rock?" I didn't think the youth population could handle Bob and the whole underground watching them.

"You know, that was a really good idea he had for a show." Bob was smiling at me. "Besides, I couldn't let that opportunity go to waste. Who knows, if I scared them enough maybe they'll do something amazing with their lives."

I was sure. Like never have sex, join a convent or monastery, or become hermits. I figured it was safer not to tell Bob that.

"Good job, you did scare the hell out of them. Constantine would be proud." I tapped him on the shoulder and smiled. My boys were nuts. "Should we try this again? Let's see what we have behind door number two."

Bob gave me a quick nod, looked around, and kicked the door open. I was starting to wonder what the doors in Texarkana were made of. Bob did that way too easily. I took a deep breath and dashed through the doorway. We entered the apartment's living room and kitchen area. The place was dark, cold, and smelled of incense and something rotten. There were potpourri bags everywhere. The place had a layer of dust over all the horizontal surfaces.

"What in the hell?" Bob said from behind me. I was starting to like the teenagers' situation so much better.

I didn't dare walk in. The place looked like a tomb or haunted house. Bob pulled out his flashlight. Nothing was moving. It was like nobody had been here in ages. I found a light switch. I flipped the switch and slowly walked in. I didn't want to disturb anything.

"Should we check the bedrooms?" Bob asked me.

I did not want to go in any deeper. Unfortunately, Bob was moving down a hallway already. Staying at the door was just as bad as following Bob.

"Bob, there's something wrong with this place," I whispered. Even talking out loud felt wrong here.

"Which part gave it away? The smell or the destroyed furniture?"

I was so busy looking at all the weird bags on the floor, I hadn't bothered to notice the furniture.

It looked like a wild beast had been loose in here. I was now in full paranoid mode. I took my 9mm in my right hand and my paint gun in the left. It looked ridiculous, but after six months in Constantine's training camp, I could shoot with either hand. Not to mention I was pretty good at holding my own in a fight, guns or no guns.

The hallway wasn't very long. We passed a small bedroom on the left and a bathroom on the right. The bedroom was used as a storage space. Boxes upon boxes were piled everywhere. Bob kept moving toward a closed door. I stepped into the room and checked in one of the boxes. I found a few empty bottles labeled "P Laboratories."

I guessed we'd found Pestilence's lost virus.

"Isis, you might want to see this," Bob said from the hallway.

"Holy Jesus Christ." I made a quick sign of the cross. That was a common Catholic prayer, where you used your thumb and index fingers crossed in the shape of a cross, and then did a cross over your body. I started at the forehead, down to my heart, then across to my left shoulder, and ended on my right shoulder. I did that on reflex when something was bothersome. This took my breath away.

A man, or what was left of a man, was chained to the bed. Not the kind of stuff in Fifty Shades of Gray. More like the stuff you saw in medieval torture chambers. He looked emaciated. Bob walked over to one side of the bed and I walked to the other side. The man was lying in his filth. It explained the temperature of the apartment and all the potpourri.

"Dead?" For his sake, I was hoping he was.

"Let's find out," Bob poked the man's leg.

The man woke up and started thrashing around, howling and trying to bite me. I jumped back at least two feet and shot him in the chest. Fortunately for him, I pulled the trigger on the paint gun. I worked for Death, but I wasn't interested in being mauled by a deranged zombie.

"Not dead," Bob spoke from his side of the bed.

I glared as I tried to get my heart rate to slow down. "No kidding," I told Bob, shaking my head. "I'm assuming we found victim one."

"At least we know she only has love for her work." Bob was right about that. "How long do you think she's been keeping him here?" That was a really good question and I had no clue.

"I don't know, but I hope Eugene can figure that one out." I walked back out into the hallway. "That girl needs some serious help."

"Isis, I'm afraid she's past that point. If you're willing to do that to your boyfriend, there's nothing you won't do to others. She needs Jesus—or maybe Buddha."

"That is too creepy." I was getting the chills here. "OK, if you call Shorty, I'll call Reapers. We need Eugene to get his lab ready for this one."

"Works for me. Do we want Shorty to take the boxes?" Bob pointed to the storage area.

"That would be great. I'm sure Pestilence wants whatever is left of her stuff back. He can come back later for those. I don't want Shorty hanging out with mummy over there any longer than he needs to." The last thing I needed was for Shorty to get attacked by the first zombie. Who knew how tough he was? "By the way, have we given Shorty a gun?"

Bob's eyes got huge. I held up my paint gun to make the point.

"Oh, one of those. You scared me for a minute." Bob needed to give me more credit. I didn't trust Shorty with the truck; I for sure was not giving him a gun. "Not sure, but I'll tell Bart to issue him one when he drops off friendly over there."

"Good. At this rate, we need all the help we can get." I pulled out my phone.

"Bart the Greatest at your service. Internationally known and ready to make all your needs into a reality."

I rolled my eyes. "Bart, what are you talking about?" I needed to start monitoring what the boys did when I wasn't around.

"Trying out my sales pitch. What do you think?" Bartholomew was a little too excited now.

"It depends. Are you opening up a dating service or becoming an arms dealer?" I was afraid of the answer.

"Neither." Thank the Lord for that one. "Still working on my products," Bartholomew replied, a little distracted.

"In that case, let's wait for the slogan till after you finish your business plan." Twelve-year-olds were easily distracted. What happened to the robot obsession?

"Okie dokie." Bartholomew was in much better spirits and not bothered at all. "So, did you find the boyfriend?"

"We found a body. Tell Eugene to get ready; he'll be getting a visitor." I was not sure how to describe him.

"Eugene is out," Bartholomew said, still reasonably cheerful. "He got an emergency call from one of his people. He took Ladybug to meet him."

"He's meeting them somewhere not in the lab?" I said, full of panic. This was not good.

"Yeah, why?" Bartholomew heard the change in my voice.

"Bart, I need you to load the coordinates of Ladybug to my phone. Try to get ahold of Eugene. Hurry, he's in trouble."

"Got it," Bartholomew replied and hung up.

"Bob, we got to go. I think Eugene is in danger."

Bob didn't need too many explanations. We were running out the door as fast as possible.

Chapter Twenty-Nine

According to Bartholomew's coordinates, Ladybug was parked at Rocky Point Park, at Wright Patman Lake. From Texarkana College, it was going to take us at least twenty minutes to get there. I wasn't sure if Eugene had that much time. Bob tried to follow the speed limit through town, but let loose once we hit the highway. I hadn't asked why he picked Storm for his truck and now I didn't need to. Storm was a force to be reckoned with. We were going at least ninety and the ride was smooth.

"Bart, tell me you found him." I had Bartholomew on the speaker system in the truck. We were hoping he had good news because we had reached Ladybug and the area was deserted.

"I tapped into one of the satellites, but I'm only getting vague information. I could send the drone out." If Bartholomew wasn't picking up something concrete with all his toys, it was not a good sign.

"No, we don't have time to wait. What do you have?"

"In your area, I got two bodies about one kilometer heading east from your direction." I started playing with the GPS in the truck to see what the terrain was in that direction.

"Isis, the cliffs are in that direction," Bob said faster than I could find it. "What's your fastest run?"

"Not pushing it, about a seven-minute mile." It wasn't Olympic running, but for being late twenties, I was ecstatic about it.

"OK, we're about point six-two miles away. You need to push it. Leave the guns and the machete; I'll be right behind you. If you're right, it might be too late for Eugene."

Bob's words were hard to handle. I liked Eugene; he was becoming family. I took a deep breath; we had no time to panic. I nodded to Bob, left everything in Storm that would slow me down and jumped out.

My sense of direction was always pretty good, but recently it was amazing. Constantine's theory was that Death's gift was augmenting all my talents. That was a creepy notion, but today, I was praying he was right. I oriented myself and took off. I needed to run over half a mile in under three minutes through rough terrain. I wasn't sure if I needed to pray to God or Death, but I needed speed.

I knew I was flying, but those were the longest seconds of my life. My lungs were burning. I felt the wind beating on my face and the branches cutting into any bare piece of skin they could find, but I couldn't stop. I jumped over logs and took turns sharper than my mind believed possible. When I finally burst through the trees into a clearing, the accountant was pushing Eugene off the cliff.

"Noooo!" I screamed. I was running toward the cliff before I could stop crying. The accountant was slipping away.

"What would you do, little girl? Save your friend or get me? It's all about the job, you know."

Did she think there was an option here? I kept moving toward the cliff as she walked away.

Eugene was dangling from a rope. The rope was tied to some limb that was slowly breaking. This chick had some serious issues. It wasn't enough to hurt people; she wanted to play with them before she killed them. Maybe she was part cat? I stopped wondering about the insanities of the accountant and grabbed the rope before it broke. Eugene was flailing like a madman. I couldn't pull him up; he was a lot heavier than he looked.

"Eugene, stop shaking," I yelled down at him. "I can't get a grip on this rope."

"Isis, is that you? I'm going to die!" He screamed the last part. It was a good thing he wasn't next to me because I had the urge to slap him.

"Eugene, shut up! You're not going to die. Stop shaking so I can pull you up."

I was losing ground. I had no traction and I was getting tired. Maybe I needed to add strength training to my running regiment.

"Isis, where are you?" I heard Bob's voice from behind.

"Bob, over here! Hurry, I need help." After so many near-death experiences I was no longer ashamed to ask for help.

Bob rushed out of the wooded area and came sprinting over to me. He was out of breath and sweating like crazy. After this, I was sure Constantine was adding more running to poor Bob's life. I felt terrible for him. He tossed the rifles over his shoulders and grabbed the rope.

"I got him. Did you see the accountant?"

We were slowly pulling Eugene up.

"Yeah, she went north," I told him as we pulled.

"Good. Go after her. I got Eugene."

I wasn't sure how he did it without dropping the rope, but he managed to pass me my M16. "Are you sure?" I didn't want to leave them alone. Bob just gave me a glare and I took off.

Fortunately for me, the accountant was a little narcissistic and underestimated people. She wasn't moving very quickly. I was able to catch up with her at another parking area in the park.

"Stop!"

She had reached her vehicle, a very sensible Nissan.

"Well, look at you. Still doing the dirty work for Death's Intern." She had a smirk on her face.

"What? Woman, please. I am the Intern."

Her mocking smile turned to surprise at my words. "Now that is delightful news. I'm impressed. Hearing Pestilence talk about her sister, I figured she was just as bad as her. Maybe all is not lost." She was inspecting me up and down as she spoke.

"I'll make sure to pass the news to Death." I refused to lower the rifle.

"It's a shame you will die, but Pestilence will know she made a mistake by passing me over twice. She'll beg me to come back. I'm the better Intern." She was truly demented.

"Lady, we need your formula, so step away from the car."

She laughed at me. "Or else what? What are you going to do, kill me?"

The accountant laughed again and got in the car and took off. I wasn't sure what to do I had left my paint gun in Storm, so I took a couple of shots at the back window with my M16. The glass exploded, but she kept driving. By the time my brain started functioning, I had started shooting at the tires. It was too late; she was gone. Oh God, what have I done? I dropped to the ground shaking. I had a panic attack and I couldn't calm down. I closed my eyes, feeling my throat constricting. I was afraid I was going to pass out.

"Easy now, Isis. Breathe. Breathe, sweetie."

I felt arms wrapping me in a hug. Tears were running down my face. Had I doomed Texarkana? The hands kept soothing my back and the voice whispering to breathe. Slowly, my heart slowed down and I looked up at the person holding me. For a moment, I thought it was my mother.

"Death, what are you doing here?" My voice was trembling and sounded distant. Now I was embarrassed;

my boss had seen me fail.

"Making sure you don't give yourself a heart attack." She was smiling at me. She took a handkerchief from somewhere in her suit.

"I failed. I had her and I failed. I couldn't shoot her. We're running out of time and I couldn't take her out." I was crying again and this time I didn't care.

"Isis, dear, your job is not to kill people. That's not why I picked you." I tried to breathe in between sobs. "Do you know why I picked you?" She asked me in the softest voice I have ever heard.

"'Cause I killed Teck," I replied feeling so useless and guilty.

"No, silly. That made you take the job. I picked you because you love people. You care about those around you with a passion that goes beyond nature."

I was pretty sure I was in shock because I wasn't following Death's words. I was a loner. What was she talking about?

"Isis, the reason you don't let people in is that you are afraid to lose them." OK, was Death reading my mind? "Isis, I picked you because you believe in the goodness of humanity. If I wanted a killer, I'd have plenty of options. Now stop beating yourself up. You'll see her again and a solution will appear. Killing her is not the way." Death hugged me tight and kissed my forehead. "Now you better get back to those boys before they hurt themselves. You're the glue that holds them together."

I wasn't sure what that meant, but Death dragged me up to my feet. Before I could speak, she wiped away my tears and turned me around. She gave me a little push, probably because I wasn't moving and sent me down the path again. I looked back to thank her and she was gone. I took a few calming breaths and started jogging back. This time, at a more leisurely pace. I wasn't sure what I was going to tell Eugene and Bob.

By the time I got back, I didn't have time to wonder what to say. Eugene was on the ground, freaking out. He was wailing and twitching like he was having an epileptic seizure. I ran over and dropped next to him. Bob looked at me in panic.

"What happened?" I asked Bob, who looked distressed.

Eugene grabbed my hand in pure horror. "Isis, I'm dying. She forced me to eat pies. I'm not going to make it. She gave me a triple dose of her regular formula."

Eugene was back at twitching. I looked over at Bob, and he was holding a picnic basket. He mouthed back to me, "Pies."

"Eugene, aren't you immune to all plagues?" I asked him.

He stopped moving, his eyes rolled back, and I was afraid he had died. Then he sat up and looked straight at me. I was ready to bolt if he turned super zombie.

"Oh yeah." He slapped his forehead with his hand. "I forgot. It was probably the stress of being pushed off the cliff." Eugene gave me a huge smile. Bob slapped him over the head—gently, just to make a point. "Ouch. What was that for?"

"For all the theatrics." Bob had a point. Eugene did an excellent imitation of the dying cockroach act.

"It could happen to the best of us," Eugene said with a gorgeous smile. Bob shook his head and I rolled my eyes. I wasn't sure if I could handle being the glue to all these dysfunctional souls. My heart was not strong enough.

"On a positive note, you got plenty of samples now." I pointed to the basket Bob was holding.

"That is true. By the way, I understand why people are going crazy over those things. They are delicious. She really could have a career in catering."

Eugene had lost his mind. I got up from the ground and pulled him with me.

"We're running out of time and you have a plague to kill. Let's go." I brushed off the grass and leaves Eugene had managed to cover himself in. He was not getting in one of our vehicles that dirty.

"Yes, can I drive?" Eugene asked.

"Nope." Bob and I said simultaneously.

"Can I have my keys back?" Eugene looked like he was pouting when he handed me my keys, but it didn't last long. "Thank you, sir."

"I'll take the weapons; you take Eugene," Bob told me. I handed him my M16 and he handed Eugene the basket. "Now that we know they won't kill you, don't eat the plague, Eugene. I'm heading to check on Shorty and the cleanup of the apartment."

"Sounds like a plan." We started walking back toward our vehicles. I was keeping a close eye on Eugene. Bob was right. He did look like he wanted to eat the pies.

"Give me that basket." I took the temptation away.

Eugene smiled sheepishly and I shook my head.

Chapter Thirty

By the time we made it back to Reapers, I was drained. The adrenaline from the morning wore off and I was dragging. Eugene wasn't looking any better. His near-death experience had him dragging, too, not to mention he was covered in dirt and leaves. I, apparently, did a horrible job of wiping him down. It wasn't my fault; a person can collect a lot of dirt when they flop around like a dead fish in the soil. My legs were sore going up the stairs. I needed a long bath and probably a shake if I wanted to be functioning again.

"Wow, you look like hell!" yelled Constantine as we walked in.

"Nice to see you too, Constantine," Eugene said from behind me.

"Wow, you look even worse," Constantine told Eugene. I turned around and laughed at him. Eugene stuck out his tongue at me. Oh yeah, he was officially family.

I walked straight to the couch and dropped down. Eugene decided to stay near the kitchen area, trying to avoid dragging dirt everywhere. Bartholomew was on his computer, typing away. He finally looked my way and then he looked Eugene over.

"Don't believe Constantine. You don't look that bad. Eugene, on the other hand, looks like roadkill."

Bartholomew looked at Eugene one more time and shook his head. "I ordered pizzas from Dominos. In the oven, grab some food. Do you need me to get you some?" he asked me softly.

"No, thank you, honey. I got it." I hauled myself out of the couch. I couldn't let him know how tired I was. We all couldn't look hopelessly defeated.

Eugene looked so lost, I felt bad. I hadn't realized he didn't know his way around our kitchen. I walked around him and pulled a couple of plates from the cupboard. I grabbed the pizzas from the oven and removed drinks from the fridge. Bartholomew wasn't kidding; he had ordered eight pizzas. Granted they were gluten-free, which meant they were all small. Still, that meant we had at least a pie per person and leftovers.

"Bart, are we expecting visitors?" I asked him as I pointed to the food.

"Not really. I was hungry and everything sounded delicious, so I ordered one of everything. We got chicken wings in the microwave as well." I had to laugh. That was the reason Bartholomew and Constantine were not in charge of cooking or groceries. Between the two of them, we got pounds of meat but no side dishes to go with them.

"Fair enough." I smiled back at Bartholomew who was blushing. "Eugene, you got plenty of options. Here's a plate. Grab as much as you like." I placed a Dr. Pepper in front of him and Eugene looked like he was in heaven.

I grabbed a couple of slices of the veggie pizza and a shake and headed back to the couch. Eugene took a chair at the table next to Constantine. Constantine was looking around the room, a little concerned.

"Isis, where did you leave Bob?" he finally asked.

"He went to check on Shorty and the cleanup of the apartment. At least that's what he told me." I answered him in between mouthfuls.

"You don't sound too convinced," Constantine said very suspiciously.

"I'm just saying. You know Bob. He'll start in one location and end up all the way across town. So, who knows where he'll go?" I also did not want to share the fact I was sure Bob was checking on the teenagers in the other apartment. Bob believed he was given a second chance at life and he was all about paying it forward. Even if the people were not ready for it.

"That's a good point," Constantine replied. "So, please tell me you at least found something besides dirt and leaves." He walked over to Eugene and swatted a leaf from his hair. Eugene tried to duck, but Constantine was quicker.

"We got pies," I told him as cheerfully as possible.

"On purpose?" Bartholomew asked.

"Not for us, Bart. We got fried pies from the accountant," I explained quickly.

"OK. I was wondering when were pies that exciting."

I laughed at Bartholomew. Since Bob started cooking, nobody in the house missed gluten. So, pies were no longer a big deal for Bartholomew. Bob made a gluten-free version of everything.

"I will start on those as soon as I'm done eating and take a shower. I'm afraid I'll get dirt in my samples," Eugene said in between bites. "Besides, I have never been so dirty in all my life. I'm even itchy."

"Let me go shower before I go crazy. I'm taking more pizza with me." He piled more slices on his plate.

"We got more than we need, so take more. Just remember, don't eat the evidence."

"Not a problem." Eugene grabbed his plate, the basket, and his Dr. Pepper and headed out the door. I wasn't sure how he was carrying everything, but he managed not to drop anything.

"I'm going to head downstairs as well. Doing one more drill with my robot before tomorrow." Bartholomew jumped up from his seat and ran out the door. I watched him go as I chewed my pizza.

"What's wrong?"

I hadn't heard Constantine sneak by. He jumped on top of the headrest of the couch and was staring down at me. This was probably how those poor patients at the shrink's offices felt—very small and scrutinized.

"Nothing, why?" I replied, without meeting his eyes.

"Right. I know your 'nothing' look, Isis, and this isn't it. Spill it before I jump on you and make you talk."

That sounded painful. Constantine was fifteen pounds of pure muscle. If he jumped on me, those tiny paws of his would feel like steel columns landing on your chest. I took a deep breath before talking and jumped on the couch.

"I had her, Constantine. I had the accountant in my sight and I couldn't shoot her," I told him without looking at him.

"Isis, since when do you go around shooting people?" Constantine asked me. He was still staring at me and I was afraid to hold his gaze for too long.

"Constantine, maybe if I had shot her, all of this would be over. Ana wouldn't be dying downstairs, kids wouldn't be fighting one another, and Father Francis could have his church back." I knew I was rambling, but the words were pouring out.

"Isis, please. Just listen to yourself for a minute. This woman has been planning this for months. The damage is done. Now she is just assessing her work. You shooting her was not going to make Ana or Joe better." Constantine was glaring at me.

"Constantine, what would happen if I freeze when it matters?" I didn't want to start crying again, but I was close.

"We were not looking for an assassin for this job. Anybody can pull the trigger of a gun. That doesn't take skill. Saving a life, helping a soul, caring for people—that is a rare gift." Constantine was still looking at me, but a least he wasn't glaring.

"Death said something similar," I said, almost in a whisper.

"You talked to the big boss, yet you still don't believe?" Constantine was shaking his head as he spoke.

"I just feel like I'll let everyone down." My eyes were misty. Constantine jumped down and sat on my lap. We were almost at eye level with each other.

"Isis, let me explain something to you. We have thousands of killers in this world, hundreds of suicide bombers, and a plethora of angry people. Today, you saved Eugene, got evidence back that we needed, found the missing boyfriend, and to top things off, you gave Bartholomew a family. You can't compare those things." Constantine made sure that I was looking at him and listening. "Every other horsemen's job is to kill humanity. You saw what Eugene and his peeps could do. Our job is simple. Take care of souls. You give them hope and respect when they most need it. Don't dismiss that."

I had tears running down my cheeks.

"Constantine, sometimes I feel like I'm not good enough for this." I was feeling overwhelmed. "I'm not a very good Intern."

"We're in luck. You don't have to be good, just be you. That is plenty. Follow your instincts and trust in your family. They trust you, Isis, and they won't let you down." We sat in silence for a moment. "When it becomes too easy to pull the trigger is the day you should panic. That's when you've lost your moral compass. You don't want to go down that path, regardless of how bad humanity becomes." Constantine looked lost in thought. Like he remembered some horrible past.

"Constantine, what happens to Interns that lose their moral compass?" I wasn't sure why that was important to me now.

"They fall asleep in the River Styx." I had no idea what that meant, but it sounded horrible.

"Good to know." That was all I could think to say.

"I recommend you take a bath and try to rest. We have a long day ahead of us."

Constantine was right; tomorrow was going to be a long day.

"I'm going to make more paintballs before calling it a day. I have a feeling we're going to need a lot of ammo."

"Good plan. I've got to call Eric. Make sure to drink your shake."

Constantine jumped off me and headed toward the computer area. I slowly got up and smiled. Sometimes, Constantine had a way of surprising me. His demeanor never changed, but his words were profound.

Chapter Thirty-One

It wasn't even five by the time I woke up. I was on edge and stressed out. Everyone had worked until at least eleven last night. Eugene was busy making more knock-out formula for the paint guns and working on his plague-killing concoction. My eyeballs were boiling by the time we were done. Bartholomew, Bob, and I left Eugene to his work. We needed sleep. Constantine kept him company. Not sure if that was good or bad for Eugene.

I didn't get any rest; I had nightmares all night. Fortunately, these were not my usual nightmares. I suffered from nightmares, which ranged from my parents' deaths to my comrades' death in Iraq to the day I accidentally killed Teck. My nightmares progressively worsened to the point that the dead were talking to me in my sleep. Sometimes, the conversations were good, other times they were screaming for help. The blessing of Reapers was having those dreams stop. Constantine believed the wards on the building were blocking them. Bartholomew, on the other hand, thought it was Death herself who ended them.

Honestly, I didn't care who had stopped them or how. I was grateful I could sleep. Constantine was also pretty sure somebody or something was making the souls torment me. That was another piece of information I was not concerned about. After meeting the devil, I was not interested in asking him or giving him any personal questions that could be used against me. So, I enjoyed the lack of nightmares. My nightmare last night was strange. I was chased by the gingerbread man from Shrek all over Texarkana. According to him, he was bringing the pie man to destroy us.

Not the most terrifying dream, so it was easy to dismiss it once I woke up. But the lack of sleep had me tense. I considered going for a run or working out downstairs, but I did not want to wake anybody. If I was stressed, I knew everyone was ready to blow. I compromised. I did a quick workout circuit in my room with deafening music. By the time I was done, I felt better. I was thoroughly awake and focused. I needed to be functioning, and the workout did the trick. Unlike the accountant, my first priority was not the job, but my family. I needed to give them structure so we could make it through the day.

By the time I made it to the loft, it was six-thirty in the morning, but the boys were ready and dressed. Bob was working his magic on the stove while Bartholomew played with some controllers nervously. I made my way to Bob so that I could see what he was making. We had a big breakfast by the looks of it—eggs, bacon, pancakes, and fresh fruit. We discovered that when Bob was agitated, he cooked. It was a better habit than cleaning guns. He did that for the first month and had all of us on high alert. I grabbed a piece of melon and kept on walking.

"You're going to ruin your breakfast," Bob told me without looking away from his pancakes.

"I'm so hungry, I doubt it. It smells amazing in here," I replied with a smile. Bob was a typical cook; he loved to know what we thought of his food.

"I got banana pancakes and they'll be done in two minutes," Bob said with a smile on his face.

"Morning," I told Bartholomew and Constantine, who were already sitting at the table. Everyone had been busy. The table was set and ready.

"Top of the morning to you." I wasn't sure if Bartholomew was watching too many military or Irish movies, but he was picking up their phrases. He put his controller away and faced me. "What's the plan?"

"Let's keep it simple. Search and destroy," I told them. Bob stopped in mid-flip and Constantine finished cleaning his face with his paw.

"My kind of plan," Constantine said with an evil smile.

"You got my attention, explain." Bartholomew was watching me with a smile.

"Simple. If the accountant has been feeding college students pies for the last couple of weeks, we're going to have a zombie-galore. Step one, we need to contain the situation until Eugene gets his plague-killer done. We need to buy him time, so shoot and move out." I waited for everyone to nod to show they were following me. "Step two, we need to shut down her pie stand and destroy all the pies. We don't need any new zombies joining the party. Third, we need to make sure we capture the accountant. The last thing we need is for her to start all of this somewhere else. Everyone with me?"

I was always amazed how things came to you when you were working out or in the shower.

"I like it. Simple, destructive, and to the point. Nice job, Isis." Constantine was smiling like a proud parent.

"Let's not celebrate just yet. We still have to execute this. Bartholomew, is your robot ready for competition?"

"Oh, trust me, Terminator is ready."

Bartholomew had named his robot Terminator. I was afraid to ask what this robot looked like.

"Good, we're going to need it. We need to get in and start scouting the park. All participants have VIP access according to the packet they gave Bartholomew yesterday." I felt like a proud parent or responsible older sister; I did manage to read his instructions. I haven't read my manual, but anything dealing with Bartholomew I paid close attention to. "Bob and I will go with you, as your robot assistants. While you're setting up Terminator, we'll check out the park. Constantine, you have aerial support. We need eyes in the sky. Just don't blow anything up, OK?" I gave Constantine a level look.

"One little fountain and the whole world goes paranoid. By the way, it was a hideous fountain anyway; the new one is so much better." Constantine had blown up a memorial fountain and half of the post office with his drone last fall, fighting witches. We learned very quickly that Constantine was trigger happy and little reminders were needed.

"Yes, the new fountain is beautiful, but the old one was pretty nice, too. So, let's keep Spring Lake in one piece today." The College Bowl was taking over most of the park and I was hoping the park would be standing after we were done.

"Fine, but nobody likes those fountains in that park anyway," Constantine said, looking very dignified. I couldn't help it; I had to smile. Bartholomew and Bob were doing the same thing.

"Any questions?" I asked the boys and they all shook their heads. Most of the time, Constantine was in charge of planning. But we found out when it came to planning around human events or significant locations, it was safer if I did it. The destruction and collateral damage were a lot smaller with my plans. Bob handed drinks all around—orange juice and hot chocolate, of course. He had a huge mug of coffee for himself. My phone went off and I almost jumped. I forgot I had the stupid thing in my pocket.

"Hi, Eric. You're up early." If Eric was calling at this hour, it was not good. I put him on speakerphone, so I could save myself from having to repeat everything.

"We got a body."

"Should we be worried?" I asked after a moment of silence.

"It meets the description of your accountant. I pulled some strings and got permission to let you come and ID the body." Eric sounded very proud of himself. Why would I ever want to see a dead body right after breakfast? I didn't mind souls at all. I enjoyed them. But dead bodies decompose at an incredible rate and they smell. Not to mention once the soul leaves, the body stops looking human and just falls apart.

"Great. Can't wait." I didn't want Eric to think I wasn't appreciative. I made a crazy face to Bartholomew in shock. Bartholomew covered his mouth, trying not to laugh.

"I'll send you the directions. See you when you get here," Eric said in his official police-officer voice.

"Thanks. See you soon." We disconnected the call and I looked around the room.

"Do you think it's her?" Bob asked me as he started bringing food over.

"I don't think we're that lucky. She's straight crazy. I doubt she accidentally fell over dead right before her huge event." I started cutting my pancakes while I spoke. Constantine was devouring his bacon and sausage already and Bartholomew was covering his pancakes in syrup. I had no idea where Bob found the recipe, but his gluten-free pancake mix was out of this world.

"Are you going?" Bartholomew asked, before popping a massive piece of pancake in his mouth.

"We can't take any chances. If it's her, we need to know, sooner rather than later. But our plan still stands. Bob, you and Bart head to the park and start scouting. I'll catch up with you as soon as I'm done with Eric."

"We got this," Bob replied when he finally started eating. We were a lot calmer now that we had a plan and marching orders. "Boss, would you make sure Eugene eats something, please? That boy is losing too much weight lately."

"After his all-nighter, he'll be tired. I'll keep an eye on him," Constantine agreed.

We all had things to do, but none of us rushed through breakfast. If the zombie apocalypse was starting, we were going to enjoy our meal together. We went over last-minute details on potential muster points. We were planning a small military campaign and we were all pretty comfortable with that.

Chapter Thirty-Two

I needed to start asking more questions. Agreeing to meet Eric at some unknown location was not a bad thing. Driving up to a police investigation with a car full of weapons was a recipe for jail time. After this past year, I needed to learn to give up my expectations of things for those expectations were always wrong. If I expected nothing, I would not be disappointed and still surprised. As I parked next to the yellow tape at the banks of the Red River in Hooks, I was in shock.

I had never been out here, but the place was beautiful. It was close to Hooks city limits heading north, away from the central town. The river was pretty high, due to all the winter rains. A sandy beach ran down along the river for several miles before turning back to the wild terrain. State troopers, city officers, and unmarked cars were everywhere, destroying the scenery. I did a quick mental check on my arsenal. I took the gun from my back and placed it under my seat. I wanted to make sure nobody confiscated my Smith & Wesson special.

Cautiously, I got out of Ladybug. It didn't take long to find Eric; he was standing by a group of men wearing diving suits. He looked up and waved at me. I waved back. I wondered how he knew I was looking at him. Maybe wizards and witches had a unique sense for that kind of stuff. I strolled around, willing myself to blend in with the rocks. It was hard; I was the only one wearing jeans and sneakers. Eric wasn't in uniform, but he still had slacks and a polo shirt.

"Thank you for coming, Isis. This shouldn't take long." Eric told me as he came closer.

"When was she found?" I asked. With the number of people here, somebody had to have reported it hours ago.

"We got a call from a man walking his dog out here. He found the body stuck in between two boulders. He couldn't reach it, so he called it in." Eric and I made our way toward the team standing around the body. "The coroner thinks she's been dead less than a day." As we got closer, the smell of decay grew stronger.

"Hi, gentlemen," Eric told his peers.

"Are you sure about this? It's not a pretty sight," one of the guys wearing a white coat said to us. Maybe he was the coroner. As I looked at his serious face, I knew I wasn't ready, but I couldn't turn back now.

"Yes, sir," I replied. I realized everyone was looking at me.

"Please, brace yourself." He pulled the tarp back from the body with one smooth motion. He was the coroner and used to seeing dead bodies. He didn't flinch like the rest of us.

Oh lord, it was a horrible sight. I took a quick step back and covered my mouth. The last thing I wanted was to puke all over their evidence. Eric was right. It was a match for height, weight, and shape. But the face was missing. It looked like an animal had taken a huge bite out of it. Eric was looking pale next to me. I was glad I wasn't the only one traumatized. As much as I stared at the destroyed body, there was no way to confirm the identity. So convenient. No way of knowing till the police department ran its tests. My gut was telling me she was playing with us. I took a few steps away before I could get a delicious whiff of the smell.

"Sorry, sir, I really can't say for sure if it's her or not," I told the coroner. "Would you be able to identify her by her fingerprints or anything else?" I was hoping those detective shows were based on some kind of truth because I had no idea what I was talking about.

"Eventually, yes. It'll take some time to go over all the evidence and go through all of our databases. But we'll get it done." The coroner smiled at me. I was sure he was trying to make me feel better. I wondered if Eric had told these people I was a friend of the family. My phone vibrated and brought me back to reality. I excused myself and took a few steps away from the group.

"Bob, what's going on?" I was so grateful for caller ID.

"Isis, we got a problem." I was pretty sure Bob forgot that we had started the week with problems.

"I'm all ears. What's up?"

"She has three pie stands here," Bob said, sounding almost incredulous.

"Three? Are you kidding me? How is she going to pull that off?"

"She's pretty smart. She hired college students to run them. According to all the kids, their delivery truck arrives at nine with all their pies.

"Of course, it does. There is nothing simple for us." I looked around to watch more people wander around carrying stuff. "OK Bob. You're going to have to hold it down till I get there."

"Is the dead body the accountant?" Bob asked in a whisper. He was probably around people and couldn't talk regularly.

"Can't be determined yet. The face is missing, as if something ate it," I whispered,

"You were right, Isis. Nothing easy," Bob replied.

"Tell me about it. Be careful and keep your eyes open." This was a minor setback but nothing we couldn't handle.

"You, too. See you when you get here." Bob disconnected. I made my way back to Eric.

"Is everything OK?" Eric asked when the others were distracted.

"We got three pie stands at the bowl. Eric, things are going to get nasty unless you can call it off," I told him without looking at him.

"Isis, I don't have that much power or connections. The mayor would kill me if I said we needed to cancel this event with no actual proof. Somehow, I doubt he'll buy zombie apocalypse as a convincing campaign."

I hated to admit it, but Eric was right. Nobody was ever going to believe we had a zombie invasion in Texarkana.

"Hey, Eric, we found a basket. Any ideas?" A state trooper was walking over toward us.

"What kind of basket?" I was afraid of what he was going to tell me.

"You won't believe it. It's an actual picnic basket. I didn't think they still make these. It looks like something went through it," the state trooper said, almost laughing.

"Show me, please." I was a little too forceful because the state trooper was staring at me. He pointed in the directions of the basket. Two other officers were examining the contents.

"Stop! Don't touch it!" I yelled, running in their direction. Eric was right behind me. I made it to the little group and looked at the basket. The basket was destroyed. My fears were correct; the basket still had small pieces of pies inside.

"Isis, what's going on?" Eric demanded.

"We got a problem. Those pies are probably contaminated, and if something ate them, this could be bad." I looked at him as I spoke. I was hoping I was wrong.

"Everyone, keep your eyes open," Eric told the officers.

"For what?" one of them asked.

"For that," I said, pointing in the direction of the vehicles. From behind the cars, three very large bobcats were walking out. "I guess we found out who ate the pies." I looked at Eric, a little scared.

"What's wrong with those bobcats? They don't look normal," one of the troopers said. He was so right; the animals were foaming at the mouth.

"They are infected and a lot more dangerous than normal ones." Before any of us could move, the bobcats charged at us. They were faster than any animal I had ever seen.

The officers pulled out their guns and started shooting. The area went wild in less than three seconds. All other officers began screaming, trying to find out what was going on. The bobcats scattered. Officers were getting attacked left and right. Everyone was shooting. This was an excellent time for me not to have my guns with me. I looked around for a place to hide. People were running and screaming. There was no place to hide. I was afraid I was going to get shot by a random bullet. I wasn't sure if anyone was aiming anymore.

I decided to head to Ladybug for cover when a large bobcat stepped in front of me. He looked hungry and was foaming even more. He had been shot on the side, but it didn't slow him down. I looked around for something to use as a weapon. Before I could find anything, he pounced. I dove to one side just in time. He barely missed my leg. I was rolling on the ground when it pounced again. I managed to grab a rock from my side and throw it at him. I hit his head but to no effect. The bobcat just looked angrier. I was crawling back when it leaped, I covered my face with my arms and braced for impact.

I heard the shot go off. I looked up and the bobcat was lying right next to me. Eric was running in my direction, holding his gun. Thank the lord, Eric was an amazing marksman. That was an incredible shot.

"Isis, are you OK?" Eric helped me to my feet.

"That was terrifying," I told him. I glanced at the bobcat. "Don't tell Constantine; I don't want to know if that little fellow is part of his family tree." Eric looked at the bobcat again and nodded. The last thing I needed was Constantine wanting vengeance. "Is everyone OK?" I looked around the giant disaster zone.

"After the initial shock passed, everyone recovered quickly. The other two are down, but some explanations will be in order." He looked at me, taking a visual inspection.

"I'm fine. But are you ready to explain that a zombie plague is loose in Texarkana and can affect anything, human and animal?" If people weren't bad enough, I wasn't ready for zombie cats and dogs.

"I'm not sure I'm ready for that. Most people here will think rabies. This is not going to help convince them about zombies." He had a point.

"I need to get back. Can I go?" There wasn't much left for me to do here and the boys needed me.

"Yeah, be careful." Eric looked worried.

"I'm heading to Spring Lake Park. We could use your help." We needed Eric and an entire unit of Navy SEALs.

"Got it. I'll meet you there as soon as I'm done here. Watch yourself, now. You're a magnet for trouble." Eric gave me a severe look like it was my fault bobcats appeared at his crime scene. I really could never win with people.

I made my way quickly across the area toward Ladybug. Officers were being treated for bites, and I made a mental note to add them to our list of potential zombies. If those cats went zombie in less than a day, I was pretty sure our troopers would be turning fairly quickly as well. Oh lord, this was going to be messy.

Chapter Thirty-Three

The drive back from Hooks on I-30 was quiet. I planned to get off at the Nash exit, swing by Reapers and change clothes. If I was going to be chasing zombies, I wanted to be comfortable. I was doing a mental recon of the park when my phone started vibrating. I answered it in Ladybug's speaker system. Bartholomew decided I needed to get with the times. The car system announced Shorty was calling.

"Hey, Shorty, what's going on?"

"Boss lady, you were not answering your texts," Shorty said a little out of breath.

"I'm driving. Trying not to die." I had picked up too many souls who had been decapitated because of texting while driving. Not the way I wanted to go.

"Very responsible of you, but we got a problem."

"Shorty, we got a lot of problems today. You need to be more specific."

"Boss lady, you remember the apartment buildings across from TC?" I made a faint grunt sound for him to continue. "Well, they're overrun with zombies."

"What? Are you sure? How as that possible? We were there yesterday and it was clean."

"I was doing my rounds and made it down Robinson and it looks like the block party from hell. You might want to hurry." I was starting to hear screams in the back. That was not good.

"I'm on my way. Can you contain the situation till I get there?" I hit the gas and started flying down I-30 to the Richmond exit in Texarkana.

"Contain? Boss lady, I barely have enough ammo to stay alive. Do you remember I'm the cleanup crew? You tag them; I'll bag them."

Shorty was starting to get loud. I liked his motto.

"I got it. Take care and don't let them touch you. On my way." I disconnected the call and drove just as crazy as Shorty. Thank God, Ladybug had a great center of gravity because I took a right turn at Richmond like an Indy driver.

Time was not on our side today. I took another sharp right on Robinson and was relieved the road was clear. Either the situation was not as bad as Shorty described it or we had time. I flew down the road and made the traffic light right before TC. That's when the situation deteriorated quickly. It was bad; it just hadn't spread. I promptly parked behind Shorty, grabbed two large paint guns, and jumped out of the car. I stayed as low as possible, to avoid the zombies.

Shorty was inside the truck, leaning on the driver's door and staring out the passenger window. I quickly tapped the window to get his attention. I was afraid I gave the poor boy a heart attack. He jumped at least two feet in the air, hitting his head on the roof of the truck. He lowered the window, holding his chest.

"Are you trying to kill me?" Shorty was somewhat yelling and whispering at the same time. It was a weird combination.

"Sorry. I thought you saw me coming." If the situation weren't so insane, I would have laughed. "Status report. How bad is it?"

Shorty looked at me then back to the scene in front. "All hell broke loose." He eyed my guns very suspiciously. "I hope you have a bigger gun."

"Bigger? Shorty, what do I look like, Clint Eastwood?" These were the biggest paint guns on the market.

"Well, boss lady, they are about to make your day. You better give them hell."

I wasn't sure if I was flattered or annoyed that Shorty gave me so much credit. He gave me a serious head nod and a fist pump. It was official; I was on my own.

"Don't die, boss lady. I got your back."

"From the truck?" I gave him a quizzical look for good measures.

"Hey, I didn't say how far." He did have a point on that.

"Fine, I'm out." The situation was not going to solve itself, so it was now or never.

I considered the best plan of attack, then decided straight on was just as good as any. Why hide? I was the only one armed. I walked around the truck and started shooting at everything that was moving. We were practicing the 82nd Airborne's model, shoot them all and let God sort them out. I didn't have time to distinguish between friend and foe. If they were moving, they were going down. I made it across the street, faster than I hoped. The parking lot of Windsor Place looked like the scene out of a horror film. Zombies were everywhere. Some were attacking one another; others were chasing the poor civilians who were still normal. Others were banging on doors. Did the accountant drop a pie wagon here?

I made it to the middle of the parking lot, shooting zombies left and right. My favorite pair of lovebirds was running in my direction, but this time they were fully zombie. I liked them better when they were naked and scared. I hope this concoction didn't have any long-lasting effects because it was the second time in less than twenty-four hours, I was knocking these two out. I sensed more than felt movement from my right side. I did a quick drop just in time for a zombie to charge at me. Constantine was probably a clairvoyant because when he sent me to take Brazilian Capoeira, I thought that was the most useless fighting technique ever. Now I was doing midair spins, trying to dodge zombies.

It didn't take long for all my little zombie friends to realize I was human. I had a new plan and hopefully, a more practical one. Make them come to me and give the humans time to run. I hope I didn't die from this. I put my fingers in my mouth and whistled as loudly as I could. The air-splitting sound made all the zombies who hadn't yet noticed me turn in my direction.

"Do you guys want to play?" I asked the crowd. I felt like a Spanish bullfighter. All I needed was the cape because every zombie on the block charged in my direction. Common sense would tell humans to duck and dodge if someone was holding a gun at you. That part of their brains was gone. They just charged.

I took three out in under two seconds. Two got past them and aimed at my head. I elbowed one in the face and double tapped him with the paintball. His friend tried to grab the other side and ended up with a roundhouse to the sternum. When they woke up to their usual selves, they were going to be in pain. I was pretty sure I broke several jaws and femurs in less than ten minutes. That was all it took—about ten minutes from the time I left Shorty till I had chased the last zombie up a set of stairs.

I walked back to the center of the parking lot, double-tapping any zombie that was still twitching. I was not taking any chances with another rebellion. My clothes were covered in sweat, and I was pretty sure I stunk. The May heat was in full effect by now. I heard footsteps and turned, guns ready.

"Hold up, boss lady; it's just me."

I saw Shorty, hands in the air in the middle of the road. I took a huge breath and relaxed.

"Please tell me I didn't miss any of them." I didn't want to chance a rogue zombie going down the streets of Texarkana.

"Boss lady, you are on fire." Shorty was inspecting the aftermath of the fight. "You are one tough lady. I'm impressed." Shorty gave me a fist bump and I returned it. I smiled back. It was easy to take them down when I knew I was only putting them to sleep.

"Shorty, you got a mess to clean up now." This was his department. He looked around the place in awe.

"I should have asked to get paid by the body count, not the hour. I'd be rich." I looked around as well and Shorty was right. There were at least fifty people scattered about.

"I'll talk to Constantine and see if he can give you a bonus."

Shorty's eyes got huge. "Can you check instead and see if I can keep the truck? I like being the cleanup crew. I'm important. I even got business cards."

I had no idea what Shorty was talking about. He pulled a black business card with red gothic letters that read, "Shorty, Reapers Incorporated, Cleanup Crew."

"I'm sure Constantine could make that happen." I smiled at Shorty as he ran over to get this truck. I didn't have time to help. Maybe he could hire more people. Before I could suggest it, my phone vibrated. I quick-checked the caller ID. It was Abuelita.

"Hi, Abuelita, what's going on?" It was rare for Abuelita to call me. Usually, she just texted.

"Isis, we have a problem."

Why did everyone's problem involve me?

"What kind of problem?" This better be good.

"The alarm system at Abuelita's is going off. I need you to check on it."

Was she serious? "Abuelita, can it wait? We got a lot of things going on today like the zombie apocalypse."

"Honey, I know that. But I have a couple of potions boiling at Abuelita's that if disturbed will send Texarkana back to the dark ages." Abuelita said that very calmly for a person brewing a bomb in her restaurant.

"That can be a problem." What else was I supposed to say after that piece of information?

"Not to mention, my security system happens to be dead."

I was confused. "What do you mean dead? Like ADT shut the power down?" How was a security system dead?

"No, honey, like as a dead SWAT member who guards the premises and notifies me when somebody breaks in. Unlike Death's Interns who can make the dead destroy things, all I can do is have my security guy send me messages."

Could I tell the dead to destroy things? I was really behind the curve today; I was not getting all the information. I might need to check on that later. "What exactly do I need to do?"

"Just swing by, check in with Dave, and see if everything is OK. He's freaking out and I can't get a clear signal." Abuelita was a medium and could talk to the dead. That was awesome.

"Got it. On my way. If you see Bob, let him know I'm running late." I looked around for Shorty to let him know.

"Will do, dear. Thank you." Abuelita hung up and I ran over to Shorty.

"Shorty, I'm heading to Abuelita's. Can you get some backup here to clean up?" Shorty looked at me like I had grown another head.

"I can hire?" I was worried, just by the sound of his voice.

"Yes, but only reliable people, and you better not discriminate. And offer them fair wages. I don't need another disgruntled employee trying to kill the rest of Texarkana." This whole thing about being an employer was complicated. I was leaving this work for Constantine.

"Boss lady. Where should I meet you afterward?" Shorty was way too happy to have people.

"Once you get this organized, swing by Abuelita's. I have no idea what's going on, but just in case, stop by. We eventually need to make it to Spring Lake Park. Got it?"

Shorty smiled back at me like a madman. I wondered if he'd been drinking. After today, I might need to start drinking as well.

"We got this, boss lady. You tag them; I'll bag them." I laughed at Shorty and ran to Ladybug. Eventually, I was going to get home and change. That was still on my list of things to do.

Chapter Thirty-Four

The parking lot at Abuelita's was deserted. Whatever had set off the alarm did not drive here. Maybe they parked their tiny vehicles in the back. Either way, I needed to get out of the car. I gave Abuelita my word, so here I was. I could be doing so many other things than checking on empty buildings. I took a deep breath to calm myself. Being pissed at the world was not going to help anyone, including me.

I strolled toward the front of the place. The sun was shining and nothing out of the ordinary was going on until he appeared. I mean, he literary popped out of thin air in front of me. He was a tall black man, built like a linebacker. He was way over six feet and 300 pounds of solid muscle. He was wearing black everything, including a shirt with the words SWAT on it.

"Dave?" I asked with my hands up, just like Shorty had done to me. I wanted to make sure he knew I meant him no harm. Granted, I was pretty sure he could crush me.

"You are real." Now that was ironic; the ghost was surprised that I was real. Only in my world. "I heard so much about you." OK, this was getting weirder by the minute. Dave rushed over and shook my hand. My hand disappeared into his and they were freezing. The typical phenomenon that happened with all dead souls.

"Do I want to know what you heard about me and from whom?" Let's be honest, if all he heard were bad things, I did not want to know about it.

"You find lost souls and take them home. My cousin finally made it to heaven because of you."

"That's our job. Not a big deal." I wasn't sure why Dave was so excited about that.

"But you are the only one that does it consistently." I knew Dave was telling me the truth. Souls couldn't lie to me, but I was lost.

"What are you talking about?" I was staring into his eyes and excitement was dancing in them.

"Finding souls is not sexy," he said. "Nobody is ever going to thank you or even notice you did it. All other Interns want to save the world, battle vampires, and witches. Yes, they save souls, but not all the time and not as much as you do." Dave took a breath. I wasn't sure what he was talking about, but I would rather find souls any day than battle crazy witches. "They work on their powers. Nobody wants to do the small, menial jobs. Why do you think they are so many lost souls left behind?"

"Because they can't find the tunnel with the light," I told him, a little meekly. Dave laughed a genuine laugh. I smiled a little. I felt better. At least somebody got my joke.

"You are truly special. It is an honor to serve you. When I'm done paying my karmic debt, would you take me home?" I wasn't sure if Dave knew that he needed to be alive to pay his karmic debt. This was his story and I was not going to break the news to him.

"As long as I'm still around, it will be my pleasure," I told him with a smile.

Dave lit up like a Christmas tree. "You mean it. Thank you. We can tell when humans are lying, even Interns." I had no clue. Good to know. "What you do matters, Ms. Isis. The souls believe in you. It might not be big, like saving a city from zombies, but it means the world to that soul."

Maybe I couldn't save humanity, but I could touch one soul at a time. That was huge and I was getting teary-eyed. This was my week to cry.

"Honestly, I thought that was the whole purpose of the job. I guess I didn't realize we had options." Maybe it wasn't a bad thing, I hadn't read the manual. Dave beamed at me again.

"You are the youngest Intern; there is hope," Dave said softly. "I know you're busy, so I won't keep you long. I got two trespassers in the shop. There is something wrong with them because nothing I tried is working. It's like they don't register there is a ghost in the room. They keep yelling your name."

I shook my head and just stared at Dave. Why did I attract all the crazies? Dave looked at me, a little sad.

"Dave, we need to get them out before they destroy the place or tip Abuelita's potions over."

"Too easy on my way." Before I could say anything else, Dave was gone. I wasn't sure what to do. Before I could move, the two thugs that had attacked me three months ago at Abuelita's were back. This time, they had a little zombie help going for them.

"Look who's here. It's about time you showed up," one of the thugs said to me. I couldn't tell them apart by their faces and I was pretty sure they weren't twins. Their faces were contorted and they looked almost like they were foaming, just like the bobcats. At least they were wearing different clothes. The one that spoke was wearing a red shirt and the other a blue. I started backing up slowly.

"Dave, what did you do?" I said to the wind since Dave was missing.

"You said you wanted them out. I whispered to them you were outside and they left," Dave told me from behind the thugs, proud of himself. I wanted to choke him to his second death.

"True, but you at least could have warned me they were heading my way."

The thugs were coming toward me.

"Sorry. I thought you were ready."

Nobody was ever ready to get beat up. What was Dave thinking?

I pulled my paint gun and pulled the trigger. It was empty. I tried the second, and the same thing happened. I had my 9mm in my lower back, but that was for last resort. These two were annoying and a pain in the neck, but they didn't deserve to lose their souls.

The reasoning was not going to work with these two. They couldn't make rational decisions when they were only humans; now it was a lost cause. My situation was deteriorating very quickly. Blue zombie was carrying one of Abuelita's large knives. That thing looked more like a sword than a knife. I needed a weapon now.

I ran back to Ladybug and the zombie started chasing me. I wasn't sure how, but every zombie here was moving with a purpose. I barely had time to get to my door when they were on me. Blue was moving the fastest. I had no idea what to do on short notice, so I slammed him with the driver's door. The reinforced door took Blue Zombie out. That was going to leave a horrible mark. I was afraid he dislocated his kneecap with that hit. At least Blue dropped down like a sack of potatoes.

That gave me enough time to grab my machete from the ceiling of Ladybug. Red ran directly at me. I wasn't in the mood to deal with these two today. I still needed to get to the park and this was not part of my master plan. I had no idea how he did it, but Red managed to grab the knife his buddy had dropped. He was petty agile with a weapon for a zombie. I had to block several swings very quickly with the machete.

"Hey, Dave, a little help over here!"

Dave was bouncing up and down like he was shadow-boxing.

"What do you need, Ms. Isis?" Dave was running in my direction, finally.

"I'm out of ammo for the paint gun. I have more in my trunk; I need you to fill it for me." I was blocking with the machete with my right hand and with my left, I passed Dave the gun. He shook his head in wonderment. "Dave, take the gun now."

He made it to my side and reached for the gun. His hand was shaking. I handed him the gun and he held it firmly in his hand.

"How is this possible?" Once again, I didn't know what Dave was talking about.

"Dave, hurry! I need the gun now."

Dave moved around the car and headed toward the trunk. Blue was starting to twitch back to life. Red kept on coming and I was not happy. I managed to drag him away from Ladybug to keep Dave focused. When I finally got a clean angle, I kicked him in the ribs and knocked him to the ground. I knew that wasn't going to keep him down for long. They just kept coming. I got distracted and Blue pulled me down to the ground.

"Dave, anytime now."

Red was getting ready to join the fight. I kept trying to get away from Blue. I was trapped by two of the most annoying zombies ever.

"Ms. Isis, cover your eyes." I had no idea what that meant, but I did as Dave told me. I opened my eyes to find both zombies out.

"Thank you, Dave." I slowly pulled myself to a standing position.

"It's not possible, how can I hold it?"

I looked at Dave and I finally understood. He was not supposed to be able to hold solid objects, which explained his hesitation. He looked at me for answers. I thought about it for a minute.

"Because I gave you a direct order. I guess it's part of Death's gifts." I didn't have a more reasonable explanation. Death's powers were still a huge mystery to me. "Are you going to be OK?" I wanted to make sure he wasn't going to freak out.

"I helped an Intern. That was awesome. Let me know if I can do it again."

Not the answer I expected, but at least Dave was back to his cheerful self. Ghosts were weird at times. My phone vibrated as I was watching Dave do his celebration dance. I wanted to scream. This stupid phone was worse than a leash.

"Hello." I didn't even bother looking at the caller ID. I just didn't care anymore.

"Isis, where are you?" Constantine sounded angry.

"At Abuelita's," I told him, as I made my way around Ladybug to close the trunk.

"Why?" Constantine asked. "Never mind. You can tell me later. They need you at the park. The apocalypse is under way."

"I'm low on ammo and I'm struggling here," I admitted to Constantine. I was becoming exhausted.

"You're just around the corner. Head over here first and I'll get you fixed." I was hoping Constantine had a plan before I passed out.

"On my way. Can you send Shorty this way? I got a couple of bodies for him to pick up. Also, have him lock up Abuelita's while he's here."

"Got it. Hurry." Constantine hung up as usual.

"Dave, I got to run. Are you good here?"

Dave walked over, smiling brightly. "Yes, ma'am. This has been a great day. You are the real deal."

"Sure. Watch the place. I'm off to chase more zombies." I shook his hand for good measure and he smiled. What an odd day.

Chapter Thirty-Five

Constantine had understated the situation at Spring Lake Park. I parked by the baseball fields closest to the entrance off I-30 and it was nuts. Our little local sociopath had been busy. There were as many zombies running around as humans. I got out of Ladybug and went to the trunk to get my gear. I finally felt prepared to face the world. Black cargo pants and combat shirt, hair in a long braid, steel toe boots, and enough ammo to take on an army. This was how you went to war. Constantine had sent me out with another shake. I had taken two before leaving the house. Eric was my hero right now. Who needed those five-hour energy drinks when you had these?

Modifications to my gear were in order. I strapped two paint guns to my legs, grabbed my backpack full of extra ammo, and hooked up a police baton in the place where my machete usually went. The screams were overwhelming and I wasn't sure who was chasing whom at this point. I finished my shake, dropped the bottle in my trunk, and pulled out my extra-large paint gun. It looked like a modified M16, but with enough rounds to take down at least one hundred of these bad boys. I did the sign of the cross one more time. In cases like these, it didn't hurt to have some divine intervention.

"Father, don't let us die today," I prayed.

"Are you talking to me?" Constantine asked in my ear. I forgot my mic and earpiece were hot.

"Sorry, Constantine, just talking to the big guy," I told him as I took a quick survey of my surroundings.

"Good call. You might need him over there."

If anybody else had said that it would have sounded condescending. With Constantine, it was just a fact.

"Constantine, where are our boys?" I looked around at the chaos.

"Bartholomew is by a field near the plane where they have the stage. Start there." I took a breath and Constantine continued. "And Isis, hurry. He's surrounded."

"Why didn't you say that first?" I demanded, as I took off running.

"No need to add any more pressure to this mess." Since when was Constantine so considerate?

Running across a field of zombies was like taking a leisurely walk across a minefield. There was no point in stealth; they were everywhere. I was convinced our accountant had fed half the town. Bartholomew was right; we had at least five thousand people in this mess. I decided to be Moses today; I was parting the sea by shooting everything in sight. At first, I didn't seem to make a difference until the humans noticed the zombies dropping.

"Get down," I screamed at a mother who was holding her baby. I wasn't sure if it was her husband who had turned, but the scene was terrifying. She hit the ground and covered her baby with her body; only a mother would do that. I took the guy and five others out around her. "If you can, get in your car and stay in. Got it?"

"Yes, thank you." The young mother picked up her child and took off. She was fearless. She would die before anyone touched that baby. I took a knee and cleared a path from my location. If she were willing to face hell for her kid, I would give her a way. When I was sure she was safe, I took off again.

I made it to the central area of the bowl. The place looked like a riot site. Tables were overturned, tents ripped apart, chairs in pieces. I wasn't sure where the humans were, but zombies were everywhere. A group of ten zombies was charging the only vendor's booth still intact. I had no idea who was there, but they were putting up one hell of a fight. I took out the first five before getting close. By the time I made it over, three more were out, and the residents of the booth took out the remaining two. I tagged them each one more time, just to be on the safe side.

"Of course, you would be here. Mayhem and destruction in Texarkana. It was only a matter of time before you would appear."

I looked in the booth and saw no other than Angelito smiling back at me. Abuelita was on the other side, facing the rear.

"Aren't you supposed to be in Florida?" I asked him, as I kept shooting down zombies.

"Are you serious? And miss all this fun? Got back last night just in time," he told me, as he threw some weird red flame at the zombies. Abuelita had said to me after last fall that Angelito's powers had manifested. She was starting to train him.

"Hey, we want them alive." I had no clue what that red stuff was, but it didn't look safe. He gave me an odd look. "Death's order." He shrugged, closed his eyes, and his ball of whatever that was changed to blue. I was hoping blue meant good. I was still firing when I heard Abuelita.

"Dear, how is the restaurant?" she asked from behind me. I looked behind and she was throwing green stuff from the opposite side.

"Secure. Shorty is locking it up."

Angelito was sweating, unlike Abuelita, who looked like she wasn't even struggling. I grabbed one of my paint guns and handed it to him. "Here you go, my little warlock. I don't need you burning yourself out in your first fight." I grabbed extra ammo from my cargo pockets.

"Thanks. This is harder than it looks. What is this?" Angelito took the gun and aimed. The boy's accuracy was scary.

"No idea, but it takes them out, and that's all I care about." I smiled at him.

"I do wonder if you are not part of the terrorist group because you're a force to be reckoned with." He gave me a quick visual inspection. "By the way, you're rocking your Lara Croft look."

I shook my head and suppressed the desire to shoot him.

"Thanks, Angelito. Love your tan." He was glowing and his mocha complexion looked amazing. I turned back to shoot five more zombies before reloading when I stopped short. "Is that Eric?" I asked

"Oh wow, he can run." Angelito and I were staring in awe as Eric sprinted across the field with at least ten zombies chasing him. "Is he being chased by the soccer team?" Angelito asked me, still in awe.

"Or the track and field team. That has to be the most traumatizing image of the day," I told Angelito as we watched them running away. That was karma for all those horrible running sessions he had put us through. At least he was running. I had no time to chase them.

"Isis, you need to hurry. Bartholomew is in trouble," I heard Constantine tell me in the earpiece.

"On my way," I told Constantine. "You two need to get out of here," I told Angelito and Abuelita.

"No way, dear. You need help. We can take a few out from here for you." Abuelita was smiling at me. "Family doesn't leave when things get messy. Go. We'll guard your rear."

She was serious; they weren't leaving. What had I done to deserve people like this in my life?

"And it is a nice rear," Angelito added and ruined the moment. I rolled my eyes.

"Just be careful and don't let them bite you."

Angelito gave me a look like I had lost my mind. "Bite me? Girl, those things are not getting near me. Go, Wonder Woman, save the day." Angelito could never be serious, even under attack.

It was hard to run with all the zombies, so I just shot them down. I wasn't sure who was a zombie or who were the regular humans being attacked by the zombies. We had blood everywhere. I heard a loud explosion from the opposite side of the park. It shook the ground.

"Constantine, what was that?" I could see flames over the trees. The sound made all the zombies in the area run in that direction.

"Bob just took out one of the pie stands," Constantine said.

"With what? A missile?" Why was I even asking? I should know by now my people did not believe in overkill.

"In tough times, we must improvise," Constantine told me very calmly.

I shook my head and kept on running.

Chapter Thirty-Six

It took me longer than I had hoped to get to Bartholomew. He was at the far end of the park, near the Frisbee golf trail. Why did Texarkana have a Frisbee golf park? Something to ponder on my next run. When I finally made it to where Bartholomew was, I was impressed. Give a boy genius unlimited funds and he will build you an eight-foot, fully functioning robot. That thing was huge. It was like a cross between Ironman and the Pacific Rim robots. No wondered he was stressing. That was a massive undertaking.

I wasn't sure what capabilities Bartholomew's Terminator had, but now he was using it to swat zombies away. Bartholomew was keeping the zombies at bay, but they kept coming. He was going to be overrun in less than a minute. I pulled my second paint gun and took off at a full sprint. If Death's gift augmented my natural abilities, I was praying for perfect aim now. I couldn't afford to miss a single one. I cleared the field in less than thirty seconds, shooting with both guns. I had never played baseball, but I had seen enough players sliding into a base to know the drill. I slid in next to Bartholomew, making sure his rear was covered. I had cleared a path that looked like a runway.

"Nice. That was a great entrance," Bartholomew said when I stood up by him.

"Practicing my moves." We gave each other a fist bump and a smile. "You're a tough man to find, Bart." I passed him my extra gun and we started taking the zombies out within his perimeter, about twenty feet wide.

"Not my idea to put the robot judging area this far. I think they were trying to leave space for the relay races." I wondered if those were the kids chasing Eric.

I took off my backpack and handed him extra ammo. I added more to my gun to be on the safe side. Bartholomew was firing, taking zombies out.

"How many people do you think she fed?" he asked rather casually.

"Probably the whole town. I wondered if she was giving them away at every school in the four states area. They just keep popping up." I glanced around and we still had humans in the area. "Why are those kids still here?"

"They think this is part of the event. They're convinced it's all a hoax and they refused to go," Bartholomew said. We watched a group of kids climbing the stage and throwing stuff around.

"They can't possibly believe that." I glanced over at Bartholomew to make sure he wasn't joking.

"The human mind can't process this kind of situation. Besides, we have years of brainwashing telling us things like this could never happen. It's easier to deny it's happening than believe in the alternative."

I looked around and wondered how it was possible not to believe. "They don't even believe in God anymore. Do you honestly think they'll believe in this?" Bartholomew was right. People only believed in the power of the dollar. Nothing else mattered.

"Bart, please tell me they are not still eating pies." I looked around and saw kids stuffing their faces with fried pies. "This will never end if we don't stop them."

"I'm afraid they were giving the pies away for free. People are turning a lot faster," Bartholomew said over his shoulder. Our backs were touching as we took out more zombies. After five minutes of straight shooting, the place was finally cleared.

"I'm pretty sure she increased her doses for those pies." I lowered my weapon and wiped my forehead. I was drenched in sweat. "Constantine, we need to blow up that pie stand."

"Oh really, now you want me to blow something up. What happened to that whole speech to behave? Oh, how the tables have turned." Constantine was dripping with sarcasm. I rolled my eyes, mentally slapping Constantine over the head. Bartholomew looked at me, perplexed. I noticed he wasn't wearing an earpiece.

"Are you going to do it or not?" I demanded.

"Of course, I am, but I can't pass up an opportunity to point out how right I am." Constantine was proud of himself. "Just a small problem: unless you want me to take out the humans and zombies, you need to clear the area." I looked over at the stand. Zombies were charging the group of kids. The madness didn't end.

"Bartholomew, what can Terminator do to draw attention? We need to get the zombies over here, so we can get those kids out. I'm open to anything." I was running out of ideas. Charging headfirst into battle was getting old. I was not made to be an infantryman.

"Yes, I've been waiting all day to try this."

I didn't realize when Bartholomew had dropped his remote control. Probably because I was busy shooting angry zombies. Bartholomew retrieved it from Terminator's feet and started pressing buttons and levers.

"Bart, what exactly are you doing?" I wasn't ready for missiles to go flying from our tall friend.

"I made some preset functions that'll run in automatic. That was the part that was taking me so long—to get the programming so it would flow. I finally got all the bugs out. We need to stand back."

I grabbed Bartholomew's gun and stepped back ten feet. I had no idea what Bartholomew was up to. "Is he going to explode?" That would be a lot of shrapnel flying everywhere.

"It's better. Ready?" Bartholomew asked and I nodded. I was ready as I would ever be. Bartholomew hit a button and music started blasting from Terminator.

"Is that Mozart La Para?" I asked Bartholomew. Bartholomew was playing a Latin Reggaetón that roughly translated as "The monsters have arrived."

"You know, it's perfect." I had to admit it, he was right. What happened next blew my mind away.

"Oh my god, he dances?" That was the understatement of the century. Bartholomew had made a dancing robot. "Bartholomew, you are a genius. How did you pull this off?"

Bartholomew was glowing. "Baby, I got skills." Bartholomew bragged and he deserved it. Terminator was amazing, doing head rolls to side steps. "You can admire my work later; our friends are coming." Bartholomew pointed at the crowd of zombies running from everywhere. I had completely forgotten the whole point of this. Bartholomew had done it, the music was blasting, and the zombies were coming.

"Bartholomew, how long can Terminator last like this?" I was hoping he wasn't going to die on us and have that stampede of zombies turn on us.

"He has three loops of dances. At that pace, he can last about forty-five minutes without needing a charge."

"You are not allowed ever to doubt yourself again, got it?" I told him as we made our way across to the pie stand.

"He's pretty impressive." That was an understatement. Bartholomew had no idea how talented he was. "I hope you don't mind; I used your running-mix music."

"I'm flattered."

We made it to the pie stand to find three kids staring at Terminator. They were probably all late teen or early twenties and drunk out of their minds. No wonder common sense wasn't kicking in.

"Dude, that is amazing!" First drunk boy screamed at Bartholomew. Who said 'dude' anymore?

"This is the best costume party ever," his drunken friend added.

"Hey, sexy, you should dance with me," the third stooge told me as he started moving. I wasn't sure if he was only drunk or high as well. Terminator had changed songs to Don Miguelo's "Llevo La Vainita."

"That's my song!" screamed my new fan. Bartholomew and I looked at each other in disbelief.

The three stooges broke out into a dance number. Seriously, I love music more than most people, but this was not the time for dancing. The boys were even twerking. Larry and Curly were humping my legs and Moe probably had an epileptic seizure. Liquid courage made people do stupid things.

"I will never drink," Bartholomew told me as he watched the horrible scene.

"That makes two of us." I tossed my gun over my shoulder and grabbed two of our dance troops by the neckline. "Bart, grab that one."

We dragged the stooges about twenty feet away. I'd rather face zombies than drunken boys. They were not cooperating at all and thought it was a game. I considered shooting them, but I didn't want to drag them.

"Constantine, hurry. It's cleared." I wasn't sure how long we could hold these three.

"Watch your eyes." That was all the warning we got.

"Incoming!" I shouted at Bartholomew. We hit the dirt as quickly as possible.

When Constantine blew things up, he did it in style. I had no idea what he used, but that little booth went up in flames with a blast. When I looked up, our three stooges were flat on their backs from the impact, as well as every zombie within the area. I wondered if there was something wrong with me, but I didn't feel too bad that the boys were out. They had that coming for being foolish.

"Bart, are you OK?" I asked him.

"Maybe we should have told Constantine the stand wasn't that big," Bartholomew told me as we slowly got up.

"Doubt it would have made a difference." I was wiping dirt from my clothes again. I had spent a lot of time on the ground today.

"You said take it out. You don't get to pick how," Constantine supplied. "Isis, enough playing. I spotted the accountant near the fountain."

"Are you sure?" I was trying to get my bearings.

"Don't question me, girl. I got the skies." Constantine hissed at me. "You better hurry. She has a basket with her." Who did she think she was, Red Riding Hood?

"Bart, I got to go. Can you hold this down?" I took my rifle and backpack off.

"Terminator and I got this." He smiled back.

"Good. Here, let's switch." We traded guns and I gave him my backpack. "Watch the stooges now. If they get wild, shoot them."

"My pleasure." Bartholomew looked dangerous. I was afraid the trio might get hit just for the hell of it.

"Constantine, give me a status." I took off running. No time to question the sanity of my decisions.

Chapter Thirty-Seven

With the amount of running I had done this week, I was ready for the Olympics or the Bataan Death March in White Sands, New Mexico. Either one was probably less painful than this. I ran at full speed toward the lake area. Based on Constantine's instructions, our accountant probably had a car on that side of the park. If I didn't catch her, she could take South Park Road, which intercepted the park. I worked hard not to hate people. Hate was a powerful emotion, but I honestly despised that woman. My friends were dying and Texarkana was in chaos because of her. A loud explosion went off behind me.

"We're in luck; Bob just blew up the third stand. Food threat eliminated. Now we need to neutralize the accountant," Constantine told me.

I made it to the lake to find the accountant passing out pies left and right. Why would anyone take food from a stranger? Probably because we were in the south and she looked harmless. I wasn't sure if I should knock her pies out of people's hands or come back later. No time now. I had no idea what car she was driving. I didn't see a Nissan anywhere. Bartholomew's music was so loud the whole placed sounded like a carnival. People were oblivious to the danger they were in.

I looked around and made up my mind. I rushed the accountant at full speed and tackled her to the ground. She at least had the decency to look surprised. We did a quick roll and we were both on our feet in seconds. I did not like how quickly she moved.

"You don't give up, do you? That's a shame, little girl. Don't you see, you're nothing but a tool? As soon as the horsemen get tired of you, they'll discard you. You're irrelevant."

Wow, Pestilence had done a number on this one. She was projecting some severe self-hate.

"OK, lady, you know I can't let you go." I needed to turn this conversation back to the present moment.

"Right. Like you have much of a choice here." She proceeded to throw an impressive combination of punches and kicks.

I blocked most, but a few punches landed on my ribs. She was a lot faster than me, but only because she had the advantage of not running and fighting all through God's creation all day. I managed to land a kick on her side. Instead of going down, she got furious. She was a lot stronger than she looked. She grabbed my arm and I'm not sure how, but she flipped me over her shoulder. I landed on my back, out of breath and hurting all over.

"I'm done with this game. You're not worth my time."

I was on the ground seeing stars, completely dizzy. She walked over to her picnic basket and pulled out a revolver. I was pretty sure she had real bullets in there and not paintballs.

"Hope you said your prayers, little one." She aimed and I couldn't even focus enough to be afraid.

Before she could pull the trigger, she got hit by a truck. I couldn't believe that had happened. The truck hit her so hard she flew straight into the lake. That was the last straw; this day was nuts. I dropped flat on the ground and closed my eyes.

"I told Constantine that boy was going to kill somebody someday." I opened my eyes again and Death was standing over me. I pulled myself up to look at what she was staring at. Shorty was climbing down from his truck and I lost it. I started laughing.

"Thank you! I have been saying that all week. I'm just glad he hit her and not me."

Death laughed as well. "That makes two of us. I'm not sure the world is ready for Shorty to be an Intern."

I couldn't stop laughing. That was a great mental picture.

"Oops. Sorry, boss lady. I thought I hit the brakes, but not quickly enough. Do you think she's going to make it?" Shorty was looking at the lake and then back at us. I wasn't sure if he was remorseful for hitting her or for getting caught.

"Not that one, dear. She has a trip planned and not where she was hoping," Death told Shorty.

"Sorry, sir, I mean Death. I know we weren't supposed to kill the zombies."

Death smiled at Shorty. "She wasn't a zombie. Just an evil apple. I'll leave you in good company, my dear. I have some deliveries to make."

Death walked on water toward the accountant. If that's how Jesus looked when he walked on water, no wonder the apostles were amazed. That was one impressive sight.

"You heard, boss lady? Death said I was good company!" Shorty was fixing his hair and ironing his shirt with his hand. "You know Death has style. That is one elegant black man. Smooth." I looked at Shorty and then at Death and smiled. I liked Shorty's version of Death. Smooth.

"Are you planning to stay on the ground all day, boss lady?" Shorty asked very cautiously.

"You might need to help me, Shorty. Everything hurts now."

Shorty rushed over to help me. By the time I was back to a vertical position, dozens of cars were pulling into the parking lot and surrounding the park. Shorty and I looked around, puzzled at this new development. I was leaning on Shorty when the doors to every vehicle opened in unison and people poured out of them. It was like watching synchronized swimming, but scarier.

"Are we being attacked by storm troopers?" For the first time, that was an accurate description on Shorty's part. They were all wearing white hazmat suits.

Eugene emerged from the front vehicle, giving orders. "Everybody move out. Tag anything that doesn't look human twice. If not sure, tag it again. Don't take any chances. Hurry, people. We're on a deadline."

"It's about time he got there." I jumped at the sound of Constantine's voice. I forgot I had my earpiece in.

"Eugene, what's going on?"

"I brought you some backup," Eugene answered me as he got close. "Damn, what happened to you? You're looking rough, babe." Shorty and I just glared at him.

"Shorty, remind me to slap him once I stop hurting."

"Don't worry, boss lady. If you forget, I got you covered." I smiled at Shorty, who was holding most of my weight.

"Who are your friends?" I asked Eugene.

"I got the CDC to quarantine Texarkana," Eugene replied with a huge smile.

"Which side?" Shorty asked, looking concerned at the large group of people running everywhere.

"Both sides, plus most of the surrounding area."

Shorty and I were looking at Eugene with our mouths open.

"On what grounds did you get them here?" I was pretty sure I was missing something.

"It was easy. I just reported a zombie apocalypse in Texarkana." Eugene was extremely proud of himself.

"What? The Centers for Disease Control has a zombie code?" I have heard everything today. I was pretty sure I hit my head when I fell.

"They do and it also helps that I'm on the board." Eugene gave me the most charming smile. "It's part of my responsibilities as a rookie. Besides, we need to administer my plague killer to both infected and healthy, and they're the experts."

"Attention, all non-zombies!"

The three of us turned in the direction of the park. Constantine was broadcasting his voice, probably using the drone. "I recommend you hit the dirt in three, or you will get blasted by the CDC. One...two...three. Don't say I didn't warn you."

"Oh good, Constantine got my message. Got to go. I must supervise the dissemination." Eugene was smiling like a kid at Christmas. "You two, tag these two and everyone on this side. Hurry now." He yelled orders at two poor individuals in hazmat suits. The two storm troopers, as Shorty kept calling them, ran up to us. Before I could see what they were doing, I was injected in the arm with some strange syringe.

"Ouch!" Shorty yelled at the guy next to him.

"Easy now, tiger. I'm still alive." I told the one fixing me.

"You're safe to go now." The guy told me and kept making his way around the park, stabbing people with shots of vaccine.

"Shorty, I'm done. Can you please take me home?" I probably looked as miserable as I felt because Shorty just smiled at me.

"Of course, boss lady. You did great today."

Shorty patted my arm and walked me slowly around the truck. I was so beat I didn't care if he put me on the tailgate. I climbed slowly into the cab. Shorty buckled me in and closed the door. The last thing I remember was falling asleep as Shorty was jumping into the driver's seat.

Chapter Thirty-Eight

It was past seven when I woke up. I wasn't feeling nearly as exhausted as earlier, but I was struggling to get out of bed. I needed to check on Bob and Bartholomew and make sure everyone had made it back OK. I took a quick shower. My hair was greasy and all matted. I usually didn't move in my sleep, so I was surprised I looked so rough. When I got out of the shower, I felt human again. I did a double check to make sure I wasn't turning zombie and didn't know it.

When I entered the loft, all the boys were around the kitchen table. Conversation stopped and they all stared at me.

"Oh, thank God. I was afraid I was going to leave without saying goodbye to you," Eugene said as he got up from the table.

"You're leaving so soon?" I was taken aback. I knew Eugene couldn't hang out with us all the time, but I was hoping he was staying longer.

"My work here is done. CDC has lifted the quarantine on the cities and are done vaccinating people. The Mistress said I needed to return to my real work now." Eugene looked pretty sad.

"Wow, the CDC moves fast." How did they get all that done so fast?

"Well, it helps when you work all night," Eugene told me.

"All night? How long have I been sleeping?" I was missing a huge piece of information.

"About twenty-eight hours," Bartholomew told me.

"What? And you guys didn't think to wake me?" It was Sunday already.

"We checked on you to make sure you were still breathing," Bartholomew told me with a smile.

"Isis, you were delirious. That's how tired you were," Constantine told me from the table. "All the running, the stress, and then the fact that you drank three shakes in one day crashed you."

"Is drinking three shakes bad?" There were side effects to those shakes. I knew it.

"Calm down now. It's nothing bad; it's the normal side effect of being wired. You were eventually going to crash. You just crashed hard. Shorty had to drag you up the stairs." Constantine was shaking his head as his spoke.

"How is Shorty? Is he OK?" I didn't remember much from the point I climbed in the truck with him.

"He's doing great," Bob told me with a smile on his face. "Working his crew to deliver former zombies to their homes and cleaning up disaster areas. He said you told him he could keep the truck. So, he's living the dream."

All the boys were staring at him.

"I thought I said I would talk to Constantine." I rubbed my wet hair, trying to remember all the details from yesterday. "Are you okay with him keeping the truck?" I asked Constantine cautiously.

"I already raised our insurance and added premium coverage to his plan," Constantine replied.

"What's premium coverage?" I didn't think I was familiar with that.

"It's like full coverage, but triple, to cover all the pedestrians Shorty is going to hit," Constantine said.

The rest of us laughed.

"Of course, he can keep the truck. I'm not going to find another cleanup crew as reliable as Shorty that doesn't ask any questions. I'm willing to pay the price for good help." Constantine winked at me.

"We won't get to see you anymore," I said to Eugene, a little discouraged. He was part of our family now. Life-threatening situations were great ways of bonding people.

"I have good news. Death talked to the Mistress and convinced her that we should continue our collaboration. Death said this was a great way of creating a unified front." Eugene was bouncing up and down with joy.

"Did that work?" I was surprised Pestilence had agreed to that.

"Death suggested you guys come one week and we come here the next. That way the burden would not fall on one organization to always travel. The Mistress freaked. Instead, she offered I come and visit every week, so you guys don't have to worry." Eugene finished with a grin.

"Wow, Death is good. I'm impressed," I told the group.

"Oh, it's payback. Death will always have the last word," Constantine told us.

"Eugene, we need to get going. I need to make sure you make it back in time for your curfew," Bob told Eugene. "Isis, your dinner is in the fridge. Eric said you're not allowed to drink any more shakes for three days. Death said you need more sleep. So, as soon as you finish your food, head back to bed. Got it?"

"Yes, sir." Normally, I would have argued about all the instructions and me not being a kid, but I was so tired I had no energy. Bob eyed me suspiciously. "I promise. I like that plan."

"Boss, you want to go for a ride?" Bob asked Constantine.

"Sounds great. We can stop by Sonic and get a blast," Constantine replied.

"Can I get a blast? I haven't had one in years." Eugene looked so young now.

"After all your hard work, you can have two," Constantine told Eugene as he headed out the kitty door. We'll even get you enough for the rest of the interns. You'll be a hero for life! Isis. Food and then bed. No delays." It seemed Constantine also had to have the last word.

"If you two need anything, call me. OK?" Bartholomew and I looked at each other and nodded back at Bob. Eugene rushed over and gave me a big hug.

"See you next week, Isis." I hugged Eugene back.

"I can't wait." I gave him a quick kiss on the cheek and he took off.

"Bye, Bart. I must hurry before those two leave me." Considering they were both downstairs already, Eugene was probably right. I wondered what Bob and Constantine talked about on their many drives.

I opened the fridge and found a covered dish with a note addressed to me. Bob left me instructions for my supper. I peeked inside the container. Bob had made me cheese tortellini. Bob was a life-saver. If I weren't so tired, I would have done a little dance.

"Bart, what did I miss while I was in my coma?" I leaned on the counter and watched Bartholomew while my food heated in the microwave.

"Nothing much. Police recovered the body of the accountant from the lake. Eugene coordinated the efforts of the CDC and made sure all victims were properly treated. Ana and Joe have recovered and are on bed rest. The media is going crazy. Pretty much all you would expect after a zombie apocalypse."

That was an excellent summary by Bartholomew. I walked over to the freezer and pulled out a pint of Ben and Jerry's ice cream. I handed Bartholomew the ice cream and a spoon.

"That deserves a celebration then," I told Bartholomew. I joined him at the table with my food. "How are the schools handling the fiasco?"

"They're already planning next year's event," Bartholomew told me as he took the lid off his ice cream.

"What? After that giant disaster, they're doing it again?" I was holding my fork in midair.

"Zombie Apocalypse II is on. College Bowl has been nixed. Terminator and I have been asked to return as defending champions in the combat dance competition." Bartholomew did a couple of head rolls followed by shaking the haters off his shirt.

"That's my bro." I gave him a fist bump and he returned it with a huge smile. It was nice to see him smiling again and at peace with himself. "I'm glad Texarkana is making the most out of this."

"Hey, if Salem can be the home of the witches, we can have zombies," Bartholomew said.

"So true." I took another mouthful and was grateful Bob loved to cook. "Tell me, what happened to Texarkana being calm and quiet?"

"We moved in," Bartholomew told me with a mouthful of ice cream.

"That's right—I forgot," I said, laughing. We were dangerous to the real estate market.

"I almost forgot. You got another package." Bartholomew jumped from the table and ran to his workstations. I got tired just looking at him.

"Here you go." He handed me a small box wrapped in white paper. I did a quick look-over and then ripped it open.

"Do you have any idea why Antarctica-Bob sent me a ceramic penguin?" I asked Bartholomew. The little thing was cute, maybe two inches tall and full of detail.

"Hey, it has your name on it and a number."

Bartholomew was right. On the back my name was written and the number 776. “A little weird, but we do work for Death.”

“That pretty much sums up everything in our lives.”

“It’s a thankless job, but somebody has to do it.” Bartholomew was full of clichés today.

“It’s not thankless. The souls appreciate it. We do make a difference. A small one, but a difference nevertheless.” I smiled at Bartholomew.

“In that case, you won’t mind heading to New Mexico on Tuesday. We have a streaker on the loose.” Bartholomew eyed me from his side of the table.

“Never a dull moment,” I said.

“Never.”

“In that case, fill me in on the details while I eat. I want to be in bed before those two come back.”

The tension in our home had vanished. I was looking forward to finding the lost souls now; I made a difference to them. I just prayed for a couple of boring weeks. I needed a break.

While Isis barely survived the madness of those zombies, this is not the end of our adventures. Are you ready for the next saga?

Elves, Vampires, and Demons, oh my! **Forbidden War** is coming packed with action, and the introduction of War’s very own Intern. Make sure to start pick up your copy.

Acknowledgments

Dear Reader,

Let me start by saying, Thank you! I'm so excited and grateful you are joining me on this world that has become the Reaper's Universe. Plague Unleashed was an absolute blast to write. These zombies were so much fun, even a bit intense as my bother pointed out. I do hope you enjoyed them as much as I did writing them.

It has been a joy to see Isis grow and become more comfortable in her role as Intern. As an older sister, my heart hurt for Bartholomew's situation, but so happy Isis has claimed him as her brother. For me, the Intern Diaries is a story of finding and growing your family. In the case of our Reaper's crew, "family" goes beyond blood, binding them through true love and commitment.

If you enjoy the story, please consider leaving a rating and possibly a short review. Your reviews help others find the books you love.

With love,

D. C.

About Author

D. C. Gomez was born in the Dominican Republic, but grew up in Salem, Massachusetts. She studied film and television at New York University. After college, she joined the US Army, and proudly served for four years.

Those experiences shaped her quirky, and sometimes morbid, sense of humor. D.C. has a love for those who served and the families that support them. She currently lives in the quaint city of Wake Village, Texas, with her furry roommate, Chincha.

Also By D. C. Gomez

In The Reapers' Universe- Urban Fantasy Books

The Intern Diaries Series

Death's Intern- Book 1

Plague Unleashed- Book 2

Forbidden War- Book 3

Unstoppable Famine- Book 4

Judgement Day- Book 5

The Origins of Constantine- Novella

From Eugene with Love- Novella

Rise of the Reapers- Novella

The Order's Assassin Series

The Hitman- Book 1

The Traitor (coming soon)

The Elisha & Elijah Chronicles (UF and Post-Apocalyptic)

Recruited- Book 1

Betrayed- Book 2 (coming soon)

Humorous Fiction

The Cat Lady Special

A Desperate Cat Lady (coming soon)

Young Adult

Another World

Children's Books

Charlie, What's Your Talent? – Book 1

Charlie, Dare to Dream – Book 2

Devotional Books

Dare to Believe

Dare to Forgive

Dare to Love

Printed in Great Britain
by Amazon

86357551R00161